EVERY THIRTEEN YEARS

JEAN KNIGHT PACE

To my siblings, for whom I would always come back.

CHAPTER 1

GRETA

The one good thing about Daddy leaving was that the screaming ended.

That's not the way Hans remembered it, but I did.

I'd hated that yelling—day in and day out. Daddy and Mama, their voices fit to shatter walls.

We remembered a lot of things differently—Hans and I. And when we did, Hans always said it was because I was practically a baby when Daddy left.

Not true.

He just said that when he wanted to be right about Daddy, which was a lot.

And why was I thinking about Daddy anyway, when I had chores to do?

I scooped up the broom. One thing about chores—the doing made me feel better than not doing. Especially this afternoon.

Hans had stormed off again—probably to play a video game at his friend's house. Mama said that's how teenagers did things —all stomps and grunts—but I didn't like it.

I liked the sounds that came from soft mosses and leaves caught in the wind. From paths made of dirt and decay that would barely make a sound no matter how many times you tromped on them.

I moved our dirty shoes out of the way so I could sweep the crusted mud they always left by the door. Then lifted my backpack off the floor, cleaning under it.

Soon as that was done, I moved on to the dishes, counters, the table in the nook where Mama liked to eat breakfast and watch the birds.

When Daddy left, things had fallen quiet. Not soft moss quiet either. Not at all. It had been a sharp silence—the type you heard at every turn, with every step, under every whisper. That silence hadn't broken until we'd moved to Grammy's old house —a maze of rooms encased in dusty wallpaper held in place by bowed ceilings and crooked floorboards.

The house wasn't much—that's how Mama had put it—but it was ours.

I thought it was perfectly *much*—big old rooms with nooks and crannies, places to play, places to hide, places to sit and read a book. Places where our laughter could finally wake up, as though we were shaking it out after a long winter.

Much better than the house we'd lived in with Daddy, which had been a tight combination of square angles and open floor plans.

This house had spaces. Inside and out. Because this house also had woods—right behind us, miles and miles of green and bark and berry. Not that we were allowed miles and miles out. Mama made that very clear with the bright orange markers she set all around our property.

Of all that deep vast wood, we owned only five acres. Though back when Hans and I had roamed together, we had often slipped through those barriers to explore the bigger woods beyond. These days, though, I stayed inside the posts.

I picked up my backpack, sorting my books—one about

birds, one about flowers, one about a little girl with no parents who lived in the woods in her own little cottage.

I always imagined those woods parting for me, just like they did for the girl in my story—branches and bramble moving aside as I walked along loamy paths. And in a way, maybe they did.

I almost tucked the backpack into its nook, and then thought better of it. My chores were done, the house empty, the late sun calling me to it. I slipped the backpack onto my shoulders, slipped my feet into my shoes, slipped a granola bar into my pocket, slipped my way out the back door.

All in a steady silence that only the woods could appreciate.

They made room for me, the woods. Like they made room for everything that was willing to muscle its way in. An insistent vine wrapping around a tree, a little sprout popping out of a cluster of rock. The woods were busy, bossy too. Like some sort of too-full Thanksgiving gathering. Everyone who wanted to come was invited, plopping down wherever they could make a place for themselves.

Just what I needed after Daddy left.

Just what I needed when the house got too empty.

Just what I needed today.

Space.

But not space away, space deep in.

I hiked farther into the woods, to my favorite place where the sunlight went green because the trees grew so thick, to the place just before Mama's orange posts that marked the edge of our property.

Hans had liked the woods at the beginning too. When we'd first moved here, he'd explored them with me—way past Mama's posts and the old barbed wire that set off the other property. The vast woods had been ours then. We'd made up games, carved in trees, played hide and seek.

And then he'd grown up. Well, sort of.

And I didn't like it.

Teenage Hans reached back toward the normal, the neat, the plain—toward the taut corners of our old life.

Which brought the yelling back.

Only now it was Hans and Mama. I hated the yelling even more with them. I was terrified that, just like with Daddy, Hans would walk out the door and never come back.

I couldn't bear to lose Hans.

I couldn't bear for Mama to cry again like she had with Daddy.

And I couldn't bear to be the only one left.

I sank to the ground, right next to my favorite tree—one Hans and I had carved our initials into when we were young, well, younger. I had a little stash of stuff there, like I was a squirrel or crow. Smooth stones, snail shells of different sizes, various feathers and interesting leaves. Like a fairy garden. Only I didn't need a fairy to come to it. I just needed a place to come to myself. Did that make me the fairy? Probably not with my short legs, all scraped up at the knees, and hair that wouldn't stay braided, plus a face that was starting to thin, but not in a beautiful way like Mama's.

When Mama and Hans yelled, and then when they finished and sprang apart like two same-sided poles of a magnet, I never said anything, never talked about it at all. But I used that quiet to organize Mama's pens and pencils and chalks. Or do the dishes. Or, if I was feeling extra still, I'd sometimes even do Hans' chores, cleaning the toilet and dusting the furniture. He never seemed to notice, though I know Mama did.

And on days like today, when it had gotten really bad and both of them had burst apart to their own separate corners of their own separate worlds, I retreated to the silent calm of the woods. Wandering. Orange post to orange post.

I knew every inch of our property, while not knowing it at all. That was the beauty of the woods—every day a different sky, every plant a changing thing, every step on different dirt than the day before. I loved that.

Today a whole cluster of mushrooms had burst out of the loam, right behind our tree. Blue-tinted tops, creamy bellies.

I plucked one and wrapped it in a tissue.

Because sometimes, after the screaming was done and the tautness of the house started to unfurl like a fern in the morning, Hans would come home and I'd show him a caterpillar or bone or something else I'd found in the woods. Usually, he'd grunt and mostly ignore them, but sometimes he'd look them up on his phone and tell me which caterpillars would turn to butterflies and which were destined to become ugly brown moths. Or whether it was the bone of a bird or snake. Things I already knew before he looked them up, but I let him tell me about them anyway.

I figured with this mushroom, he could tell me if it was a type we could eat or if it was one that would kill us dead in minutes. And to be honest, this time I had no idea.

Usually after he looked something up, he started to feel better. And maybe after that we'd play a game of Scrabble. Just like we used to, before he was a teenager, and before I was whatever this awkward version of the old me was.

Because I was growing up too.

Mama was starting to talk puberty. She didn't need to. At age twelve, I could feel it coming for me—claws out—the moodiness, the acne, the uncomfortable conversations. When I much preferred soft silences.

Which is why, as opposed to Hans who never went into the woods anymore, I spent more and more time there.

Until one day I didn't.

CHAPTER 2

GRETA

The police officers parked in the long drive that led up to the house. Stiff uniforms, guns tapping their sides as they walked past the bright pink azaleas, the pots of pansies, right up to the front door.

I raced out of the dense thicket of mulberry trees, ignoring the mosses under my feet, splashing through the miniature streams that trickled through our yard from the rain the night before. Ran straight to the back of the house and up the steps—my heart hammering like summer thunder.

Had something happened to Hans?

I ran through the back door, my hair unraveling, and my mind with it—imagining every horrible thing that could have happened to my brother.

Except that he was right there. Alive and well—and peeking around the corner, trying to hear what Mama was saying to the officers. Which I found strangely comforting. Because something about the way he was doing it let me know that his heart was hammering just like mine.

When he saw me, he squared his shoulders and gathered his courage and walked right in. "Is it Dad?" he asked, facing Mama.

It took her and the officers a second to register the question.

"Oh, no," Mama said, as I trailed in, still just listening.

"It's actually about the woods," one of the officers said, looking from Hans to me. And then staying on me, since it was clear by my dirty knees that I was the bigger problem where woods were concerned.

"You really need to take precautions, Annika," one of the officers said to Mama. I recognized him a little. Mama had known him in high school.

"Oh, you don't have to tell me that," Mama said, with a big sigh behind her voice. "Thanks, officers."

After they left, she turned to us, saw all the questions in both of our faces. "We'll talk about it after dinner."

"Sounds important enough that we should talk about it now," Hans said, his voice taking on that ready-for-a-fight tone.

"If that's what you want," Mama said, settling onto the couch, and motioning for us to sit beside her.

I wasn't at all sure it was what I wanted, but Hans plopped down, arms folded angrily across his chest, as though Mom had already done lots of things wrong.

"So it's not about Dad?" he grumped out. He'd stopped calling him Daddy as soon as he'd started high school.

"Not at all," Mama said.

At least there was that, I thought to myself, still not sitting.

"It's about the woods, just like the officers said." She sighed, like the woods and words were things too heavy to hold. "You know those 'No Trespassing' signs?"

We both nodded. They were right at the edge of our property, just behind Mama's orange posts. The signs were stapled to a dying barbed wire fence that the forest was trying to reclaim —wrapping its weeds in spirals around the poles, working away at the rust, tugging its tendrils through the pocks and gaps and holes of the metal.

"Well, it's no secret that no one really knows who owns that property," Mama said. "But it's huge."

"Someone has to know," Hans said. "There's paperwork, and taxes. You can probably look it up on the assessor website."

"Okay, we do *know*," Mama said. "A couple by the name of Schmidt. And apparently their taxes get paid every year. But no one actually *knows* who they are. They never come here or take care of the property or anything."

"This still isn't *news*," Hans said.

"Truly," Mama began, her voice taking on enough of an edge to rival Hans' tone, "nothing I'm going to tell you is exactly *new* or *news*. Which is partly what makes it a little scary."

And then I sat down. I knew what was coming.

"Thirteen years ago, a teen boy disappeared in those woods," Mama said.

"You're right," Hans said. "That's not news. Everyone knows that, and there are a million stories and conspiracy theories."

Mama ignored Hans and continued. "We were in Michigan at the time, for a stint at a job your father was trying." Mama turned to Hans. "You were in preschool back then."

Hans opened his mouth to say, I can only assume, that this was also not news, but Mama cut him off.

"But it also happened thirteen years before that," she continued. "Back when I was a teenager. That time it was a girl, almost my same age. And really sad. I didn't know her because we'd always been in different classes—she was more of a music and theater kid—but in a small town like this, everyone knew or knew of the family. And, as I'm sure you've all heard, that disappearance is also unsolved."

This time Hans didn't say it wasn't news. Instead, he leaned forward like he was actually curious and asked, "Did they find her, Mom? The body?"

"No," Mama said. "Nor do I think they ever will. Those woods are thick and deep."

Again, Hans opened his mouth. Again, Mama held up her hand. "But it's not just that those crimes happened. It's that every thirteen years for the last sixty-five years, a child has gone missing in those woods."

"Since the fifties?" I asked.

"Yes," Mama said. "Every thirteen years. In May."

Hans and I looked at each other. It was April 30th.

"The police think it's a serial killer. And this is their year."

"But if it's a serial killer, he's probably dead," Hans piped up.

"And he could be," Mom said. "It's so bizarre. Every thirteen years. Those woods. But he could still be alive. If he was just a young adult at the time of the first murder, he would be an old man by now, but not necessarily dead, or even disabled. And then there's always the possibility of a copycat crime. As you so helpfully pointed out, Hans," Mama said. "*Everybody* knows. This is usually such a safe town. But, well, for now, it's not. There's a notice in the paper and there will be a public service announcement on the news and social media. But the police are going around personally to warn families near the woods."

Mama took a deep breath, and I felt it coming—felt it like a noose. "For the next month, you two are forbidden from going into those woods."

"But Mama," I sputtered.

"I'm sorry, Greta girl, but it's really very dangerous. You have no idea how awful it was all those years ago. It's bad enough to read about it, to talk about it, but when you actually experience it as a town—it's just terrible."

Mama shuddered, and there was nothing more I could say.

CHAPTER 3

HANS

Someone forgot to tell the cops and, well, every grown-up alive, that the best way to get a bunch of teenagers to do something is to tell them *not* to do something. If they want to make the thing even more appealing, then they should attach a creepy story to it.

The parties started right after the news broadcast hit.

The first one on May 1st—a Maypole party, the kids called it. Out in the woods. I assume it was just a bunch of beer and making out. And everyone came back, safe and sound.

That only stoked the fire.

Soon kids were going out every night. I'd never heard about so many parties, especially in the woods. In fact, at our age, most kids barely gave the woods a thought. Not when there were dances and dates and hookups, or at least some really good video gaming in your basement—plenty of distraction.

My distraction went by the name of Savina Johanson. Smart as a whip and as hot as a forest fire. She had hair like dark chocolate, which she tipped in purple. I liked that too. Her nose was a perfect triangle, her lips round but level—not plumped like some of the other girls had started doing.

Creamy white skin that softened around deep chestnut eyes. The kind of girl you could imagine as a princess in a tower. And quite often, when I should have been doing my homework, I did.

We had pre-calc together. Which is where I'd heard a few of the other girls whispering about the final party. Tonight.

Now I waited behind Savina at the drinking fountain, enjoying the view.

When she came up for air, she smiled.

I made an effort to smile back, though my brain felt all wobbly, like it couldn't wrap itself around the idea that she was actually making eye contact with me.

"Hey, Hank," she said. That's what everyone at school called me. And Dad too. Only Mom and Greta hung onto my German birth name.

I opened my mouth to say, 'Hi,' which I hope was the sound that actually came out. Truthfully, I felt even more stun-gunned that she knew my name.

She didn't seem to notice my completely immobile status. "You going tonight? To the end-of-the month party."

"The one in the woods?" I managed to croak out.

"Yeah," she said. "To celebrate May 31st. Guess that sicko killer is dead by now."

I nodded.

"So you going? I think it's going to be a bonfire. Hotdogs, marshmallows, nothing too wild."

I wanted to ask her if I seemed that tame—like I needed reassurance that there would be marshmallows. I felt pretty confident that the party wouldn't end with just marshmallows, but I was still in stun-gun status, so all I could stutter out was, "Not sure my mom will let me."

Yeah, way to play it cool, Hank.

She smiled then, this slightly wicked thing. "I mean, I think that's kind of the point."

Another stupid grin from me, which was apparently the only expression I had in my arsenal.

"I'm not a big rebel either," she continued, "but my dad thinks the whole thing is a bunch of garbage. And a party to celebrate the demise of a serial killer seems like a good reason to head to the woods."

I didn't point out any of the problems with this argument, like that we didn't actually know the killer was dead, or even who he was, or that there could be copycats. I just nodded away. After all, I'd already made a big enough mama's boy of myself.

Savina's twin came up behind her, shoulders slumped, one foot dragging a bit behind the other. He took a drink from the fountain without looking directly at me, or anyone else.

But Savina was enough smiles for the both of them. "Plus, at midnight it won't be May anymore," she added, leaning against the wall. "So, if May freaks you out, come in June."

Greta chose that moment to appear by my side, waiting for her ride home. She always walked the block from the middle school to the high school. I wondered how much she'd heard.

"Oh, hey Greta," Savina said, and I think even Greta was stun-gunned that Savina knew her name, and Greta was never stun-gunned about anything.

"Hi," she answered back. "Were you talking about the woods?"

I shot my sharpest eye daggers into the side of Greta's head, but Savina answered, "Yeah, a little."

And maybe Greta appreciated that Savina didn't lie about it, because she somehow managed not to say anything too embarrassing. "You ready to go?" she asked me.

I nodded, a quick thing.

Savina smiled like she thought me taking my kid sister home was the cutest thing in the world. Which I hoped translated to also being the hottest thing in the world.

"See you in June," Savina murmured.

And those lips.

I was still thinking about them eating marshmallows when Greta said to me, "You know there's a psychopath living in the woods, right?"

"Only for a few more hours," I replied.

"How you gonna talk Mama into it?" she asked.

"I'm not," I said.

CHAPTER 4

GRETA

I'd been reading about killers all month. Well, one killer. *The* killer.

Nobody had a name, or any potential names for the killer. Nobody had a description. Nobody even had a story of unknown people they'd seen in the town or the woods.

In fact, it turns out that with serial killers, it's usually someone in your town, or an adjacent town—someone you might just see at the local Publix every Saturday buying a bag of grapes and a gallon of milk.

If the killer was the same person and not a copycat, it'd have to be an old person. I tried to think of all the octogenarians I could and came up with precious few. A few of the ladies who had been Grammy's bridge buddies before she'd died. But most of them were in wheelchairs, and weighed all of ninety pounds. Besides them, I could only think of the old man who still worked at the corner store, and an even older man who was the greeter at Walmart. And he was missing both arms.

I knew there were more, but it seemed like most of them spent the day hanging out at home, not wandering the streets of Millersburg, much less preparing to kill and then hide a body.

Copycats seemed much more likely. The first few could have been done by the same person, but then another person—just as twisted—heard of the story and took up the job.

But, again, for that person to be someone we knew, hanging out in the barbershop and just waiting to commit a murder in thirteen more years—it was a stretch.

Maybe they came from out of town to do it. Maybe they copycatted all over the country in the same way people went on tour to sing. That certainly didn't help narrow it down.

All anyone knew, and it was precious little, was that kids went into the woods. And kids didn't come out.

No one ever found anything either. No clothes, no trinkets, no hair, no fingerprints, no blood, no bones, no notes. Not even a footstep or crumpled bit of grass. In fact, the only marks that anybody seemed to leave were from the search parties that looked for days, then weeks—hunting for a kid who seemed to have simply vanished.

For the last disappearance, they'd hired a few professional trackers. Eccentric experts who looked for things in woods for an actual living. Even those guys had found a whole lot of nothing.

Nothing.

That was the creepiest of all.

Some thought the cases were suicides. But even then, where were the remains? You couldn't hide *yourself* if you were dead. And we didn't have a lot of cliffs or gullies or rivers to fall into.

All Millersburg had was Sparrow Creek. And good luck vanishing in it. It was all of ten feet wide and only about four feet deep. Surely if anyone had tried to drown themselves in it, they would have washed up in someone's backyard, probably still breathing.

So far, I hadn't found a single theory that stood up to any scrutiny.

All I'd found were sad families. Sad obituaries. Sad stories from friends.

Five kids.

Benjamin. He was the first. Benjamin Jarrison Howard. Born in the forties, died in the fifties. Or at least vanished.

For a second, I played with the idea that these kids were being kidnapped or trafficked. Or maybe just runaways.

In the grainy picture of a yellowed newspaper obituary, Benjamin certainly didn't look that happy. Standing there in a pair of overalls like an old farmer with a young face. He held something in his hand and stared straight at the camera, like he was daring it to mess up this shot.

Then there was Shelby. Her hair long and flat, wearing a miniskirt—all knees and stork legs and embroidery across her chest. She was the oldest of the five—a sultry look in her eyes, which I was guessing were blue from how light they looked in the newspaper photo.

Melissa. The 80s. And you could tell. Hair permed, bangs frizzed until they stood up at least three inches from her forehead. High-waisted jeans, zig-zags on her shirt, big earrings.

I touched my own naked ear.

She was a kid who looked a little younger than me, but like she was trying to appear older. She and Shelby seemed like good options for runaways, though I had no evidence for that at all, except that they had a look that said they wanted to be some-where else.

The same look Hans sometimes had.

I pushed that thought away.

As I looked at the school picture, it dawned on me that Melissa's family would have lived in our town, would have known both my Great-grammy and Grammy and maybe even Mama as a baby. Were any family members still here? Mama had said most families eventually left after the killings. Which made sense with so many memories to torture them in a small town.

The fourth kid was named Larisa. The only black kid to have disappeared. During the nineties. In her picture, she was wearing high-tops and a geometric shirt. As well as a bright smile. She was probably just a year older than me at the time. But way cooler. At least in the picture. Also happy. At least in the picture. This was the girl that Mama had known.

And then, Edgar. A kid in a band uniform, holding a trumpet. Starched and stiff, his hair plastered to the side, like no amount of wind would be allowed to move it.

A boy who was a teen before Hans had even started school.

The picture had a military air. Formal and serious. I wondered what he did when he wasn't playing the trumpet. Did he smile more? Did he have a cell phone—one that flipped open? Had he been learning to text on it?

Or had he spent his time sitting in his room with a music stand and that shiny instrument, mastering scales and Sousa and steps? According to his obituary, he'd been really good.

Which meant there would be people here in this town, right now, who would remember hearing him play in the marching band. Something about that made me feel really sad.

Five kids. Happy-looking, sad looking, serious or smiling.

Kids whose ages ran the gamut from me to Hans. No wonder Mama was freaked out.

I sat staring out my window into the woods, trying to see through them—a thing I knew was impossible. They weren't woods with paths and sunlight and meadow. They were deep and thick. Tall trees with a canopy that blocked the light. Vines and roots wrapping their way along the forest floor. Fairy tale woods if ever you saw them.

Which was what made the woods so alluring—the way you could hide there, disappear there, not worry about someone watching over your shoulder.

And that, I realized as I looked away from my window, was exactly what a serial killer needed.

CHAPTER 5

HANS

Mom saw me messing with my hair that night—adding some gel, flipping it over. That's all she needed to start in on me.

"I heard about that party and I know it's going on. Don't even think about it. May is still May and serial killers are still serial killers."

"What are you talking about?" I said like I had no idea. "I've got too much homework to do anyway. It's gonna be a wild night of math." The only reason I didn't raise my voice was because I wanted her to believe me. Besides, I *was* planning to get a jump on my math homework before heading out. The perfect half-truth.

She looked me over, my button-down shirt, my good jeans. "Hans Jonas Becker, you may not go to that party tonight."

"I wasn't asking to," I replied, the crick of anger stabbing into my voice. "And don't call me Hans. You know I hate it."

Maybe I would have listened, maybe I would have skipped the party, waited till June. If it hadn't been for Mom's own little secrets. By which I mean: William.

Sure, we'd been hearing about him for weeks. In little passing bits at first—someone new at work, so nice to have another pair of hands on deck, yada yada. I admit that I didn't even notice it, until one day I found a doggie bag in the fridge. "What's this?" I'd asked.

"Oh, I just grabbed some breakfast with a co-worker," Mom had answered.

It was the word 'co-worker' that tipped me off. She never called them that. The other nurses had names and she used their names. We knew them all anyway. Mom had grown up in this town and every nurse at the hospital treated us like their own little babies.

"What *co-worker?*" I'd asked.

"I've mentioned him a couple of times," she said, not making eye contact with me. "His name is William."

Greta had popped in, like some kind of tween secret agent. "Was it a date?" Greta had asked, pouring herself a bowl of cereal.

Mom had cleared her throat. "Just breakfast."

Okay, great. Fine. Except that she'd cleared it again. "I actually, well, I asked him if he'd like to come here this Sunday for dinner, meet you guys."

"I hope he said 'no,'" I shot back.

"He didn't," she answered, her jaw tightening.

Which meant that I had to meet him—and hate him—in person. From his uptight name (no nickname either) to his uptight khaki pants to his uptight wire-rimmed glasses, which he pressed back against his nose with his pointer finger every forty-five seconds. Nothing like Dad. No, this guy had brown mousy hair, brown droopy eyes, crooked nose, and pink lips.

Way too pink for a dude (I could practically hear Dad saying that too).

He was holding Mom's hand when they came in, and they were laughing. I had to grit my teeth to keep from punching him in the face.

Greta had watched them, smiling, all night. And asked questions.

William was some kind of internist—not even a real doctor or a gritty nurse. Something in between. Which is basically how he could be described on every level.

After dinner, Mom invited him to watch a movie, and even though he made eye contact with me, and I knew he could see the daggers, he accepted that invitation. He and Mom sat close.

I left.

Though Greta stayed. I was glad about that too—ha, try making out with Greta right there.

They didn't. He went home after the show. I was watching them, spying like a little kid from upstairs. And I caught him stealing a little peck on Mom's cheek.

She went back into the kitchen and did the dishes and hummed show tunes. I hated show tunes. Dad had liked old-school hard rock and lots of rap and Mom always complained that he listened to the explicit lyrics in front of us.

I'd flopped onto my bed and stuck my headphones in and listened to my 'Dad playlist.' And when I'd woken up in the morning, still wearing my blue jeans, with a film on my teeth, I'd had to hustle to get ready for school. Mom hadn't even woken me up.

So, yeah, if Mom could have a secret relationship with a secret boyfriend, then why couldn't I let myself into the woods for an end-of-May bonfire?

Of course, I had to wait until she left for work. Which was later than usual. Tonight, she only had an eight-hour shift, instead of her usual twelve.

I tapped on my math book, fidgeting with my pencil, waiting for her to leave, and looking out the window every four minutes.

Sure enough, there was a nice plume of smoke rising up from the woods. The party was still going strong. Perfect.

Honestly, the fire looked close enough to our actual property that it would hardly be breaking the rules at all.

Not that breaking the rules would be hard. Mom's shift at the ER took her away till seven in the morning. Which meant the only person I had to avoid waking was Greta.

I flipped my pencil over, erasing the series of numbers I'd just written.

For some reason, it made me feel guiltier to think of sneaking out on Greta than it did to think about sneaking out on Mom. I penciled the correct numbers in, shaking off the feeling. The last thing on earth that someone like Greta wanted to do was crash a high school party, or any party for that matter. She was happier talking to trees than people.

I glanced up again, just to make sure the smoke was still there.

It was.

I wondered what Savina would be wearing. She had this black top I really liked—tight along the shoulders and chest, slim at the waist. For a moment, my pencil hung over the equation on my paper and I pictured her in it—the light of the fire dancing up her face, reflecting off of the dark eyes, catching the deep colors of her hair—the chestnut browns that hid under the near-black. She would look down, shyly, when I came over to sit beside her, and when she glanced back up, her lips would tilt just so, and then… my pencil broke. And with it, the spell of her face.

I heard Mom putting on her shoes, shuffling around her bedroom, looking for her purse like she did every night.

Fifteen minutes later, I slipped into my favorite jacket, pocketing a pack of gum. I could still see the plume of smoke coating the stars above it.

I paused at the window. It'd been a while since I'd gone into the woods. Months actually. Maybe longer. I wondered if the old "hieroglyphics" that Greta and I had scratched into the trees were still there—little markers to show us the way back home if we ever went past Mom's posts (which I'd often talked Greta into) and got lost. Of course that was forever ago. The trees had probably grown over the shallow markings or the animals had scratched them away or the poison ivy had surrounded them.

Not that it mattered. I knew how to get home. I'd been out in the woods a thousand times. Even if it *had* been a while.

Still, as I grabbed my wallet, I couldn't help but remember what Greta liked to say—that the woods moved, never staying the same, never respecting the lines and boundaries people tried to create.

Even Mom's orange posts were already becoming lost to the movement of the woods—choked in vines and bleached by the sun.

CHAPTER 6

GRETA

I listened to him walk down the stairs. Checked my clock. Eleven. One hour before the window of serial killing closed. I had to agree that it seemed close enough. Though I expected Mama wouldn't agree at all.

I'd heard them arguing. I *always* heard them arguing.

And even though Hans had told Mama he'd just be doing math all night, I had a feeling he wasn't hanging out in the kitchen for a power snack.

A suspicion that was confirmed in the gentle opening of the back door, in the soft way Hans closed it behind him—not a single creak or click, not even to lock it. Usually, he thumped his way through the house, as though determined to make an imprint with every stride.

Not tonight. Tonight, Hans slipped into the darkness, crossing the tree line with the grace of a shadow.

Losing him like that, into the night—after he and Mama had argued—that's what did it for me. I grabbed my little backpack, filled it with granola bars, and shoved a water bottle into the pocket as I walked.

I didn't need to be quiet like Hans. The house was empty now.

But I tiptoed my way through the halls anyway, slowing as I passed Mama's room, exactly like I would have if she was there. Once outside, I shut the back door without a sound, just like Hans. But when my feet hit the grass, the dewing blades grazing my ankles, I sprinted.

The soil and leaves and dirt ate up the sound, and I realized that I was a shadow too. I glanced at my phone. 11:10.

Hans wouldn't get to the gap in the fence before I did. *No one* could get to the gap in the fence faster than me, especially in the dark.

"I know what you're doing," I whispered when I finally saw his hunched shoulders bending forward, looking for the space where the fence had rusted apart.

And I had to admit that the way he jumped back was mildly satisfying.

For a minute, his eyes dilated in the darkness, like an animal taking in the danger. And then the sigh in his posture. "Greta? Mom would lose her crap if she saw you here."

"If she saw *me* here?" I asked.

"I told her there was a party," he said.

I lifted an eyebrow, though the effect might have gotten lost to the darkness.

"What are you doing here anyway?" he asked. "Following me?"

"I was here first," I pointed out.

"Yeah, I noticed," he grumbled. "Anyway, go back home. Aren't you tired?"

I shrugged, even though I was, in fact, incredibly tired. To combat it, I stuffed a bite of granola bar into my mouth.

"Go on, Gret. Get some sleep."

"You're going to that party," I said. "And Mama told you not to. And you told her you wouldn't."

"I told her I wasn't asking her permission," he said. "Which I didn't. Besides, May is nearly over, so I'm barely even breaking a rule."

"You've got forty-five minutes of rule-breaking left," I said, glancing at my phone. "In this time zone, of course. Who knows what rules serial killers follow?"

"Exactly," Hans replied. "For all we know, the killer is from Georgia and it's already June."

I took another nervous bite of my granola bar, the crumbs dropping onto my t-shirt and then to the ground. I brushed them away. "Hans, can't you just wait? We promised her. When the cops came."

"I didn't actually *promise* anything," he said. "I don't really remember what I said, but *saying* something isn't the same as a promise. And if you're so worried about it, call her."

We stood there, staring at each other in the darkness.

I dropped my eyes first. "You know I missed the woods more than you did," I murmured.

"Well, it's almost June, so you're about to get them back," he answered, looking at the line of smoke.

"Am I?" I whispered. And the wind must have been blowing it the opposite direction, because the fire looked close, but I couldn't smell it at all.

Hans shrugged. "Look, Gret, go to bed. I'll be back later. You won't even hear me come in."

I glanced back at our house, tiny in the distance. It looked almost darker than the woods now, with every window curtained, every door closed. I felt a deep ache between my shoulders, looking at it. "Can I come?" I asked so quietly Hans had to lean in to hear.

"I really don't think that's a good idea," Hans said. "And not because of any serial killer."

"Then why is it a good idea for you?" I asked, looking away from our house.

"Because I'm older, obviously."

"So older kids can do dumb things?" I challenged him.

He pulled out his phone and glanced at the clock. 11:20. He must have decided that didn't give him enough time to argue because a few seconds later he grumbled, "Fine. Come if you want. But try to keep up."

I glanced at the line of smoke. It really did look close. If we were lucky, it was just past the fence.

Easy peasy.

Except that it wasn't.

CHAPTER 7

HANS

We snuck past the orange markers, shimmying through the gap in the old barbed wire and then thrashing our way through weeds that seemed to have doubled in the month of May.

Greta tripped every few steps, until I reached out and took her arm, trying to steady her. By the time we stumbled onto something that felt moderately like a path, the fire seemed to have moved farther away. It still didn't look far, but definitely not as close as I'd thought it was.

11:30. When I glanced back at Mom's boundary, I couldn't see it, not a single stab of faded orange post.

"Is it weird that I wish it was midnight?" Greta said, rubbing her neck and upper back.

"It is somewhere," I muttered. "You said so yourself."

Nervously, she followed me through the trees, slipping along the thin line of erosion we were using to guide our steps. I wondered if she'd ever crossed Mom's posts after I'd stopped coming to the woods with her. Did she know these woods any better than I did? I glanced at the line of smoke. At least Greta knew a lot about trees and navigation and animal paths and stuff.

Which could be very useful, since when I looked up again, the smoke felt a little thinner, a little farther. Like we were going the wrong direction. Not only that, but a mass of clouds was beginning to cover the stars, inking over the moon, threatening rain.

"Come on," I said. "I want to get there before it rains out."

We walked another half mile, and I swear it felt like the line of smoke was walking away from us. I could still see it, even through the thickening clouds, but it felt every bit as far away as it had when we shimmied through the fence.

Greta nibbled away at her granola bars one after the other—the oat and honey version of chain smoking.

When I was pretty sure we'd logged at least another couple miles, I pulled out my phone. It said 11:45, which couldn't be right. I stopped, turned a circle.

"Distances are difficult to track," Greta said, which I didn't consider helpful. "You know they've done studies..." she continued.

I held up my hand. "I don't have the energy to hear about studies right now, Gret. And you *know* we haven't been walking for just fifteen minutes."

She gave a brief nod and went back to her granola bar.

"Maybe my phone is catching a cell tower from a different time zone," I said. It was common enough here near the state border when Georgia was Eastern time, but we weren't.

She didn't answer, except to add, "Also, people usually walk in circles, even when they don't think they are." She turned around, a little hopefully. "Are we back home?"

"No," I answered, an edge to my voice. She was on her third or fourth granola bar by now, nibbling at the edges like a mouse. "But no matter what, it's got to be at least midnight, probably well past. So we've missed the killer's deadline. After all, it's Alabama, not California."

She crinkled her wrapper and shoved the trash into her pocket. "The deadline was for when the kids vanished," she said, her voice a tinny line as she stared into the dark trees all around us. "We don't actually know when the kids got killed. None of the bodies were ever found."

"Jeez, Gret," I replied, trying my best to keep my language in check.

And then we stumbled onto it—a black charred circle, abandoned marshmallows and beer cans surrounding it.

But not a soul.

I stood for a second, feeling that stun-gun feeling. Had we missed it? Had they really ended it just after midnight? Maybe since it wasn't May anymore or something. But in the distance, through the low-hanging clouds, I could still see that line of smoke. It finally looked a little closer.

"This was probably an old one," I said, the realization hitting me. "They've been doing these parties all month."

"I'm cold," Greta murmured, pulling her jacket tight around her, a few more crumbs falling to the ground. "And all scraped up." She rubbed her upper back, just below her neck, and I noticed a scratch where a branch or maybe even the barbed wire had gotten her when we crawled through. "Also tired."

"I know," I said. "I'm tired too." And I was. Really, really tired. But we were almost there. "Come on," I said. "You can lie down by the fire when we get there."

That would serve me on a couple levels. It would keep Greta warm, happy, and sleepy. Which would get her out of my hair. I'd been so focused on getting to the bonfire that I hadn't really thought about how fantastically uncool it would look to show up with my little sister. Whatever. I would just claim she followed me. Which wasn't a lie. Besides, Savina's twin followed her everywhere, and we all knew he was a little slow. How was this different? Greta was younger, but smarter. They should get along just fine.

I tore through the underbrush.

Greta tripped, and I turned back, helping her up. "Come on, Gret. It's not far. At this point, it's probably the best and safest place we can be."

"Because you don't know how to get home?" she said. No sass or meanness in her tone. Just truth.

After a few seconds, I asked, "Do you?"

She shook her head. "Let's just get there."

"'Kay," I replied, holding out my hand. She took it, like when we were younger. I'd been trying to make her feel better, but I had to admit that her smaller hand felt nice in mine. "Your fingers are ice cubes, Gret."

"I thought it'd be warmer," she replied.

"Yeah, me too." I glanced up as a low cloud covered the moon completely, heard the distant rumble of thunder. Cursing, I dragged both of us through the woods. Maybe I should have just cowboyed up and asked Savina out on an actual date instead of doing this weird thing. But it was too late for that right now.

A flash of light seared the sky, followed by the crack of thunder. Greta sniffled, just a bit, in that hidden sort of way. The same way I used to when Mom and Dad were yelling at each other and I didn't want to be heard.

The next rumble was a lot closer. A streak of lightning that shot down in front of us, one of those pretty ones. It was a lot less pretty when you were alone in the woods with your little sister.

But we were still doing okay, because right after the flash, I smelled it—actual smoke. "Almost there, Gret."

She dragged her legs, practically sleepwalking beside me. But she must have smelled it too, because she gave me a little smile.

"Bonfire or bust," she said.

"Bonfire or bust."

❧

BUST.

When we finally arrived at the source of the smoke, it wasn't a bonfire at all. Just an old, abandoned house. One side smoking, like it had been struck by lightning.

I let a big swear slip from my mouth. "Sorry, Gret," I mumbled. I knew she hated when I cursed, since it reminded her of Mom and Dad and yelling.

"'S okay," she murmured, gazing at the house.

It wasn't big, but what it lacked in width, it made up for in dilapidation—tall and rickety, moss growing along the shingles, vines creeping up the edges and snaking under the front door. It stood two stories, the bottom half almost twice as big as the skinny top, which looked like it'd been pasted on with Elmer's glue. Two chimneys piped out of the lower half—one at the front, one at the back.

The front door had a chunk missing from the bottom, like mice had been picking at it for ages, and right above the front door, an abandoned bird's nest hung in a crooked corner of the ancient awning.

"Whoa," I said, just as another crack of thunder opened up the skies. The rain crashed down in sheets and waves of water, deep-south style. Grammy used to say it was like God dumping out His wash bucket. Which was exactly what it felt like as we dashed for the house, the rain pelting us with the force of thousands of tiny needles.

We hunkered under the crooked awning, barely able to see through the rain to the forest we had just come from. Greta and I pressed as close as we could to the front door, its paint peeling off in ribbons onto our clothes like grated chocolate. "Who even paints a door brown?" I asked, dusting the flecks of old paint off my clothes.

"I like it," Greta said, sniffing at the door, then the air. "It smells sweet."

"Rain always smells sweet," I grumbled.

She sniffed again, staying under the ledge of the roof and walking along the house to the place that was scorched.

"Greta," I hissed, following her. At the scorch mark, the varnish of the wood had bubbled up like burned caramel, and I had to admit, it *did* smell sweet, sweeter than rain.

"It's nice," Greta said.

"Great, now let's get back under the awning before the rain gets even worse," I said, sounding more like Mom than I cared to.

I tipped my gaze up at the sky, looking for a break in the clouds, a glimpse of moon, something to indicate that this storm was going to pass quickly so we could go home. The party, if it had still been going, was definitely over now. And all I wanted was a hot shower and my warm bed.

Greta stood up on her tiptoes and peeked into one of the windows, the glass wavy and old, like it had been hand-blown a hundred years ago. I was surprised it wasn't cracked or broken out by the wildness of the forest.

"Should we go in?" she asked. "To get out of the rain."

"Definitely not," I said. "It doesn't exactly look structurally sound."

She nodded, scooting her way to another section of the wall and looking in a new window. "I guess we better call Mama," she said, not looking at me.

"Are you kidding?" I asked, just as another streak of lightning fired up the sky and another burst of rain exploded through the forest.

Greta scampered back to the awning, doing her best to stay

dry. "I think we've got to," she said. "Blame me if you want. Say I went out into the woods."

"Yeah, like she'll believe that," I grumbled. But I got out my phone. There were times to man up and deal with the consequences. And this kind of seemed like one of them. But when I held my phone up, the screen was black. I flipped it over, pressed the power button. Nothing. "That's weird," I muttered. "I charged it before I came. Something must have been running and sucked up the battery. You got any service?"

She pulled out the ancient phone she'd inherited from Mom. It barely worked in the best of times, and was only really reliable when there was Wi-Fi. So...not right now. Still, she clicked it on—hitting Mom's number. It pulled up for a second, trying to dial, then died, her screen black just like mine.

"Maybe she has her Find My Friends on," Greta said with a small voice.

"Even if she did, it wouldn't work with our phones dead."

The rain hadn't let up at all, pelting the ground in hard, angry splashes. Greta was starting to shiver in earnest. We were wet. We were tired. And it looked like we might have to wait for the morning sunshine to find our way home

I pressed gingerly on the door. Something sticky smeared onto my fingers, but the door creaked open. I wiped my hands on my wet jeans, then brushed away a few cobwebs.

"Come on," I said. "Let's go in."

"I thought you said it was structurally unsound," she replied. "And what if another lightning bolt hits the house?"

"You know better than I do what the odds are of that. So I'm cutting our losses. Let's just try to stay as dry and warm as possible."

She didn't argue. If anything, she perked up a little at the prospect of going inside.

I stepped through the door, into the darkness.

CHAPTER 8

HANS

Without our phones, all we had for light were the irregular flashes of lightning that illuminated the house every few minutes. I tried to gauge whether the storm was getting farther or nearer, but it seemed to have settled right over top of us.

Greta knocked around the room, exploring it. A small table stood near an old rocking chair, and she felt around on the table.

"Gross. Don't touch that," I said.

"Looking for candles," she replied. "An old house like this should have some."

"An old house like this doesn't have anything but the occasional rat."

"Wrong again," she answered, holding up a long white candle. Just as a flash of lightning sent a blinding light through the window, making everything look pale and dead.

"Put it down, Gret. We don't even have matches."

"Of course we do," she said, digging through her little backpack. "I always have some."

A few seconds later, the candle was burning.

I had to admit, I appreciated that tiny amount of light. At least until I looked around the rest of the room, which appeared unsettled and abandoned—like someone had just been here and left. Except that *just been here* felt like a hundred years ago.

The table where Greta had found the candle was covered with scraps of molding fabric, rusting needles, and an iron candlestick, which Greta picked up, jamming the candle onto it.

"Well, that's nice," she said.

"Is it?" I asked, turning toward an old fireplace. Leaves and twigs had blown in through the chimney, filling most of the fireplace with debris, though you could still see streaks of ash at the bottom of the hearth. To the left, a few rotten logs rested in a cast iron grate. Around the fireplace, the wood of the floor was slightly bowed and charred, like the fire used to get too hot.

"Too bad we probably can't make a fire," she said.

"Yeah, I think that chimney is full of a hundred years' worth of leaves, and probably a family of raccoons or something."

Greta held up her candle and we both took in the rest of the room. The only other piece of furniture was a broken bench that someone maybe used to sit on while they put on their shoes. In fact, two boots still rested under the bench, standing upright, all cracked black leather and decaying laces.

Greta picked one up, inspecting it. "Hans, look at this. It must be ancient. And such a tiny foot. Like mine." She held it up to her own foot.

"Put that down," I growled.

"Why?" she asked, giving me an annoyed look, made worse from the glare of the candle. "It's just old stuff. I think it's amazing. How have we not found this house before?"

"Things get lost in the woods," I said. "Kind of like us. Now let's find a place where we can sit down that doesn't involve too many dust mites or spiders or roaches or mice. As soon as it's dawn, we can make our way home. I think our house is to the east, so we'll just follow the sunrise."

"That sounds nice," Greta said, sleepily.

"Sure does," I grumbled. "You take the rocking chair." I blew off the dust, or some of it, and Greta sneezed. "And I'll find a place on the floor."

"'Kay," she said, settling into the chair and placing the candlestick on the table beside her. "This is where someone must have done her sewing. I feel like we fell back in time. It's kind of cool."

"Yeah," I said, not because I thought it was, but because I just wanted her to be quiet and try to sleep.

"And look at that." She pointed to the wall where an old cuckoo clock hung. "Do you think it still works?"

"Nah," I said. "The little door is all broken, and the hands aren't moving at all."

"Too bad," she said. "It'd be nice to know what time it is. What time does it say?"

I squinted in the dim light. "11:00-something maybe. It's hard to see. You can look in the morning."

She nodded, curling up in the rocking chair.

"You better blow the candle out," I said, trying to position my head comfortably on the floor.

"Take my backpack," Greta said.

"Thanks," I said, cramming the mini backpack under my head. It was a little soggy from the rain, but still softer than the floor. "Sorry I got us stuck out in the woods."

"I like being stuck in the woods," she answered. "And I was the one who followed you. Good thing though," she said, smiling at the candle. "What would you have done without me?"

"Whatever," I answered back, teasing. "It's just like camping with Dad."

"I never camped with Dad," she said.

I stared at the ceiling. "Oh, yeah. I guess you were too little."

"How was it?" she asked. "Camping? Dad?"

I propped up onto my arm. "Do you really not remember him?"

She shrugged. "Some things, but I was just four when he left."

"I know," I said. "What do you remember?"

She squinted into the darkness. "The color of his eyes. Gray-blue. Just like yours."

"Yeah," I muttered. Sunshine hair, stormy eyes. Exactly the way our mother liked to describe me. "My hair was the same as his too."

She looked at me, shook her head. "Nah," she said. "I'd remember his hair if it was."

"What else do you remember?" I asked.

"Piggybacks," she said.

"That's it?" I asked.

"Basically," she answered.

"He used to dance with you," I said. "Swing you around the room. I was always a little jealous because he said I was too big." And a boy. But I didn't add that part. Something inside of me wished I didn't remember it at all. Boys didn't get to dance. Boys wrestled. Which had worked out I guess, since these days—now that I was nearly seventeen—I didn't want to dance anyway. At least not with my parents.

"He screamed a lot too," she said.

"But not at us," I added quickly.

She cocked her head to the side, like she was trying to remember, like she thought I might be wrong. But I didn't remember him yelling at me, not once. Just him and Mom—back and forth—sometimes for days on end. Or at least that was how it felt.

And then, one day, the screaming ended. He'd walked out, and hadn't come back. I was nine at the time.

Mom replaced her screaming with crying. "Do you remember how you used to pat Mom on the back when she was crying?" I asked.

Greta nodded, her head barely moving in the darkness.

"Like you were the mom," I murmured.

"Just for a bit," she answered.

"Yeah," I murmured. I hadn't patted Mom on the back. I hadn't comforted her at all. I'd just hung back, waiting for all of it to end, waiting for Dad to come back, to apologize like I'd heard him do a thousand times. But he didn't. Not that day. Not that week. Not yet. It'd been eight years.

"She did better," Greta said. "After a while."

And now it was my turn to nod in the darkness. I honestly didn't remember any kind of divorce settlement, but there must have been something. Mom had moved us to the old house by the woods that used to belong to her grandmother—our great-grammy. She'd started working nights at the hospital. Before Dad left she used to work one shift a week while we'd gone to our Grammy's house, which was really a condo downtown.

We never went there now. A couple years after Dad left, Grammy had died from cancer.

Then it was just me, Greta, and Mom. And our great-grammy's house with a million rooms and peeling wallpaper and an old servant staircase where Greta and I used to play hide-and-seek, back when we played things like that.

"Remember playing hide-and-seek?" I asked.

"Of course," she answered.

"Kind of feels like that now," I said. "Even though that doesn't make sense since we're both together."

"And not hiding on purpose," she replied, with a little laugh.

I smiled in the darkness. "'Night, Gret."

"'Night," she answered, sucking in a breath to blow out the candle just as we heard a scratching outside of the door.

"It's just an animal," I said quickly, trying to convince myself as much as Greta.

But then the animal started to whimper, and the whimper

sounded a whole lot like a human girl. Greta cast a quick glance at the tiny boots, then shook her head like she was shaking off a thought.

I cleared my throat. The crying got louder, followed by a soft, deep shushing noise.

"Hello," I said, because I couldn't just ignore a crying girl, even if part of me was worried she was some kind of serial killer's trap. And I could tell by Greta's wide eyes that she was thinking the same thing.

The crying stopped.

"Hello," I said again, a little louder.

And then the door burst open. "Hank!"

In the dim light of Greta's still-lit candle, I could see the black eyes and blacker hair. Dripping wet.

"Savina?" I said into the darkness.

She spilled into the room, rain-soaked and tear-streaked. "I'm so glad to see you. We were at the party and it started to rain and we got lost."

I looked past her. Her brother was skulking in the shadows of the room, looking down at his shoes, his hands thrust into his pockets. "Oh hey, Gideon," I said.

He nodded, still not making eye contact.

"It's so good to hear your voice," Savina gushed. "You have no idea. We've been walking around in the rain for at least an hour, probably longer, but I can't tell because our phones died."

I looked outside. Had it been that long?

"Yeah," I said. "We never even found the party. We just skipped the fun part and started with the getting lost."

"We?" Savina asked, glancing around and then jumping back when she noticed Greta.

It *was* mildly terrifying. In the rocking chair, Greta looked a little like a deranged granny, with her small frame and the candle lighting up odd lines in her pale face.

She gave a little wave.

Savina laughed nervously. "Girl, I did *not* see you there."

"I'm closest to the candle," Greta replied matter-of-factly.

And I couldn't be sure in the dim light, but it almost felt like Savina blushed. "Yeah, I just heard Hank, and I guess I was only focused on him."

"Plus, you didn't expect me to bring my little sister to a midnight party," I said, giving Greta a look.

"I followed him," she replied, without the tiniest bit of apology in her voice. "And we found this cool house."

Savina and I exchanged a quick glance. "I have to admit I'm glad you did," she said. "I was too scared to go inside until I heard your voice. But I guess you probably heard me, uh, freaking out." She blushed again.

"It's kind of a freaky thing to get lost in the woods," I said. "Honestly, I'm impressed you knew it was me."

And I could pretty much swear that Savina blushed a third time.

"It's cozy," Greta said. I wasn't sure if she was serious, or teasing Savina, or trying to torture me.

"It's something," Savina said. "And it's dry." She glanced around, squinting in the darkness, then shaking her phone like that would make it turn on. "Man, my dad is going to *kill* me."

"Join the club," I said. "I guess that's better than a serial killer."

We all laughed.

Until the cuckoo clock on the wall began to chime.

I jumped, Savina screamed, and Greta hopped off the rocking chair, grabbing the candle. For the first few cuckoos, we all stared. Then Gideon walked toward the clock, his head cocked to the side.

For one brief moment, I thought he was going to take out his fist and pummel the thing to the ground. Maybe that's because that's what I wanted to do.

Instead, he stared into the eyes of the cuckoo as it sang out its song, then adjusted the door that was broken. A little nest was under the cuckoo bird, and it was broken too, a small blue egg resting in the ceramic straw.

Greta stood nearby, holding up her candle. At the eleventh cuckoo, she looked back at me. The bird let out one more cuckoo and tried to retreat back behind the miniature door. Only it got a little stuck, the bird halfway in and halfway out. Gideon fiddled with it, but it wouldn't budge.

"It says it's midnight," Gideon said, the first words he'd spoken—that slow lilt to his voice. Greta's eyebrows bent toward each other, looking slightly haunted in the candlelight.

"I can't believe that thing still works," Savina said with a nervous laugh.

"I mean, clearly it doesn't," I added. "It's got to be way past midnight."

"Well, yeah," Savina replied, staring at it. "Obviously."

But none of us moved, watching the clock as it slowly ticked toward 12:01.

I shook myself out of it first. "Should we try to get some sleep? It'll probably be dawn in a couple of hours and we can make our way home. We don't live too far," I said. "Our house is to the east, so we'll just follow the dawn."

"Poetic," Savina replied.

I looked out the window into the black night, rain still pounding away, the windows dripping with sticky tears. At least I hoped we didn't live too far. At this point, it was impossible to know how far we'd come, since it was impossible to know what time it was, or anything else.

Greta settled back into the rocking chair, still watching the clock, the minute hand now ticking steadily. I wasn't sure if she'd blinked.

"You trying to win a staring contest?" I asked, hoping to make her smile.

She turned to me. "One of us should stay up," she said, her

voice soft but heavy, her excitement at the house worn out by the midnight cuckoo. "As a lookout."

"Shouldn't be too hard," I replied, blowing out the candle for her. "Since I'm not sure any of us can sleep on this floor anyway."

She nodded and I tried to smile reassuringly. "Go to sleep, Gret. One of us will stay awake."

But no one did.

HANS

Day 1

I bolted up in a sweat, the first light wobbling through the wavy windows. Greta. The woods, the serial killer, the cuckoo clock. It had made a sad, squeaky chime. A sound that hadn't woken anyone else. Greta was still asleep on the rocking chair, snoring softly.

Savina and Gideon looked fine too, curled into little balls facing away from each other, their sides rising and falling in a nearly synchronized rhythm. Breathing. Everyone still here. Everyone alive.

Of course.

I released a little puff of relieved breath, and sat up, cracking my back.

The stupid cuckoo clock now said six fifteen. Yeah, totally broken—what clock chimes at 6:15? Somehow, though, the bird had managed to slip back inside its little doors. And outside it did *look* like 6:15.

I couldn't remember falling asleep, but something in the rhythm of the rain, in the perfect darkness of a house in the middle of a forest—it must have lulled all of us to sleep.

But now we could go home.

"Gret," I murmured. "Wake up. It's morning. Come on, let's get moving. Maybe we can still beat Mom, hop into bed. When she gets home, we'll just tell her we don't feel well and need more sleep. It'll be like we never left."

Savina stirred at the sound of my voice. Her brother, I noticed, had already rolled over and was looking out the window into the orange dawn.

"Man, every bone in my body hurts," I grumbled.

Savina shifted to her stomach and pushed up. "You can say that again." She walked over to her brother and put a soft hand on his back. "At least the rain stopped."

Around the house, little birds were singing as the light of the sun changed from an early peach to a morning daffodil.

"Let's go," I said.

Greta glanced at her unlit candle, burned over halfway down, then back at the cuckoo clock. "Yeah, let's go," she said, all the adventure washed out of her voice. "I'm starving."

"No more granola bars?" I asked.

"All gone," she mumbled, picking up her small backpack from the space where my head had been and taking out a water bottle. "Who stayed up?" she asked.

"Well…" I said.

She glanced at me. "You promised…"

"I didn't," I answered, cutting her off. "I just said…"

"That you would stay up."

"That we wouldn't be able to sleep anyway. Which apparently was wrong. But it's okay, Gret. Everything worked out. Let's just go home."

"Okay," she said softly. Her hair was tangled on one side where the curls had fallen out of the worn braid, forming little knots along the side of her face and neck. "You really think we'll beat Mom?"

"Maybe," I said, even though it seemed unlikely. But at this point, I didn't care. I was just glad we'd be going home.

Gideon opened the door, Savina following. Greta took a gulp of her water, then swung her backpack over her shoulders, giving the candle one final glance. I waved her toward the door, trying to hurry her along, then turned my back on the messy house, glancing down at the broken bench with the little pair of boots underneath it.

Except there were no boots.

I stopped right in front of the door and Greta practically tripped into me.

"What's wrong?" she asked.

"Nothing," I said, moving swiftly through the door and pulling Greta behind me. "Let's just go home."

CHAPTER 10

GRETA

Something was definitely wrong. And not just with Hans, who kept looking over his shoulder and all around every five seconds. But with the whole thing.

There really were studies where they would take people hooked to GPS out into the woods and tell them to walk a straight line. They never could. Circles, figure eights, swirly loops of all types. But mostly circles.

I had always wondered why they didn't just walk toward or away from the sun. But apparently, that wasn't as easy as it sounded.

Because after walking for over an hour, we found ourselves right back at the path that led to the house. Right back where we had been last night. It looked different in the day, prettier for sure, but the same path.

A long line of mushrooms circled the back part of the property and stretched deep into the woods, like an arch of toadstools standing guard. A short distance from the mushrooms I could see an abandoned garden, full of weeds and surrounded by a fence that must have been white once. There was even an old shed for ponies or goats. It had a tall door with cast iron bars from top to bottom, a rusty lock still hanging off of it.

"Oh no," Hans said. Savina stood beside him, her brother at her elbow, looking up into the trees instead of over at the house like the rest of us.

"How?" Savina asked.

"Studies have shown…" I began, but Hans cut me off.

"Here's another path," he said. "A different one."

Savina nodded. "How'd they do it back in the day? You'd think the sun would steer us better."

Hans must have been stressed because he didn't bother to answer, even though he'd been crushing on Savina for over a year, and she was clearly trying to lighten the mood.

She kept trying too, all the way through the next hour. Until we wound up back at the house again.

Hans looked almost gray. Like he was going to cry. I'd only seen him cry once, and it was the day our dad hadn't come home. I looked away from him, staring at my shoes, at the ground. It was then that I saw them. "Hans," I said.

"Hang on, Gret. I'm trying to think." His voice definitely had a wobble—a wobble I was pretty sure only I knew well enough to notice, but still a wobble.

"Hans," I repeated.

"Greta," he said, turning on me like he was going to start yelling—the tone of voice he always took with Mama when they argued. "I know you're hungry, but it's going to have to—"

And then he stopped. He stared down, right where I was staring. "Are those—?"

"Yeah," I said. "Remember how I kept eating those granola bars."

"Crumbs," he murmured. "Greta, you and your insatiable appetite are heroes. We'll follow them home. Might be a little roundabout, but you were eating practically the whole time, right?"

"What?" Savina asked.

"Greta was chomping on these granola bars all last night while we walked," Hans said. "And look." He pointed at the ground. "A little mushy after the rain, but we can still follow her trail."

"Guess that's as good an idea as anything," Savina said.

Gideon was still looking into the trees—watching the birds who were singing and playing, oblivious to all the human drama down below. For a moment, he looked like the woods himself— that strange combination of something always there, but ever-changing. And then, like everyone else, he turned his gaze to the crumbs.

Fortunately for all of us, I was an absolute slob, so there were crumbs about every five feet.

It was slow going, but it was going. Another hour, then two. I passed my water bottle around and we all took sips. How many miles had we walked?

As the sun started to turn downward from its high point in the sky, we came to a dense thicket of trees. I didn't remember it exactly, but there was something about it that looked familiar.

Maybe it was that every tree was laden with fungi. It reminded me of the partial fairy ring at the house, that army of mushrooms curving through the woods.

Just past the trees, the crumbs stopped.

We all stopped too, Gideon leaning against a tree, watching a group of crows, pecking at a place on the ground.

"Oh no," Savina said.

"Get away," I shouted, waving my arms at the crows.

Gideon stepped back, as though I'd lost my mind. Maybe I had. On every side, there were birds of all kinds, touching down, eating the crumbs.

"Calm down, Gret," Hans said, though he had that gray look again, the one like he might cry. "Let's just retrace our steps.

They couldn't have eaten all the crumbs. We just have to catch the path again."

But we didn't, couldn't.

My stomach rumbled, making an earnest plea. Gideon's was growling too. I could hear it. Neither of us complained, though Hans cast guilty glances at me every few steps as we walked through the woods. Looking for crumbs that weren't there.

All at once, Hans stopped. His face full gray, all the color washed away. When I came up beside him, I saw it too. The old house in front of us, crooked, still smelling faintly like smoke and sweetness, despite all the rain.

Hans put his head in his hands. I saw him, could almost feel him sucking up the breaths.

"Maybe not a path this time," Gideon said in his slow drawl.

None of the rest of us said a word. We just followed Gideon through the woods, over thick branches and patches of vine and bramble that tripped and scratched us. One branch hit right below my neck—the same place I'd hurt the night before—and stung. When I reached to touch it, I could feel the line of a welt.

The sun had turned dark yellow, still high, but tipping toward the horizon.

I sucked up a sniffle. If Hans could hold it in, then so could I. But Hans must have heard. He took my hand, seemingly without thinking. "It's okay, Gret. We'll just follow the sun…"

"It's too late."

"We'll go away from the sun, then," he said.

I shook my head, all through another mile, then two, another hour. Until we came to the house again.

Hans realized it with a curse.

The little path to our left, the curve of toadstools that marked the property's edge.

My stomach growled and my legs felt like logs, stomping along the same course over and over again. Hans had gotten through the day without crying, but I wasn't sure I was going to make it. My stomach grumbled again, even louder, and I cleared my throat, trying to push away the tears before they came gushing out.

Gideon dug into his pocket, pulling out a warm and crumpled leftover bag of marshmallows. He held it out to me, looking away.

"There are just a few," Savina said, by way of apology, looking a little embarrassed at the mashed white mess.

"For you," Gideon said.

"Thank you," I said.

He nodded and Savina turned toward the setting sun, which was undeniably low in the sky.

"One more try," Savina said and I heard the tremor in her voice too. She looked at me with a wobbly smile, her eyes glassy. She reached down to touch my shoulder. Just as a man walked out of the clearing.

We froze.

The man was old, maybe eighty or ninety, which under normal circumstances wouldn't feel threatening. But we were all doing the math in our heads—I could almost hear it— because a person of that age...

He was carrying a basket—a small wicker basket covered with a blue cloth—and limping along toward us. I watched like it was slow motion—the man reaching toward the cloth, about to remove something.

Hans grabbed my hand. Savina took my other hand as well as her brother's. Hans took a breath like he was about to say something, just as the man called out, "Hello there. Could you all help me with something?" He reached into the basket.

"Run," Hans shouted, drowning out the man's voice as the four of us tore through the woods hand in hand, not caring if we ripped through blackberry bushes or ran over poison ivy.

It wasn't an hour this time, not even close. Just a quick twenty minutes before we found ourselves back at the house.

Hans turned to run again. A different direction, any direction.

But the rest of us stopped.

It was Savina who broke the silence, her glassy eyes turning to full-on tears—the same sobbing we'd heard the night before. Her brother cradled her in the crook of his arm, awkward, but gentle as her shoulders heaved up and down.

"I'm sorry," she said through the tears. "This is so embarrassing."

"It's okay," I said, patting her back just like I used to with Mama.

Hans turned and slumped to the ground, his shoulders rounded forward, the gray look in his face, all the way to the eyes. "They'll send a search party," he grumbled. "They probably already have. It's been a whole day. We just...we just have to wait it out and they'll find us soon enough. They've got dogs and helicopters and—" He lifted his head, then stopped talking.

I turned to see the thing he was staring at. A little corner of blue, peeking out from behind a tree. He jumped up and grabbed my hand again, like we were going to run, like he was going to drag me whether I ran or not.

But I resisted. There was something about the blue. So still, not even a breeze to catch and move it.

"Wait," I whispered.

Savina went silent, unfolding herself from the crook of Gideon's arm. We all stared at the fabric. And the thing that rested beside it, nearly white as bone and just as still. A hand.

"Let's just run," Hans hissed.

I shook my head. "Wait."

It felt like hours, the sun sinking another inch until it was a bright orange ball on the horizon.

It was Gideon who finally took the first step forward, the second step too. Savina came up beside me and took my hand, like I was eight, not twelve, and we all watched Gideon. One step after the other. Maybe we should have tried to stop him, but that bone-white hand drew all of us to it. It hadn't moved, not a millimeter.

"He's dead," Gideon said, the lilt to his voice just as steady as always.

Hans strode toward Gideon, then stopped abruptly, a few paces away from the body. "Are you sure? It could be some sick trick."

Savina and I were inching closer and we could see it too—the nearly white man, his mouth hanging open, eyes empty and half-closed, body slumped against the tree. The basket lay discarded beside him, a little brown card sticking out past the edge.

Gideon took the card. "Please deliver these to my sister at the cottage in the woods. She needs them."

Savina took the card. "Something's on the back." She tipped her head to the side. "Huh, German. *Wenn die sechs weg sind, wird der rest leben.*"

"Do you know what it means?" Hans asked. "You're taking German at school, right?"

Savina nodded slowly. *"When the six are gone, the rest will live."*

"Well, that's not creepy at all," Hans said.

"Was he the killer?" Savina whispered, as though he could still hear her.

"We are NOT going near that house," Hans said. "It could still be some kind of a sick trap."

But Gideon was on his knees by the body, examining it, his hand on the man's chest, then neck. "Stiff," Gideon said. "Dead for a while."

"How long has it even been?" Savina asked, then looked at the sun and sighed.

I squeezed my lips together, feeling the pinch of my stomach, the hunger biting in the back of my throat. I walked over to Hans and then a little farther to where Gideon knelt.

"Stay back, Greta," Hans said.

"He's dead," I said, lifting the blue cloth to look into the basket. "And these are eggs. Just eggs."

Hans and Savina moved closer, huddling over the basket. The eggs were different sizes, different colors—each unique—as though collected from a variety of birds in the woods. Beige, gray-blue, olive green, whitish-pink, and two speckled ones—one dark and a tiny one that was bright blue.

"No wonder the birds stay high up around here, with this nut job stealing all their eggs," Savina finally said.

I glanced at her. She made jokes when she was nervous, and I liked her for it.

Hans was looking at the man now. Due to Gideon's examination, the man had slumped to the ground, one hand extended out into the dead leaves.

"Stop touching him, bro," Hans said. "The cops'll see your fingerprints. It's bad enough that we're already going to have to tell them all this. When they find us."

Gideon shrugged, but Savina looked slightly alarmed. "Do you think this man was the actual killer?"

"Could be," Hans said. "Who knows? He's the right age. Plenty creepy. Hanging out in the middle of the freaking woods. But he needs to update his catch-the-children game with some candy or something. Who's gonna go for a basket of eggs?" Now Hans was the one making nervous jokes.

"There's no weapon," Gideon said, matter-of-factly.

"Maybe he was just a delirious old man," Savina said. "Trapped in the woods like us."

"Well, hopefully we don't get trapped for quite so long," I said, trying out my own little nervous joke. It didn't land. Everyone except Gideon stared at me with a look of horror.

"Just kidding," I said, holding up my hands.

"Not the right time," Hans replied, backing away from the body.

The sun hung halfway below the horizon now. It hadn't helped us find our way home. Rather, it seemed to have led us back again and again. To the old cottage. Just as dark, just as dusty.

The night before, I'd wanted to explore it. I'd wanted to come back after we'd gotten home and gotten a nap. It would have been my own special place in the woods.

I didn't want that anymore. In fact, I wasn't sure I even had the courage to turn around and look at it. But I knew the house was there; we all knew it was there. Waiting. Behind us.

Once again, it was Gideon who took the first steps.

❧

"Do you think he lived there?" Savina asked. "The old man?"

We had trailed behind Gideon and then stopped, still in the woods, the three of us now staring at the house from the shelter of the trees.

It definitely looked different in the day than it had at night. In fact, if we hadn't all been so spooked, it might have even looked charming—despite the peeling, mud-brown paint on the front door.

Woodpeckers had hammered generations of pock marks into the exterior wood, but the foundation looked solid, cemented together with brick and broken bits of quartz. It sparkled. Much like the roof, which was made with some type of thin stone that caught the light of the setting sun—except for the places where pieces had cracked or broken. In those spots, old mortar baked in the sun, exposed in clumps and drips, like a badly iced cake.

"Truthfully," Hans said. "That house didn't look like anyone had lived in it for a hundred years. The fireplace hadn't been used for forever, or any of the stuff. Even the dust hadn't been disturbed. So I would say no, he didn't live there. But I do wonder if that psychopath thought someone did. If he kept coming here, looking for someone—maybe he was just some kind of weird deranged guy. Or a killer who became deranged. Criminals who have done terrible stuff have to be pretty messed up mentally."

"Or maybe he was messed up mentally and did terrible stuff, not understanding," I said.

Hans didn't even grace me with a reply, but Savina—who was still holding my hand—gave it a squeeze.

"Or maybe he was just a lost old man with dementia," she said. "Someone who hadn't done any horrible stuff at all, but who was very confused. Do they still have that retirement home near the woods?"

Hans shook his head, which I wasn't sure was a reply or not.

We watched Gideon make his way to the little clearing in front of the awning, the same awning Hans and I had hunkered under the night before. I glanced back at the eggs, my stomach grumbling. Releasing Savina's hand, I retraced my steps.

"Greta," Hans' voice rang out sharply.

I picked up the eggs.

Hans bolted back to me and just about smacked them out of my hands. "Put those down!"

"No," I said.

Savina looked from us to her brother. "Greta, maybe just put them down. We can't deliver them to anyone. That man was just…troubled."

"There's nobody in the house," Hans said, swiping at the basket and trying to get it out of my hands.

"No kidding," I said. "Which is why I'm taking these stupid eggs."

"And what, exactly, do you plan to do with them if you can't give them to that man's fake sister?" Hans asked, facing off with me.

I stared back. "I plan to eat them," I said. "If we can't find anything else. I know it's gross, but I don't know how long we're going to be here. I don't know how long it will take the search parties to find us. The woods back there are huge. We just wandered for a whole day and didn't even begin to find our way back. I don't know how long it will take to be found, but I'm taking these in case it's a while. We don't have to eat them today, but if we get hungry enough, we can."

Gideon had wandered to another exterior corner of the house, inspecting the burn like I did last night, and waiting for us.

"She's right," Savina muttered. "Whether he was a killer or not, they're just eggs. Regular bird eggs. You can't very well poison regular eggs." She peeked into the basket. "I mean, it kind of seems like he thought he was helping someone with these eggs. Like, maybe he had Alzheimer's or something and thought he was going to save a sister who has probably been dead for years. That's how it goes with diseases like that."

Hans grunted in response. "Then those eggs are probably rotten. Especially if he's been walking around with them for months."

"They might be," I replied. "But we'll know as soon as we break one open to cook it."

Hans shook his head, almost like a dog shaking off the water from a pond. "Fine," he said, a tiny bit of the gray leaving his face. And then he started to laugh. "Heaven forbid you get hungry, Gret. At least you've got your priorities straight."

"We could be stuck here for a week," I said, following Gideon into the clearing.

"I mean, you're not wrong," Hans said. "It's just, here I was worried cause there's a dead guy sitting there by a tree—a dead guy who's probably killed a kid every thirteen years for who knows what reason. And you're like, 'But there are eggs.'"

"It *would* be nicer if he'd tried to trick us with candy," I said.

Hans laughed louder.

"Now if we can keep from dying of thirst," Savina said, holding up my nearly empty water bottle.

But Gideon was waving us over to something he'd found—a short stone structure near the back side of the house.

"No way," Hans said, walking over to the ancient well. "No freaking way."

"There's water," Gideon said as we came up to him. He pulled a bucket from the dark depths. "Clean water."

But instead of laughing more, a little piece of the gray crept back into my brother's eyes.

"This place is just too weird," he said.

CHAPTER 11

GRETA

We poured the water from the bucket into my water bottle—as clear as the stuff from the tap.

"Impressive," Savina said.

Hans didn't respond. He was too busy scowling. And staring at the burnt side of the house—the part that smelled like blistered caramel.

He took a couple steps toward it, sniffing, then looked up at the sky. "Gret," he said. "Remember how we found this place?"

"Um, yeah," I replied. "It only happened last night." Though it did feel like forever ago.

"No," he said. "No, I mean. Remember why we found it, when we'd never found it before in all the time we've spent in these woods—remember what we were following?"

I looked at the charred wall. "Smoke," I said, still a little confused about where he was going with all this.

"And Mom will have called the cops. Savina and Gideon's dad too. The whole town will be combing the woods. But this is just a little place that no one can see or find easily. Unless…" he paused. I wasn't sure if it was for effect, or if he was thinking it through.

"There's a fire," Savina answered before me. "It's a great idea. We'll get a fire going. It'll warm us up. We can sleep on the grass, which is better than that creepy house with the hard floor. And people can see smoke. Even at night."

"They can smell it too," Hans said, staring at the burnt caramel wall. "How many matches do you have left, Greta?"

"Almost the whole pack," I answered.

Which would have been great. Except that they'd been in my damp-from-the-rain backpack all night and all day. Most of the cardboard sticks were soggy and difficult to hold in order to strike, much less light. I tore them off one by one, laying them in a careful row to catch the light from the setting sun, hoping one of them would dry enough to light.

When I was almost through the entire matchbook, I found two that were dry, side by side at the back of the pack.

Which was good, because the gray had begun creeping back into Hans' face. "Don't light them yet," he said. "Let's get the fire ready so we don't waste them."

But the matches weren't the only things that were damp. Gideon and Savina gathered drippy twigs and straw while Hans found a few thin, sodden logs.

"It's all wet," I said, holding one of the matches.

"Just light it," Hans growled.

I did, the small flame fizzling against the soggy kindling, refusing to catch, not even nibbling along the edge of a leaf. A few puffs of smoke. Not big smoke like we needed either. Just some sad little hiccups.

"Hans," I said. "I know you wanted to do this outside, but…" I sucked on my lip, nervous to finish.

He closed his eyes, knowing what I was going to say.

"Inside the house…" I began. "Well, you know there was that fireplace."

Gideon turned, just like that, and began walking toward the

front door. Which was honestly pretty impressive, even though nobody said it.

He didn't knock, or politely nudge the door. Just banged in like the house belonged to him. "There's wood," he called through the door.

"It's a little rotten," Hans mumbled, staring at the dark open maw of the door.

"But dry," Savina said, even more quietly.

"I only have one more good match," I added. "At least until these others dry. *If* they dry."

Hans' shoulders hunched forward and he jammed his hands into his pockets. "Okay."

And, really, what else was there to say?

CHAPTER 12

HANS

By the time we got inside, Gideon had already dug half the leaves out of the chimney, setting them to the side in a careful pile. The perfect kindling.

At school, everyone always talked like Gideon was slow, and I'd always just accepted that as true. To be fair, he moved slowly, talked slowly. But so far, it seemed like he was the only one of the four of us who actually had both the guts and the calm to open a freaking door and clear out a chimney.

I kneeled next to him, pulling twigs out of the mess and arranging them in a separate pile. There didn't appear to be any raccoon families living up the chute, or mice, or squirrels for that matter. Our first win of the day.

We still had a little light coming through those wavy windows, but it wouldn't last for long. "Greta," I said. "Why don't you go see if you can find some more candles? The fire will be nice in this room, and maybe that's all we need..."

"But it'd be nice to have some candles in case it's not," Greta finished for me.

"I'm going to the kitchen," Savina said. "Greta isn't the only one who's starving, and I'm not quite ready to dig into those eggs." She glanced sideways at the basket that Greta had set on the little table by the rocking chair. "Maybe there's some canned food or something that's still good."

"Check the labels," I said. "Dying of botulism is probably the only thing worse than just plain starving to death."

"Noted," she answered. "Though I doubt any food I find will have labels. I imagine it's all home-canned."

"Here," Greta said, lighting the candle with the final match.

She brought another soggy-ish match to us and handed it—not to me—but to Gideon.

"This one's pretty dry," she said. "Try it. If it doesn't work, we can use the candle to light things."

Which was also a great idea. Because the candle would stay lit easier and longer than a match.

Though we didn't need it. Gideon made quick work of the damp match—striking it against the bricks of the fireplace, then lighting the leaves he'd put at the bottom of the pile. "Like smoking meat with your dad," he said.

And I felt like I should add something, but couldn't think of anything, because I'd definitely never smoked meat with my dad.

Truth be told, I hadn't seen or talked to my dad at all in over three years. So I settled into my job of stacking on leaves and twigs, then eventually one of the old logs, which was only a little rotten. What it was, however, was light.

"Gonna burn fast," I said.

"There's probably something behind that shed out back," Gideon answered.

"Guys," Savina called from the kitchen, her voice pitched up a notch.

Gideon jumped up and rushed her direction, leaving me to follow him. Again.

She'd placed Greta's little candle in the middle of an old table that was surrounded by three stools.

"Look at that thing," she said, pointing to the inside wall.

We turned obediently. And I don't know what I was expecting—a monster or something. What I was not expecting was a huge brick stove that looked kind of like a pizza oven. A few black-white coals lay in the bottom, and it still had the paddle someone must have once used to slide bread inside.

"This thing is huge," Savina said. "You could cook a whole pig in it."

"Maybe once someone did," I answered. "Or lots of bread. This floor kind of feels like the type of floor where someone baked and never cleaned—all sticky and dusty and yuck."

"It's so weird in such a little house," Savina said. "Like, whoever lived here couldn't have been rich."

"But might have hunted," I said. "They'd need somewhere to cook the meat."

"Yeah, true," she said. "Not how I pictured an old cottage, I guess. But cool."

"So, food?" I asked, realizing how hungry I actually felt.

"The cupboards are proverbially bare," she said. "I did find some old herbs. This one's lavender—that's easy. And I think the crushed flowers are chamomile. These big leaves smell savory."

"Sage," I said, my fingers touching hers as I rubbed the leaves in her hands.

"But as far as actual food for our actual bellies…"

As she said it, she opened a cupboard. From it, she pulled out four mugs and a little earthen container. "One for each of us. There's a tea kettle, and we could at least heat the chamomile." She reached up for the final container, removing the lid. Then stepped back. "Gross."

"What is it?" I asked, moving close. Inside was some kind of crystalized yellow stuff. It looked almost like butter that had gone off, but it didn't smell like butter that had gone off.

Gideon came between us, wiggling his way in. He squinted at the jar, then shoved a finger in and sucked it off.

"Gideon!" Savina said.

"Honey," he answered. "Crystalized."

"Huh," Savina said. "Honey lasts forever. They've even found it in ancient Egyptian tombs—still edible."

"Yum," I said sarcastically.

"It really is," Gideon said, working all the sticky sweetness off of his finger.

And just like that, we all had our fingers in the honey pot. Mine brushed against Savina's, and I must have been hungrier than I thought, because I didn't even pause very long to think about how nice her fingers would have felt in mine. Instead, I just jammed my own honey-crusted fingers in my mouth. And it *was* good. Sweet on my tongue, soft in my belly.

"We're like naughty children," Savina said, looking up into my face. I smiled, gazing down into those cocoa brown eyes.

And then Greta's voice, breaking the moment. "Jackpot," she called from somewhere that sounded distant. I glanced at the honeypot, hoping there was a little left, realizing that—as opposed to Gideon, who was always keeping track of his sister —I'd completely forgotten that mine was somewhere in the house looking for candles.

"Where are you, Gret?"

"Attic, I think," she said. "There's an old bedroom up here too. Full of dusty quilts and clothes and stuff. Also, about a thousand candles."

I turned the corner out of the kitchen, hitting my toe against the bottom stair of a narrow staircase she must have gone up. "Geez, Gret. Glad you didn't die."

I shimmied up the staircase, my shoulders barely fitting, even though I wasn't exactly built like the Hulk. At the top I passed through an equally narrow door into a skinny little room that I had to hunch in unless I stood in the exact center where the roof was tallest. One tiny bed sat crookedly near the window, piled high with several old blankets. I could only imagine the number of mold spores growing inside them. Next to it, a dingy cot had practically rusted into the floor. At the other end of the room, beneath a second window, I could just make out a trunk, padlocked shut.

I eyed it suspiciously, wondering if the body of a kid would fit, though you'd think that if there was a dead body, the place would smell a little more…ripe.

From the window, the last rays of the setting sun cast a red glow onto a table that must have been for washing. A small, wide pitcher rested on top of it, a mirror nailed into the wall—though it wasn't really a mirror, just a piece of metal that had been used as a mirror.

"This place," Savina murmured, coming up behind me, close enough that I could feel the warmth of her body.

"Wild, huh?" Greta said. She stood on a wooden stool in front of a broken wardrobe. "Candles," she said. "Also, lace, crochet hooks, and yarn."

Savina took a step closer to me. Her brother waited at the bottom of the stairs, maybe worried he was too heavy for the rickety steps.

"Looks like we've set up house," I said.

"Now let's just hope it's only for one more night," Savina replied, her shoulder brushing my arm.

The fire was crackling hard when we returned to the bottom level, heating the place up.

"Nice," Savina said, high-fiving her brother. "This place was freezing."

"It's weird for May," I said. "I mean, June."

"Easy to lose track of time, isn't it?" she said.

"Feels like time has stopped," I answered, instantly wishing I'd chosen my words differently.

"What's this?" Greta asked, noticing the honey pot. She set the candles down in a messy pile.

"Oh, it's honey," I said. "We saved some for you." I cleared my throat, pretty sure we'd eaten more than we'd saved.

She scooped it out without a thought, just like Gideon.

"I'll make tea," Savina said. "Might as well make the best of it. And we should probably boil that well water anyway."

She filled a copper teapot and, after examining the fireplace for a minute, hung the teapot on a sharp iron hook that was screwed into the bricks near the fire. "Pretty sure that's how that is supposed to work," she said, smiling at the set up.

Greta held up the honey pot. "There's a little left," she said. "You could use it for sweetener."

"No, you eat it," Savina said, sounding as guilty as I felt.

"I already had some," Greta said. "Let's use the rest for the tea. It'll make it better."

And it did.

We filled each mug with a bit of honey, then dropped in some of the little white flowers. Savina poured the boiling water over the concoction, the steam lifting into our faces along with the scent. And for that little moment, with the fire crackling and dusk settling, it didn't feel so bad.

Hardly enough food for a bunch of teenagers, but sweet and warm and better than a whole lot of nothing—or Greta's eggs, which were the other option.

We let the teas cool enough to drink and then scooped out the flowers with a tin spoon Greta found in the kitchen.

"You know what they don't have in this house," Savina said, as we all sat around the fire, the smoke carrying steadily up the old chimney as the tea warmed our bellies.

Greta glanced at her.

"That's right, girl," Savina continued. "No bathroom. Easy problem for the boys to solve. Trickier for us."

"There's an outhouse in the back," Gideon said.

"I think I'll take my chances with the trees," Savina answered. "Hundred-year-old poop feels a bit much, even under the circumstances." She looked at Greta. "Should we go find us a ladies' room?"

Greta nodded.

"Should we, like, stand guard or something?" I asked.

"Please don't," Savina said.

By the time they got back, it was fully dark outside, but the fire was getting the house a little too hot. We scooted away from it, closer to the kitchen. "Hope we don't burn the place down," I said.

"Least not with us in it," Savina replied. She sat close to me, and heat or no heat, I didn't move away a single inch.

Greta looked at the eggs, which were sitting on the sewing table by the rocking chair. "Maybe I should move them to the kitchen where it's cooler."

"Too bad there's no refrigeration here in the middle of nowhere," I said.

"Or plumbing," Savina added, picking up a hand off the dusty floor and rubbing it against her jeans. "This place just peels off under your fingers."

"Here," I said, pulling a clean, albeit ratty, tissue from my pocket. I'd planned to hand it to her, but she held out her hand as though waiting for me to clean it. I paused, then cradled her hand in mine, rubbing the tissue along her fingers, cleaning the dust and a few lines of sticky grime.

Gideon looked away.

Greta picked up the egg basket. And Greta's hand must have been shaking from hunger, because the little blue napkin fell off and the basket wobbled slightly. "Hans," she said, her voice small.

"Yeah?" I asked, not wanting to move from the spot where I was still holding Savina's hand, our shoulders nearly touching.

"One of the eggs…"

I frowned at her, and it was Savina who stood up first. "What do you need, Greta?"

Grudgingly, I hauled myself off of the floor and peeked into the basket.

Most of the eggs were still, just like eggs should be. But one of them—the beige one—was wobbling slightly, as though something was inside of it, working to hatch.

"That's weird," I said. "Surely it can't be viable."

"*Is* it possible?" Greta asked. "Did we get it warm enough that...? It doesn't really make sense."

"Maybe. If that old demented man gathered them today," Savina said, unable to tear her eyes off of the shaking egg. It rocked back and forth, the movements getting bigger by the second. "Maybe if they were about to hatch. And then the warmth, the heat, of the living room."

"A hundred degrees," Gideon piped up.

"That's what it'd have to be," Savina translated. "According to Gideon anyway. And he's usually right about these things. It's not that hot in here, is it?"

I shook my head. "It can't be, or we'd all be sweating."

"I'm sweating," Greta grumbled.

The little egg rocked back and forth, and a soft pecking began, a little tap tap against the shell. A sound that became bigger and bigger. Until—

"The door," I said.

We all looked at it, like a banshee was the one politely tapping away at the old sticky wood. Greta looked at me. Savina too. Even Gideon stayed where he was, close to the hot fire.

I glanced at all of them, one more time, then said, "It's about time." I turned to the door. "Hello," I called, just like I'd done when Savina and Gideon had arrived. "We're in here. I'm glad you found us."

No one answered, though the tapping persisted. I glanced at the egg, which rocked and rocked, wildly now.

"Maybe they can't hear me," I mumbled.

In three strides, I was at the door, motioning subconsciously for everyone to stand back. Which was ridiculous. Because it was obviously someone from the search party who had seen the smoke.

Although I couldn't help but think as my hand clamped onto the doorknob, that we still didn't know if the dead man we found was actually the killer. Or just some guy who had wandered, confused, from his old people facility. If he had just been a random guy with dementia, then a killer could still be out there. Or a copycat.

"Who is it?" I said, my hand on the sticky doorknob, holding it tight, my voice much stronger than I felt.

No answer, but three more knocks, and then it stopped. Though 'stopped' is the wrong word. Because whoever was on the other side of the door slumped into it like they'd just passed out.

I looked back at the girls and Gideon, a question in my eyes. *Do I open it?*

Just as a small voice whimpered through the crack under the door. "Hello."

Not the voice of a serial killer.

I threw open the door, and sure enough, a little kid was slouched against it, his face white, his hair full of twigs and brambles.

Savina rushed to him, dragging him in. "Is he hurt?" she asked. Not to me, but to her brother, who had lumbered over and was inspecting the kid, just like he'd done with the dead man earlier.

The boy had some kind of toy or something clasped in one hand, and in the other, he was holding little bits of the peeling wood from the door.

Eyes still closed, he jammed the wood chips into his mouth, chewing vigorously.

"Don't eat that," I grumbled, but the boy ignored me and swallowed, finally opening his eyes.

"I'm cold," he said, looking at the fire.

Savina and Gideon moved him closer to it, Savina glancing at the empty honey pot.

Greta brought over one of the mugs with a bit of water in it. The boy chugged it, then held the mug out, asking for more.

"How did you get here?" I asked.

"Don't know," he said, his eyes glazing over. "I got lost, and then I was so hungry. And I came here." He picked at the wooden floor with his fingernails, trying to scrape bits up and shove them in his mouth like they were pretzel sticks.

"Stop that," I said again. "Nothing here is even clean."

He shoved the wood bits into his mouth anyway.

"Greta, get him some more water," I said.

She poured more from her water bottle into the little mug. He chugged away, like he was in a drinking contest.

"Don't make yourself sick," I said, just like my mom used to after I'd thrown up—that point where you feel okay and want to toss back a whole Gatorade, but if you do, you'll be barfing again in five minutes. I paused on that thought of my mom— remembered her wiping my head with a rag, helping me feel better every time I had a fever.

It almost seemed like Greta was thinking the same thing, because she brought me an old rag from the little table, then poured more water into the mug.

The boy was slouching against Gideon's body, which looked incredibly hot for both of them. I swathed the rag over the boy's forehead, wiping the beads of sweat that were starting to form. His eyes closed as I did, and for this terrifying moment, I thought he had died, just like the old man. But then he started to snore. Savina made a little pillow for him with her sweater, and we let him rest on the floor.

It was nearly impossible in a room that hot to tell if he was feverish or not, but every once in a while, I'd swab the wet rag over his face, and every once in a while he'd moan in response.

We were so caught up with the boy for the next few hours that we failed to notice that the egg in Greta's basket had quieted, everything still.

Except for the cuckoo clock, which only ever seemed to chime at midnight, or whatever it thought midnight was.

Even though it had happened the night before, I still jumped when the first chime struck. We all did. Well, all of us except the sleeping boy. At each chime my muscles wound tighter. Twelve, just like last night. I laid the rag over the boy's forehead and we all settled onto sweaters and jackets, trying to get comfortable.

"Anybody else want to try the rocking chair tonight?" Greta asked.

We shook our heads. The fire had reduced to mostly coals. And every once in a while Gideon tossed a few damp leaves on, which smoldered and smoked without creating too much more heat.

"Pull him away from the fire," Savina said as we settled onto the floor. "It's not good for him to get too hot."

Obediently, Gideon and I scooted the boy away, a few soft moans and some garbled snoring his only response.

Day 2

THE NEXT MORNING, I woke at *exactly* the same time I had the morning before. 6:15, according to the cuckoo clock. This time, after the squeaky chime, I swear I heard the little door open and close, sealing off the cuckoo bird for the rest of the day. Man, I felt a lot like that little bird. My mouth felt like sandpaper had settled along all my teeth.

I took a swig straight from Greta's water bottle, swishing the water around to try to get the nasty feeling to go away. My stomach rumbled aggressively, and even though the others were still asleep, I could hear their stomachs grumbling too.

The boy was right where we'd left him, his face tipped to the side, hair swooping across his eyes, rag shifted to his cheek. Without realizing it at first, I watched for the rise and fall of his chest. When I felt sure he was still alive, I placed a hand on his forehead, just like Mom used to do with me. He didn't feel unusually warm. That was good.

When I looked up, Gideon was staring. "Not dead?" he said.

"Not dead," I answered.

He nodded to the door. "Gonna get some wood."

I nodded back. With the boy there, it didn't seem like we could strike off into the woods again, especially considering we were all getting pretty hungry ourselves. Plus, when you were lost it was usually best to stay where you were. That seemed even more true considering we had a fireplace with a forest's worth of old wood at our fingertips.

I stood, stretching, and then made my way into the kitchen to double check that Savina hadn't missed some cans somewhere. Honestly, botulism was feeling more and more like a risk I'd be willing to take.

I was trying to be quiet with the cupboards, but Greta made her way in a few minutes later and Savina after that.

"Ladies' room," Savina said, heading outside with one of the old rags in her hand.

"Hopefully they find us today," was all I answered.

Greta joined me in the food search, but all we found were a few chipped plates and some tarnished silverware.

"Where's Gideon?" Greta asked, pulling out a large steak knife.

"Out getting wood from the shed. Hopefully," I answered.

"Prolly better bring in some of that damp wood," the boy said, popping his head in the kitchen, like he woke up in a weird house with teenage strangers every day. "It'll dry better in the house, by the fire."

"You're feeling better," Greta said, trying to hide her own surprise at seeing him up, moving, talking, even telling us what to do.

"'Course I'm feeling better," he said, and his accent—it was deep south, old country. "I been eating." With that, he picked at a chunk of exposed plaster by the doorframe and tossed it into his mouth like it was a piece of cake.

Savina walked in at just that moment, her eyes widening, as though we were all in some weird cartoon. In almost any other circumstances, I would have laughed. Instead, I turned to the boy, "You really shouldn't."

"That's good," the boy said, scraping more off.

Savina gave me this little eyebrow look, like *What should we do?*

"Hey," I said, taking the boy by the shoulder and steering him away. "Maybe instead of eating the actual *walls*, we should go look outside or something. I think I saw a garden. Let's try that before the plaster."

With a little resistance, the boy allowed himself to be led toward the back door. He took a swipe of peeling paint as I shoved him ahead of me.

Greta stayed in the kitchen, opening more drawers, but Savina followed close behind me, her hand just brushing mine.

"That kid's a little wacked," she whispered, pulling me close.

The kid stopped abruptly, staring straight up at the sky. The sound of a bird trickled down to us and he took something from his pocket, aimed, shot. And missed.

"Too bad he's not a better shot," Savina said. "Apparently, he's brought a...slingshot." She looked at the little device in the boy's hand. "You know, it's not a bad idea, killing a bird. Though I'm pretty sure even Gideon doesn't know how to pluck and gut one."

"Yeah," I said. "Maybe just as well to stick with the garden. You know some things grow year after year, going to seed and then coming back."

"What?" She giggled as the kid took another shot at a faraway bird. "You don't want to eat peeling woodchips?"

"Maybe we're all gonna be gnawing on floorboards by the time this is done," I grumbled.

"Or at least breaking into Greta's eggs," Savina added.

We both looked at each other. Eyes locking. "The egg," she said.

As if on cue, Greta came from the house, the little basket in her hand. "I think it's dead," she said. "It's not moving anymore."

Along one side of the egg that had been moving was a long, thin crack.

"I'll be darned," Savina said. "It sure tried to get out. And who knows, maybe it's still alive. Maybe it just needs a break." She looked up to her brother, who had come up behind Greta, a stack of wood in his arms—as though none of us wanted to hang out alone. "Of course, I'm not sure anything could really hatch well without better conditions."

"It pipped," Gideon said.

"Either way, maybe we'll just plan to not eat that one," Savina said, smiling at Greta. Still smiling, even when things kind of sucked.

My mom had once said that when you were dating someone you should always take them camping to see how well they handled it. Not that my mom was well-equipped to be passing out dating advice. Still, it was nice to see Savina smile. It was always nice to see her smile, but it was extra nice right now. Even though we literally ate honey and chamomile for dinner, even though some weird kid was here and clearly not quite okay.

Having been unsuccessful at killing any birds, the boy

headed back to the house, a hungry look in his eyes as he stared at the mossy awning.

"The garden," I said, blocking the boy from going back to gnaw on the house.

Gideon set the pile of wood down and focused his attention on the ancient garden latch. With a swift movement, he gave it a good kick, breaking it instantly.

I was impressed. I think we all were, except maybe the boy, who was still gazing at the house. The gate swung open and Greta went in first.

"What's your name?" Savina asked the boy, trying to distract him.

He paused, like he hadn't thought about the question for ages. "Friends call me B.J.," he answered, fingering the gate, as though it looked like a pretty tasty treat too. In the end, he seemed to think better of it, and followed us in.

The garden really was a good idea. On the far side, we found a little raspberry bush. The berries weren't quite ripe, but they were getting there. We found the pinkest ones we could and tossed the tart berries into our mouths. The boy—B.J.—was still casting backward glances at the house, but even he ate a few of the berries.

It was Greta who found the carrots. And Gideon who told us we could eat the green tops as well. Which we did. Right from the dirt. We washed them with water from the well and then every bit of anything we knew was edible went into our mouths.

I watched the boy, worried he was going to start eating dirt. But he didn't. Just quasi-clean carrots like the rest of us, only glancing back a few times to gaze longingly at the splintering doorframe.

CHAPTER 13

GRETA

Gideon kept the fire going, like he'd been born to live in an older time. Hans, not so much. He kept glancing at his blank phone, hoping something would appear. Though by the second afternoon, he was checking less, resigned to his internet-less fate. He shoved his phone into his pocket and, just like B.J. had suggested, he brought some wet wood in from outside so it could dry by the fire.

We kept it going all day, that fire, Gideon piling wet leaves on it to get maximum smoke.

Plumes billowed out of the chimney and you could smell it from any point in the yard. It seemed like it would attract the attention of even the most incompetent search party.

The only problem with the fire was that it made it absolutely stifling in the house. Last night had been hot, but not too miserable since the temperature had dropped a little. But by the time the sun hung high in the sky, I began praying for rain again, just so we could get some relief from the heat.

Especially since it wasn't much better outside. In the muggy, tall grass, my whole body felt sticky. And my sweat was like bug heroin—that's what Mama always said—well, she said that I was too sweet to resist, but it meant the same thing. With all that sweat, the mosquitoes seemed to sniff me out. I counted seventeen bites so far.

I reached back to smack one on my neck and felt the faint scab from the scratch just above my shoulder blades.

"They not getting you?" I asked that kid. B.J.

"Who?" he asked, like I'd been accusing him of something.

"The mosquitoes," I answered.

"Naw," he answered, settling down in the grass as though to prove the point and watching the clouds roll by. "The skeeters never much bother me."

Probably because he wasn't nearly sweet enough.

All he did was toss that stone into the sky and catch it when it fell back down again. He never missed. It was hypnotic, that tossing, and I watched him for several minutes, transfixed.

He was right—somehow the bugs didn't seem to bother him much; the heat didn't seem to bother him much; the hunger didn't seem to bother him much; even being lost in the woods didn't seem to bother him much.

I plopped down beside him. The stone went up; the stone fell down. Almost at perfect intervals. He was a good catch, even if he wasn't a great shot.

"You play baseball?" I asked.

"Nah," he mumbled, still tossing, still catching.

"You should," I said. "You'd be good."

"Always wanted to," he answered. "Pops wouldn't let me. Didn't have the money."

Pops. Who even says that? "Oh," I said, picking at a blade of grass and shredding it into thread-like strands. "Sorry."

He did a little shrug thing, still catching the stone. "And I always have to help in the fields anyway."

"The fields?" I asked.

"Yeah," he said. "Outside town."

"Oh. How far?"

Another shrug. "A ways."

He still wasn't looking at me.

"So, how'd you get here?" I asked.

"Walked," he said.

"Right," I answered. "But…" I modified my question. "Why?"

"Wanted to be alone."

I could understand that. It was usually why I came to the woods too. But with this kid, it sounded like, even lost and hungry, he'd still kind of like to be alone. Except that he'd been nearly fainting from hunger last night.

"How long have you been lost in the woods?" I asked.

"Can't remember," he said.

I looked around for Hans or Savina or even Gideon. Someone to help me get some information out of this kid. "You came here on purpose?" I asked.

"Sure," he answered. "So did you."

"Yeah," I replied. "But I mean, you…you ran away, didn't you?"

"I just wanted to be alone," he repeated. "I was tired of the fields, tired of the farm, tired of my pops."

I nodded.

"I didn't really mean to stay," he added quietly, still catching that stone. The rhythm of it making me almost sleepy.

"What about your mama?" I asked.

"She died," he said, and for the first time the tossing stopped.

I opened my mouth to try to say something, but I was too slow. By the time a single word had formed in my throat, he'd gotten up and walked away.

I watched his back, trying to guess his age. Ten, eleven maybe. I had to admit he looked like a farm kid with a single dad. The old jeans, the slightly too-long hair, the untamed cowlick at the back.

As he walked back in the direction of the garden, he wiggled away at a piece of quartz at the foundation of the house, digging in with his fingernails until a bit finally came off. Then, giving it a little toss, he threw it into his mouth, gnawing and sucking, like it was a piece of hard candy.

Still chewing, he went back to the garden, but not to dig for more vegetables. Just to stare at the dirt while he chomped on his piece of rock.

The kid was touched, as Grammy would have said. I felt sorry for him anyway.

I stayed there in the grass, watching and thinking. Until another mosquito bit. Number eighteen.

By the time we headed back to the house, we were all itching and scratching. All except B.J., who must have that blood type that doesn't attract mosquitoes, because they still weren't bothering him even though it was nearly dusk.

I glanced for the millionth time at the sky. Still clear. I was surprised we hadn't seen a helicopter, or a small plane, or any other signs of a search party. No one stomping through the woods. No one calling our names. Everything around us as silent as a museum after hours.

How had no one found us yet? After all, we'd managed to find each other.

We all gathered in the kitchen, around the table. And when we did, it felt like we should be gathering for supper. We should have been. But unfortunately, all we'd found in the garden were a few carrots, some dandelion greens, and one lonely turnip. Which we'd already eaten. It had tasted a little like dirt and a little like radish, but we'd eaten it anyway, cutting it into five equal pieces with a dull paring knife Gideon had found in the kitchen.

B.J. had only nibbled at his, which—considering he ate rocks —didn't speak too highly of turnips.

I ran my tongue over my teeth, which felt gritty and gross. Mama would lose it if she knew I hadn't brushed them for two days.

"How are we supposed to brush our teeth?" I asked Hans, who was slamming cupboards open and shut.

"Really, Greta," he said, all grumpy. "That's what you're worried about right now."

"I've been using the hem of my shirt," Savina said quietly. "You just get it wet and rub it along your teeth—like using a washcloth. It's not perfect, but it's better than nothing."

My stomach grumbled loudly and Hans slammed another cupboard.

"Here," Gideon said, pulling something from his pocket. "It's not much," he said, letting the sentence hang there as he set the little lumps on the counter.

Five ugly button mushrooms stared back at us.

"We could each have one," Gideon said. "Or not. Up to you guys."

"They look safe," I said. "Normal."

"I went mushroom hunting a few times with my dad," Gideon replied. "These look like *agaricus*, similar to what you find at the grocery store. Edible."

Savina was the first to take one. I followed suit. Hans looked at B.J. "You want one?"

"Gross," B.J. answered.

And with that, any generosity Hans was feeling vanished in a puff of teenage grouch. He broke the final mushroom into four and gave each of us a piece, popping his share into his mouth.

We all chewed for several minutes, longer than it seemed such a small amount of food should take. But the mushrooms were earthy and rubbery, though somehow chalky at the same time. They took a while.

"It'd be better cooked up with a little butter and salt, that's for sure," Gideon said.

"Don't worry about it," Hans said. "Thanks, man. It was nice of you to share."

Gideon shrugged his shoulders in that awkward, slightly

hunched way. But he was smiling. And so was Hans, just a little. And my stomach warmed to see it.

"Okay," Savina said, swallowing the last of her mushroom with a dry gulp. "It's time for a plan. Tomorrow, should some of us go out as a search party while the others stay back?"

"But how will we find our way back to the house?" I asked.

"Seems like we can't *not* find our way back," Hans grumbled.

"I don't want to be separated," I said, my voice wobbling more than I wanted it to.

Gideon nodded his agreement. "Even if we found someone," he said with that slow drawl. "What if we couldn't find our way to bring them back here?"

"We could at least describe the place," Savina said with a big gesture at the rickety old room. "And we know kind of how far it was from the bonfire."

"Do we?" her brother asked.

They did this little twin stare-off thing, and I realized that they didn't know how far the house was from the bonfire, that they'd wandered in circles just like us.

"We didn't find the bonfire spot when we went back out," Gideon said. "Didn't even stumble into it."

"What do you think?" I asked B.J.

He shrugged, tossing that stone up a few feet, catching it again.

We all stared for a moment, hypnotized. Savina snapped out of it first. "Then what are we supposed to do? I'm hungry," she said, and her eyes were kind of dark and kind of glassy at the same time. "And I'm tired. And I'm hot. And I'm scared. It's been two days."

She cast a glance at the eggs.

And then we all did.

The cracked one to the side was still not moving, but right beside it, another one—blue-gray—had begun to wobble, just a bit, back and forth.

Hans stepped toward the basket of eggs, then Gideon, followed by Savina.

I was last. And B.J. didn't come over at all, didn't even seem to notice or care.

"This feels impossible," Savina said. "For that man to have given us viable eggs about to hatch, all from different birds."

"And for them to try to hatch, just from the heat of the house," Hans added.

Though it was *sweltering*.

We all seemed to feel it at once. I reached up to wipe the beads of sweat from my forehead. Gideon took a swig of water from his mug. Hans blew out a puff of breath.

But B.J., he just broke off a piece of the countertop—broke it like it was nothing more than thin toffee, and popped it into his mouth. Tossed his stone, caught his stone. Plunk. In his other palm.

We all stared.

"I'm seriously so hungry that I'm starting to not feel well," Savina said, choosing to ignore B.J.

"And hot," Hans added. "It's hard with the heat."

"Maybe we should sleep outside tonight," Gideon added. "Except the bugs…"

"Why do you do that?" I asked B.J., unable to concentrate on anything else. "Why do you eat the house? You're going to get sick."

"I'm not the one who feels sick," B.J. said.

The light was fading, and Savina swiped the candle from the counter, lighting it with a swift movement. "Let's just all get some sleep."

"Not tired," the boy said, tossing his stone.

"Okay, you do what you want," Savina answered with a snap.

One by one, we wandered away from him, back to the room with the fire.

"It's so hot," Hans murmured.

"To be honest, I'm starting to feel a little chilled," Savina whispered. "Almost like a fever."

"Take the rocking chair," I said. "It's more comfortable." I expected her to argue, but instead, she nodded, settling into it, turning to her side, like she had the night before on the floor.

I took a spot by Hans, trying to get comfortable on the hard wood. Before I even closed my eyes, I could hear Savina's measured breathing. She was asleep.

Not only that, but when the cuckoo went off at midnight—again—she didn't stir. In fact, I noticed she'd pulled a raggedy quilt over her shoulders. Hans, on the other hand, had taken off his shirt. Still, his skin was dripping sweat.

"This place," he grumbled, settling back down, asleep in moments.

I sat, watching Hans' sweaty shoulders, counting his breaths to try to calm my own. What if we all got sick? What then?

Taking a couple of rags from the table, I poured water from my bottle onto them. I wasn't sure Hans would approve, but I swabbed the damp rags over his back, just like Mama would have. Hans didn't wake, just murmured in his sleep, which made me feel a little better.

I tucked my knees into my chest, staring at the cuckoo clock. It seemed to have stopped ticking again and I was glad for the silence, glad for the near darkness, glad for the solitude.

Though when I turned to check on Gideon, he was staring back at me, wide awake.

"Have you slept?" I murmured.

His only answer was to scoop a wad of leaves onto the coals, along with a bit of water from his mug to create smoke.

It mostly went up the chimney, though some came into the room. Gideon coughed, and I wondered if that was partly what was making all of us feel sick—the smoke, maybe even the fire. Who knew what kind of leaves we were burning. Were they toxic?

I lay back onto the floor. It was something we could talk about in the morning.

"Try to get some sleep," I said, just like Hans had a few nights ago to me.

Gideon nodded and tossed in another handful of leaves.

B.J. wasn't in the room. I figured he was still in the kitchen, or maybe even sleeping outside, on account of his resistance to mosquitoes and all.

CHAPTER 14

HANS

Day 3

6:15. Per the cuckoo. Same as the other mornings.

Except there was no denying something was wrong with me this morning. I was soaked in sweat. Even the spot on the floor where I'd been lying was damp and sticky. I pushed myself up from the floor, looking at the sunrise, resenting the sameness of it all.

My mug sat beside me, along with some rags. I took a swig of water, then a huge gulp.

Gideon was already awake, but he was staring at the fire, instead of out the window.

Savina was still dead asleep. *Dead.* I tried to wash the word—the thought—away as soon as I had it. Gideon must have sensed it too, because we turned to look at her at the same time, waiting for that rise of her shoulders. It took a bit longer than I would have liked, but she was breathing. Under a disgusting rag quilt that she'd draped across her body. I wanted to take it off of her, give her something else, but beneath the quilt, we could see that she was shivering. Shivering. And there was nothing else in the house to keep her warm except more old blankets.

I watched her for another minute—her face pale, her lips flushed, spots of pink in her cheeks and on her neck. Still beautiful.

I cleared my throat, turning to Gideon. "Probably ought to let her sleep," I said, just as he offered to warm some water for tea for her.

"Good idea," he and I said at the same time.

And then we laughed. It felt foreign to share a laugh with a kid like Gideon, foreign but good.

I turned around to see if Greta was still asleep, but her spot was empty except for an abandoned sweater. "Gret," I called nervously, my smile flattening into a tight line.

A clatter of tin, and she rushed into the room. "Hans," she said. "You've got to see this."

She pulled me up and I grabbed my t-shirt as she took me through the kitchen and out the back door.

The sun was almost blinding, which normally I'd love, but all I could think this morning was how hot it was going to be by noon.

"Maybe we should move the fire outside," I said. "Now that the wood is drier. We can let the fire die in the house and—"

Greta was standing at the corner of the house. Huge chunks of wood and brick had been cracked off and eaten. From the bottom to about my shoulder. A terra cotta drainage pipe used to run down the side, but the bottom had been cracked off and was full of little nibbles, like when a mouse gets into the pantry and goes to town on some crackers. In fact, bits like crumbs littered the area around it.

"He needs help," she whispered.

Just as the boy walked around the corner, looking healthy as a horse and tossing that rock.

I reached out and snatched it as it fell.

He swiveled his head toward me. The rock was flat and almost perfectly smooth, but there was a little nick in one edge that my finger bumped into—maybe for where he loaded it onto the slingshot.

I handed the rock to Greta, who ran her fingers over it, just like I'd done.

"Did you do this?" I asked the boy, pointing to the drainage pipe.

"'Course," he said, no apology or worry or anything in his voice, though he cast a quick glance at his stone in Greta's hand before looking back at me. "Tastes like gingerbread. A little stale, but otherwise good."

"You've got to stop," I said, feeling my voice creep up a notch. I wiped the sweat off my forehead before it dripped into my eyes.

Greta interrupted. "Are you feeling okay?" she asked the boy softly. "Being here has been difficult for everyone. Maybe you could look around the yard with me for something else to eat."

"You are not going anywhere with this kid," I hissed under my breath.

"Okay," she whispered, "but we've got to get him some food."

"I don't need any food," the boy said. "I feel fine." He patted his belly for emphasis. And then snatched the stone from Greta's hand.

"I'm checking the kitchen again," Greta said.

I didn't have the energy to argue with her. In fact, I resigned myself to trailing after her, back into the house. Maybe there *was* something we had missed. At this point, I definitely would have even taken my chances with botulism.

Or the eggs.

But even as the thought crossed my mind, even as I turned to the basket, I could hear it, the rocking. What had been a small movement the night before had grown so that the egg now wobbled furiously.

Greta heard it too. She abandoned the open cupboard, and together we peered into the basket, watching the little blueish-gray egg as it tilted back and forth.

"I'm cooking the rest," Greta said, grabbing a cast iron skillet off of the wall. "Before they all crack."

"You can't, Gret," I said, my eyes still glued to the rocking egg, my ears straining to hear the little tap, tap that had just begun. "That lunatic gave us a bunch of viable eggs somehow, and it's so hot in here. They're all going to hatch, or try to. What did Gideon say? A hundred degrees—I can believe that."

"It's not a hundred degrees," Greta said, looking at me with concern. "It's a little warm, but—"

The egg tilted to one side, then rocked to the other with an aggressive crack. Just as a scream erupted in the other room.

Greta and I rushed to it. "Savina!"

But it wasn't Savina. She was barely stirring in the rocking chair, her eyes fighting to open.

Right by the door stood a total stranger—a girl who was looking at Gideon and screaming her head off.

She turned to us and the noise got louder.

Greta covered her ears, Savina tossed off the quilt.

But it was Gideon who went up to the girl and placed a hand solidly over her mouth. "Stop. Making. That. Sound."

I'd never heard him speak like that. Low, clear, almost menacing.

The girl stopped.

Gideon didn't move his hand though. The girl's eyes, above his hand, stared—wide and blue.

Gideon looked back at me like he was asking for backup.

With the banshee wail ended, I could see that the girl was about my age, and...not hard to look at—honey brown hair, blue eyes, and wearing a short skirt with sandals. A strange outfit for the woods.

"Gideon is going to take his hand away," I said, my own voice low, though I was trying to keep it level and calm like Greta would have. "If you scream again, he'll stop you. Please, just don't. We're lost and we're trying to find our way out of the woods. Do you know how we can get out?"

Gideon removed his hand and she opened her mouth like she was going to scream again, but her lips just hung open, revealing small white teeth.

"He looked like a bear," she said, pointing at Gideon. "Hunched over by the fireplace. Like I'd walked into a house with a bear."

I looked at Gideon with his dark hair and dark clothes. I mean, maybe I could sort of see it, but not really. If anything, with his greasy hair and dirty clothes, he looked more like our little serial killer. Which was what the girl *should* have been worried about. "Well, he's not," I said. "Now how did you get here? Was there a path?"

"I ran," she said, like that was an answer to the question. "I was supposed to meet someone in the woods and my mama caught me leaving and we had a fight and I ran out here, into the woods. It was so dark and I was terrified of bears. You know we have them here. And then this house. And there he was, crouched in the corner. Like he was trying to scare me. And I was just so tired and so frightened."

Savina got out of the rocking chair, her skin ghost-white. "We're all tired, babe. He's my brother, not a bear, so let's just take a step back." Her voice soothing as silk, though underneath it, you could sense the bite of irritation. "We're all trying to make our way out of this house, well, the woods. We've got a fire going so a search party can maybe find us. And there's another kid here…" She looked around for B.J. "He's lost too. I never really believed in this stuff, but maybe there's an energy to this house or something that brings people here when they're stressed. Who knows? Just, let's all stay calm. Which direction did you come from?"

"East," the girl said without missing a beat.

"And where is that?" Savina asked.

The girl motioned to the door, but the sun was rising on a different side of the house.

"That's not east," I grumbled under my breath. This girl with her pretty face and mini skirt and hysteria were clearly not going to be much help.

The girl stared at the fireplace, her little mouth still open. "Finally," she said, walking to it. "Something to eat."

We all swiveled in the direction she was moving, hoping to see a pot or jug of something we'd missed. But there was just the mantle, with the empty crock of honey that we'd all eaten that first night.

Our shoulders sagged as she picked it up.

"It's empty," Greta said. "Sorry. We can check the garden again or…"

But the girl had lifted the crock. She brought it down with a thud on the stone mantle. A little crack ran along the corner of the mantle, chipping off a rock that I had to admit in my hunger looked a lot like butterscotch candy.

It fell into her hand and she stared at it for just a second before popping it into her mouth.

"Doesn't taste empty to me," she said.

"This house," Savina murmured.

"Let's get some fresh air," I said. "See if there's something to eat for breakfast in that old shed."

Savina nodded, taking Gideon by the arm, as we hurried through the kitchen, past the blue-gray egg that was no longer shaking, and out the back door.

❦

B.J. WAS STANDING at the garden gate, just staring and tossing.

And suddenly, I knew what he reminded me of, just a little. A non-playable character. The pulse of the stone, the perfection of his catch. Like something out of a video game. Until he looked at you, all of that fury in his eyes. Although even that felt just a little...the same.

I tried to remember if I'd seen him smile since he got here, or make any other expression at all. Maybe when he'd first arrived, slumped against the door. What had he looked like then?

I couldn't quite remember. Only that he'd seemed sick.

"What should we do about the lock?" Savina said, bringing me back to the problem of the shed and breakfast.

But Gideon had already picked up a stone. With a heavy swing, he struck the lock. Bits of rust fell to the dirt like crumbs from a cookie, and for just a second, I wondered if one of the new kids was going to come over and shove some of *that* in their mouths.

But no one did. The new girl hadn't even come out yet. She was still in the house with...I whipped my head around, relieved to see Greta coming out of the back door, carrying the little basket of eggs.

"The blue-ish one is cracked," Greta said, rushing over to me. "And look—this white one. It's rocking."

"Gret," I said. "I just can't right now."

The new girl popped her head out the door. "What are you —?" she began.

"We're trying to find some breakfast," Savina interrupted.

"In the house there's plenty of—"

"Would you like to help?" Savina asked, the slightest edge to her voice. "Um, what was your name again?"

She got a blank look. The same blank look that B.J. had given us when we'd asked him.

"Shelle," the girl finally said.

Gideon hammered harder at the lock, each strike banging into my own head as sweat dripped into my eyes.

Greta stared at the long-legged girl through narrowed eyes, like she was trying to remember something and it kept slipping away from her. Then she glanced down at the egg. "It's cracking," she said, as Gideon got the lock off the shed and we all stumbled in.

My foot hit something and I tripped over it, just as Savina screamed, Gideon slumped down against the wall, and Greta's white egg pipped.

CHAPTER 15

GRETA

A body. Splayed out starfish style, mouth open like a fish too.

Savina's scream turned to a sob, but I could see the girl's torso, moving in and out, in and out. I set down the eggs—the eggs that had stilled—and laid the little blue handkerchief over them.

Gideon shuffled toward the girl. But this time I beat him to it, reaching down to touch the girl's neck. Yup. Pulse.

Gideon stared at her face while Hans stood frozen, that insane new girl gripping his arm, her nails practically digging into him.

"She's alive," I whispered.

Gideon poked and prodded the body.

"She's alive," I said, louder. And when I did, the girl began to stir, rubbing her head, smacking her mouth like it tasted bad.

Savina downgraded to a soft whimper. Hans dragged the other girl—Shelle—over so they could have a look.

"Hey," I said to the newest girl. She sat up suddenly, a mat of straw and leaves and dirt in her hair. "Hey, how did you get here?"

And then the girl began to cry.

She really went at it. I patted her back and Savina staggered over—her face so white at this point, it practically glowed in the shed.

"Maybe we should get some of the candles," I said, then squinted at the shed. "Actually, that might be dangerous with all this straw. Let's just…"

Gideon found a little flashlight, right next to the girl. "Here," he said. And sure enough, it flickered on with a weak yellow light. The first modern light we'd had for days.

Seeing it, the girl stopped bawling, and stared. "Where am I?" she asked.

I looked to Hans, who shrugged, Shelle's hand still on his arm.

"I wish we knew," I said. "We're all lost, somewhere in the woods. We were looking for some food in here and we…we found you. Do you know how you got here?"

She chewed on her lip, not even bothering to dust off the hay that was all over her. "My house is by the woods too," she finally said. Then, "Can I have my flashlight?"

"Your flashlight?" Hans asked.

"Yeah, I think so," she answered. "I…this is so embarrassing. Sometimes I sleepwalk. It's, like, really bad. There's a name for it I can never remember, though my mom says it, like, 70,000 times a week. We've tried all kinds of different things—my, um, comfort animals, warm baths, even medicine. Nothing seems to work." She looked around, cradling the flashlight like she was hoping it'd turn into one of her comfort animals. "Never wound up anywhere this weird though. The closest was the hammock in my back yard."

"Yeah, well," Hans said. "This is not the hammock in your back yard, though I wish it was."

"Me too," the girl said, real quiet. I felt like I should hold her hand or something, but she had shifted to her knees, standing up kind of wobbly, like a baby fawn. Her hair was a mess of knotted curls—way worse than mine—full now of straw dust. It was also probably the ugliest hair cut I'd ever seen. Truth be told, it reminded me of this kid in my class who got a mullet with this perm on top. I tipped my head to the side, looking at it in the light from the doorway. It *was* a perm, the girl's hair—the curls too tight and uniform to be natural. They formed a little triangle at her shoulders. And her clothes. Bright pinks and yellows. High-waisted jeans that looked white washed in places, the cuffs bound up tight along her ankles.

"I'm starving," she said, looking at me with bright eyes.

"Join the club," Hans grumbled, shaking off Shelle's hand for the umpteenth time. "There's not a whole lot to eat here. We seriously just ate a handful of mushrooms for dinner last night."

He stopped at the sentence, looking around at all of us—Savina's white face, Gideon's hunched shoulders and greasy hair, my little basket of eggs, his own sweat-soaked shirt.

"Oh, man," he said. "The mushrooms. They made us sick. That makes so much sense. Maybe they even affected us mentally too. The screaming, the panic, the eggs. The way we all watched her just eat a rock."

"I didn't eat a rock," Shelle said. "I'm not insane."

"What'd you eat then?" Hans asked.

"Just a piece of candy I saw on that mantle," Shelle replied.

And Hans, he laughed. It felt a little unhinged, but I could practically see the tension sliding off of him. "Yeah," he said. "Okay. So, no more mushrooms. I'm feeling better already now that I know what caused all this—" He waved his hand around. "—hysteria."

"But we still just found a girl in the shed," I said in a small voice. "That's reason for a little hysteria."

"Yeah, sure," Hans said. "But you know what I mean. Like, we all really just kind of lost our crap a minute ago."

Savina managed a weak little laugh.

Gideon didn't. Instead, he hung his head, not looking at anyone. "Sorry," he mumbled. "I could have sworn they were just regular button mushrooms."

"No worries," Hans said. "We're all trying to find food. But I think mushrooms are just too tricky, so maybe we won't experiment with them again." He looked around the dark, empty shed. "Now that we're all calm, let's have another look in the garden. It's big, and maybe we missed something. If we did, we'll eat, and if not, well, hopefully they'll find us by the end of the day."

Savina was helping the new girl dust herself off. And I was still staring at her. There was something…

"What's your name?" Hans asked, turning to her.

A small beat, and then, "Missy."

I realized I'd been waiting, expecting her to say a different name. Mushrooms, I reminded myself, just the mushrooms talking.

The boys left the shed to go dig around in the garden—well, at least Hans and Gideon did. B.J. stood at the gate, tossing his stone and chewing on a bit of straw.

Shelle stood in the doorway of the shed, gazing at Hans adoringly, like she was happy to just watch his muscles or something.

"Come on," I said, pushing past her. "Let's see if we can find some food." I paused to glance at the lock that Gideon had forced off. If the shed had been locked, how had the girl gotten in there? The windows were high and too thin for someone to crawl through. Well, probably. I bent down to examine the abandoned lock. Maybe it hadn't been locked. Maybe we'd just assumed and then gone banging it off, when we could have just unclicked it. What was the word Hans had used for our behavior? *Hysterical.* At any rate, we definitely hadn't been thinking straight.

"Bingo," Hans said as I got to the garden. He held up another turnip. "And we can eat the greens, right?"

Gideon nodded. "For just about anything. In fact, maybe you girls should go look for more dandelion greens. Those are pretty nutritious."

Savina turned from the garden, Missy following—and talking a mile a minute—still cradling the flashlight.

"Mmmm, would you look at that," Missy said, then trotted out of my sight. Shelle followed like she was Juliet abandoning her Romeo.

These kids, all found at the house, barely able to remember their names. "Can I stay with you?" I asked Hans, suddenly not wanting to lose sight of him.

"If you want," he said. "Long as you help us dig around." He cast a slightly accusing glance at B.J., who was now scuffing at the dirt with the tip of his shoe, staring at the opposite corner of the garden, where a poison ivy vine wound up a decayed post. That part, I noticed, hadn't been touched yet. Several green, leafy tops were popping up through the soil.

"Another!" Hans said, holding up another turnip like a trophy. "Anything that looks green or lumpy," he continued. "Dig it out."

I plodded over to the poison ivy corner. "You gonna help?" I asked B.J., who had followed me.

"Not hungry," he answered and I just about wanted to kill him.

"Fine," I mumbled, kneeling in the dirt, as far away from the poison ivy as I could get while still reaching the top of one of the plants. I grabbed it a little gingerly, and tugged. A tuft of green came off in my hands, but the roots stayed firmly in the ground.

"You've got to take them close to the base," Gideon said, coming to kneel beside me.

I nodded, as though Mama never made us weed her little flower beds. But I let him talk, if for no other reason than that he was pulling at the tops closest to the poison ivy, which meant I didn't have to.

"Well, would you look at that," he murmured.

He held a crooked white root in his hands.

"What is it?" Hans asked, coming over. "Looks like an alien carrot."

"Parsnip," Gideon replied. "A whole patch of them."

"You don't think the poison ivy leaves have gotten the oils on the parsnip tops, do you?" I asked.

He shrugged. "Probably not, unless someone brushed against them, which I'm guessing hasn't happened for a very long time."

I took a parsnip by the base of the greens, giving it a solid tug. Hans was right—they looked like alien carrots—all pale and bent and hairy. But it was oddly satisfying to pull something up from the ground that we could actually put in our stomachs. Before today I might have been scared to eat something as weird as that. But now, now I was so hungry that I was starting to feel weak, and crooked white roots were starting to sound good.

At any rate, it was more satisfying than trying to wrangle the new girls into being productive. I was glad Savina had gotten stuck with that job.

"Stop it!" I heard her saying from behind the house. "That is *not* edible."

Hans, Gideon, and I all glanced toward the sound of Savina's voice. "We don't need another mushroom debacle," Hans muttered, trying to be quiet enough that Gideon didn't hear.

But it wasn't mushrooms. From my little poison ivy corner, I could see that the new girl, Missy, had ripped off the edge of one of the shutters and was holding it in her hand like a cookie. I had to admit that, from this distance, the faded yellow shutter looked a lot like a wafer, or maybe a sugar cone, especially with bits of it bleached lighter from the sun. My mouth watered.

And even though Savina was trying to coax it out of her

hand, Missy held her grip on it, like she had no intention of letting it go.

"What's your problem," Shelle said to Savina. "She's just hungry."

I plucked another parsnip from the ground, glad to be far away from the girl drama, while Hans stood up, dusting off his knees, so he could go help Savina. Gideon followed him.

"Did you find any dandelions?" Hans called to them, trying to sound casual.

I looked down at the little mound of disturbed dirt in front of me. We'd dislodged six parsnips and something else—I bent down to get a better look, but it was just a flat, gray rock, about double the size of a quarter. With a small nick out of the side.

I glanced up.

B.J. had stopped tossing his own stone, and was staring at me, that same look, a look I suddenly recognized. Daring me. Daring me to get it wrong.

I shook my head. It was just the mushrooms, some kind of chemical enzyme messing with my brain.

But B.J. was walking toward me now, not blinking, not tossing. I saw it—the stone in his hand, so similar to the stone in my hand. No, not similar. Identical.

I shook my head again, but there was no shaking it off. B.J. *Benjamin.* "It's you," I whispered, holding up the stone. He held up his.

A flash of sunlight glanced between the stones, blinding me. And then he was gone.

I shook my head one final time and glanced down at my hand. It was still there. The stone. Gray, chipped, old and buried. Until now.

Not wanting to, but unable to stop myself, I dug deeper and deeper into the soft earth, earth that had been covered for decades by parsnips and poison ivy. I moved as much dirt as I could, covering the parsnips that had felt so valuable just a few minutes ago.

"Hans," I called, my voice cracking as I dug deeper. "Hans!"

"What now, Greta?" Hans said, coming over, wiping the sweat that dripped from his face. "I don't know what's wrong with these kids."

I looked up at him, as my fingers brushed something hard, deep in the soil.

"Greta, what's wrong?" he said, rushing over to me. His own face flushed, shining with sweat, even though it was only moderately warm out. Hans glanced around. "Where'd B.J. go? Did something happen? Did he do something to you? Where is he?"

"He's dead," I said, holding up the flat stone.

"What?" Hans asked. "Greta, where is he? What are you talking about?"

"The first victim," I responded, plunging my arms back into the dirt, up to my shoulders in the hole I'd dug. "Benjamin Jarrison Howard. The first victim of the killer."

I sucked in my breath, wrapping my fingers around the thing, things—the hard things I'd found deep in the dirt. "And he's buried right here."

CHAPTER 16

HANS

I dragged Greta inside by the fire, splashing water over her face, cleaning her hands. I couldn't see any blood anywhere, which was good.

She was still gripping the stone, B.J.'s stone, but the bones she'd found—I'd made her abandon those outside. Probably just the remnants of somebody's dead pet. An old lady's old cat from a hundred years ago.

"Here, drink," I said, and Greta obeyed, but it didn't bring any color back into her cheeks. It didn't stop the tears that were rolling down her face.

"He lived here," she blubbered. "The killer. He buried that kid. I found the bones. And somehow B.J., he…he…manifested or something."

"Okay," I said. "I think this is still the mushrooms speaking. Try to think," I said. "Did you see where B.J. went?"

"Benjamin," she corrected me, then popped up into a sitting position, her back straight as a board. "Bring me my backpack. I'll show you."

I obliged, even though I didn't want to. "Just lie down, Gret," I said, as I grabbed her backpack. "Just rest. You're hungry.

You're tired. We all are. Exhausted. But we've got water, so that's good. Drink some more." Sweat was pouring off my face as I said it, and I took a few swigs of water too. We didn't need all of us hallucinating.

Greta grabbed the pack as soon as it was close enough and dug through it, tossing out wrappers and an empty pack of gum. "Look," she said, holding up a little homemade book. Inside, she'd pasted old newspaper clippings and internet articles. "Look," she said again, stabbing the first page.

And there he was—blurry, black and white. But undeniable. Benjamin Jarrison Howard. Same height, same hair, same build. Same expression on his unhappy face.

I rocked back on my heels.

"We're not both having the same hallucination," Greta said to me, as Gideon walked in, his own face looking white.

He'd rescued the parsnips, but he had something else he was carrying in an old sack, something heavy.

"What is it?" I asked, even though my stomach was already sinking into my knees, even though I knew.

"That wasn't a cat," Gideon said.

"Oh, man. Get the girls in here," I muttered. "This is…I just wish we could leave."

But Gideon didn't have to get the girls in, because Savina rushed in right then, carrying Greta's basket of eggs, the other two girls trailing behind her.

"Are you okay?" Savina gushed, kneeling by Greta.

"No one's okay," I answered for her. "Greta found something out there, in the garden."

"I hope it was more than bits of the house that everyone keeps eating, because we really need something real," Savina said.

None of us smiled.

"She found the first victim of the serial killings," I said. "He was buried in the corner of the garden."

Savina looked at Gideon's face first. He held up the sack.

"So this is the house, the house where the killer lived," Savina said. "We've got to leave."

Greta, I noticed, wasn't looking at her. She was looking into her basket of eggs. I peered over her shoulder. And the first egg, the brown one we'd thought had tried to hatch—it was lying cracked fully open, but empty.

"I think I'm gonna be sick," Greta said.

I grabbed a bucket from near the door and shoved it under her face as she leaned over it, though nothing came. Even so, I stroked her hair back, just like Mom used to do, wiping Greta's neck with an old rag from the table.

"Just sip it," I said. "Just sip the water. Someone will come soon. Someone will find us."

I looked up to see the new girl, Missy, snatching a piece of the doorframe, a sliver that looked just like licorice in the fading light. She popped it into her mouth.

I looked outside. "Is it already afternoon?"

"Nearly dusk," Savina said, sitting beside me.

Greta had fallen asleep in my arms.

"How do the days go so fast?" I murmured.

"Well, a lot has happened," Savina answered, stroking Greta's hair.

I stared at the cuckoo clock, which was stuck at 6:15. "Let's eat those vegetables—the parsnips—and then go to sleep. When we wake up, we'll start another fire. This one *outside*."

THE SUN SEEMED to sink way too early for June.

Soon enough, everyone had gathered around the fire in the hot living room, Greta still sleeping, Gideon leaning against the wall near the wood. We'd put the sack in a cupboard in the kitchen—out of sight.

Savina settled down beside me, casting worried glances at Greta, while the other girls fiddled with the things on the table.

"Ooooh, yarn," Shelle said, reaching over and wrapping a strand around her fingers. "Cat in the cradle, anyone?"

"How do you play?" Missy asked.

"Don't you know?" Shelle said. "Here, let me show you. I can make the most beautiful flower patterns. I just adore flowers." In half a minute, she'd gotten Missy's fingers all wound up and was teaching her a game with the yarn, where you wrap it over your fingers and make different patterns.

"How do you do it?" Savina asked, scooting closer to the girls.

"You don't know how to play either?" Shelle asked. "I thought everybody did. I do this just about every minute of the day, especially when I'm bored or nervous. You gotta do something with your fingers."

Savina was trying to figure out the next pattern. "I do think I've seen something like this on YouTube."

"Your what?" Shelle asked.

"You know, on my phone," Savina said.

Shelle gave her a weird look. "I gotta admit, I sure do wish I had a phone right now. I could call Harry."

"Who's that?" Missy asked.

"Oh, just a guy," Shelle said coyly.

"Boyfriend?" Savina asked.

"He's so dreamy," Shelle replied.

"What's he look like?" Savina said.

"Mmmm, blond hair. Crew cut. Real nice. Square jaw, perfect nose. Blue eyes you could swim in." She closed her eyes, seemingly to take a dive into the memory, then popped them open, doing a complicated twist with the yarn. "What about you, Savvy? You going with any boys?"

"Me?" Savina said.

I leaned in, listening the best I could, while trying to appear to not listen at all. I took my lead from Gideon, staring into the fire, even as every part of me tipped toward Savina.

"Um, no. Not really," she murmured, looking down at the yarn, her eyelashes dark against her white cheeks.

"What's your type?" Shelle asked.

"Don't know that I really have a type," Savina said, tangling the yarn. "I guess I like tall guys."

"Well, duh," Missy said, trying to jump into the conversation with the older girls.

Savina grabbed the opportunity to jump out. "Have you got a boyfriend, Missy?"

"Nah," she said. "Mama wouldn't even let me go to the movies with a boy, even though one asked me once, real cute with a note he folded into a rose. But Mama said one of us had to be old enough to drive, or we were too young."

"Can't say I totally disagree," Shelle replied. "It's real nice once he can drive."

"How long have you been together with your boyfriend?" Savina asked Shelle. And normally, this would not at all be the type of conversation I would eavesdrop on, but with Savina involved, it totally was.

"Seems like forever," Shelle answered. "But we're technically not an item, not going steady anyway." Shelle glanced at the intricate yarn around her fingers. "Not yet." Outside and far away, an owl hooted. All at once, Shelle cocked her head to the side. "You know, I was supposed to meet him in the woods. Harry. That's where we always met. He always gave me a wild-flower. I loved the flowers from the woods. Anyway, this time, I thought he was going to ask me to be his girlfriend..." She squinted at the memory. "But then I got lost."

For a few moments, her eyes grew big and shiny like she might cry. Then it passed and she laughed. "Hope he hasn't found some other girl by now."

"Well, if he has," Savina said, "he would have been a terrible boyfriend."

"Easy come, easy go," Shelle replied.

"It's only been a day," Savina said.

"Is that all?" Shelle said.

"I know, it feels like forever," Savina said. "But, yeah, you came here last night. He's probably looking for you with the search parties. Worried sick."

"You think?" Shelle asked, the shiny look back.

"Of course," Savina answered, messing up the yarn and plucking it off her fingers. "How do you guys do this so easily? Your turn, Missy." Savina handed the wad of yarn over, and scooted a little closer to me, gazing down at Greta's sleeping face. I noticed that Savina still wasn't looking great either, her own skin pale, even her lips.

Greta groaned in her sleep and I tried to adjust her on my lap to make her more comfortable, though truthfully, my butt was killing me from sitting on the hard floor and I was so hot I wondered if I might be sick too. Plus, I need to do a little of my own business.

"Here," I said, shifting Greta over to Savina. "You want to take a sister shift?"

"I'd love to," Savina said, moving closer and taking Greta's hand. It hung limp and I paused before getting up.

"She'll be alright," Savina said, looking up at me, her eyes black and shining against the dim light of the fire. "She made a big discovery out there—a big, terrible discovery. And, well, after all this." She motioned around. "None of us is feeling well. Everybody's hungry. And then there's this floor…" She shifted.

"Tell me about it," I said. "I'm gonna go get her some more water. I'll be right back."

Savina nodded, then reached out, touching my forearm, her eyebrows dipping together slightly in concern. "Hank," she said. "Or…Hans—that's what Greta calls you, right?" She moved closer to me, our faces only inches apart, and murmured, "Don't go far. Just…stay close."

"Yeah, sure," I said, my tongue a little thick.

I crawled over the sticky floor to grab Greta's water bottle and her in-case-she-throws-up bucket. And there, under the broken bench, I saw several clumps of mud. Mud that I was almost sure hadn't been there before. Was someone coming and going? And if so, who? And how? And when? And was this still the house of a serial killer? I swallowed the acid that kicked into the back of my own throat. Then scuttled out of the front door, looking right and left, trying to see any traces of a person who might have been here. But there was nothing.

Outside, the air felt cooler and I gasped it into my lungs, trying to cool my hot face, my body. I refused to believe I had a fever. After all, that was the last thing we needed. I was probably just hot from the fire, or from Savina's touch, or from worrying about Greta. Or maybe from seeing that mud on the floor.

I walked a few paces farther, toward the well, staying as close to the house as I could.

All around, the sky looked low and dark, nearly pitch black, the stars covered by clouds. That, plus the smoke that piped dutifully from Gideon's fire.

How had no one found us yet? I rinsed the bucket, then filled it with fresh water, splashing some of it onto my own face.

Gazing into the black silence of the woods, I wanted to scream. *We're right here!*

CHAPTER 17

GRETA

I woke to the cuckoo clock, chiming at midnight.

Everyone must have been getting used to it—that or they were all deep-bone tired—because nobody else woke up.

I rubbed my back, trying to swallow the disgusting taste stuck in my throat. How long had it been since I brushed my teeth? I rolled over, feeling for my backpack, then digging into it for my water bottle. My fingers brushed the little book. The book I'd shown Hans.

Hans, the book, the day before.

B.J.

I sat up, immediately feeling a little sick again, my head spinning, my throat thick. I opened my water bottle, hands shaking, and tipped a bit of water into my mouth—just a sip like Hans had said, like Mama used to say. But I couldn't stop at a sip—so thirsty. I guzzled the rest, all the way to the last drops. Even after it was gone, I wanted more.

Getting up without a sound, I tiptoed toward the kitchen, trying to avoid tripping on anyone as I went.

Shelle slept in the rocking chair, a little ball of yarn in her lap, a strand of it wrapped around her fingers in an intricate pattern. Missy was cradling her flashlight on the floor. No sleepwalking yet, which was good. Though maybe if she could have sleepwalked her way out of here and back to her house, we could have followed her.

Gideon was sprawled right in front of the fire, Savina near him, the quilt draped over her body. Hans was the opposite, limbs splayed open, shirt off, like he was trying to get cool. I wasn't the only one who needed water, apparently. I grabbed a rag so that I could get it wet for Hans, drape it over him, like I had the night before.

I stumbled into the darkness of the kitchen, feeling around for the bucket of water. Under my fingertips, the counters felt sticky, bits of wood peeling at the edges. Like every other surface of this house.

Without thinking, I picked at a piece of it, just a bit, the same way B.J. had picked at the doorframe the night we'd met him. Or, well, his ghost.

A little bit of the wood stuck to my finger and I held it up to my face, trying to see it in the darkness.

And I knew I shouldn't. I knew it was madness to eat a house. But I figured it couldn't be madness to taste it, to try to understand.

So I popped it into my mouth. Expecting the scrape of wood as it moved across my tongue, expecting the chalky sawdust flavor, expecting varnish and rancid oil.

Instead, I was surprised to feel the wood melting in my mouth, a sweet dark flavor that wasn't wood at all.

"Chocolate," I murmured.

A FEW NIBBLES MORE, that's all I took. It was all I needed. Having something in my stomach made me feel better than I'd felt since we got here, satiated even though it was so little. I didn't even need more water, and made my way back into the living room.

Settling back onto the floor, I was asleep in minutes.

When I woke in the morning, a parsnip rested by my side. They'd saved it for me.

"Hey, sleepy head," Savina said. She was trying to be chipper and not succeeding. "Saved you some grub."

"Thanks," I said, nibbling at the parsnip. It was woody and grimy, with a bitter kick. Eating the food I knew they'd given up so I could have it, all I could do was gaze into the kitchen, at the peeling counter, the memory of the taste filling up my mouth, begging for more.

What else did that kid eat? The sides of the house, the door frames, even the floor. Everything. I thought about the way the house smelled when we'd first arrived. Like burnt caramel.

"We're thinking of taking the fire outside this morning," Savina said, her voice drooping with her pale face. "Hans is really hot with it inside." She looked at me. "Is it really that hot?"

"It's warm," I answered, a chunk of parsnip sticking in my throat so that I had to choke it down.

"Any ideas for food?" she asked. "I think the garden is basically exhausted as far as resources go."

"Do you want the rest…" I held out my parsnip.

"Oh, no, Greta, you eat it. I know we're all starving."

Except that for the first time since arriving here, I wasn't. I took another obliging bite. "Have they checked the shed where Missy was for more food?"

"Yeah," she said. "Nothing. Looks like a place where animals used to be kept. Once upon a time…"

She gazed up, looking out the window at a stack of wood made by the boys.

I dug at the floor when she looked away, scraping a bit of the surface into my fingernail. And then I put it to my mouth. Sure enough, even that sliver of floorboard tasted sweet, buttery. I tucked the rest of the parsnip into my pocket. "I'm going to go check upstairs, in the attic. Maybe there's something we missed."

"Yeah," she said, still staring out the window. "We've got to be missing something. Hans was also talking about going out to look for your house again. He and one of us." She paused. "And, I don't know, maybe we should."

Her eyes glassed over like they often did. I never would have pegged her for a crier, but she was definitely the weepiest of the four of us. I knew I should reach out and give her a shoulder squeeze or maybe say something comforting, but all I could think about was the honey butter flavor of the floor.

"It sucks, staying. On the other hand, I'm afraid for anyone to go," she said, her voice small.

I nodded. "Maybe Shelle could try to retrace her footsteps or something." It was about all I could manage in the idea department.

"Nah," she said. "Those two girls can hardly do anything except talk about boys and dolls and yarn and who knows what else—like they don't even understand the danger we're in. Oh, and I caught the younger one licking that post this morning." She sighed.

I licked my own lips, my gaze drifting to the post.

"Okay, look," I said. "I'm gonna head upstairs and see if I can find anything to eat at all. Some cans. Maybe jerky. Candy." My voice tipped up on the last syllable, and I cleared my throat.

"Yeah, keep dreaming, Greta, though I can't blame you—candy does sound nice."

She had no idea just how nice it sounded.

I left her in the kitchen, sipping water from an old mug, and hurried up the steps. Looking down, I realized that even the stairs looked suspiciously like peanut brittle. I shook my head, letting myself into the tiny room, and slinking around the bed.

Along the wall, supporting beams jutted out on either side. I reached out a hand, fingering the nearest one, the swirling wood almost like a bit of...Before I could stop myself I was licking it, just like Missy had done with the post.

It tasted like a lollipop, root beer flavored. I gnawed bits of it. A little chunk broke off in my mouth and I sucked on it, feeling much happier and more full than I had from that parsnip.

Looking around the room, I noticed the chair—soft with a bit of stuffing coming out at one of the seams.

I wandered to it like I wasn't going to do what I was absolutely going to do. When I got there, I dug my fingers in, hoping the stuffing would taste like cotton candy. But the fabric wasn't tear-able, or edible either. Just old cotton or polyester or something. I spit it out.

So it was only the house. I turned to the walls and found a small crack like it'd been replastered at some point. I could dig my fingers in, pry off just a bit. Biscotti. Crisp and buttery. I broke more from the wall, working bits of it off and gobbling them up, caring less with each bite if I got caught or not, if I'd gone insane or not. It was just too good and I was so hungry.

Working all of my fingers into the crevice I'd created, I broke a piece of board away from the wall. I sighed, about to dig into the most perfect breakfast I'd ever had when I noticed the hole I'd made extended deep into the wall. I nibbled at the plank, realizing I'd need to cover it up so Hans didn't notice how huge it was, a hole with bits of insulation or something coming out.

I leaned forward to look at it. It wasn't just an opening from the missing wood, but an actual hole, like a compartment built inside the wall.

I paused in my chewing, then hid the piece of wood-cookie under the cushion of the chair so I could come back for it later.

Maybe the hole was just a gap, a place where a mouse had pulled out the insulation to make a little nest or something. Yes, obviously, because there were little pieces of wood and a bit of yarn. Just like that ball of yarn downstairs, the one in Shelle's lap. I tipped my head to the side, feeling almost like a mouse myself.

Inside the hole I found other things too—a squirrel hoard probably—I'd read somewhere that they liked shiny things. And this hole was full of shiny things. A metal barrette, a couple of bobby pins, even a piece of ivory or—I reached in to take it out —a bit of bone. A scrap of bone among a pile of ash.

I pulled everything out, frantically tugging at the yarn— practically a whole ball's worth. I wrapped it up around my fingers, trying to remember the way Shelle had it over her hands this morning, the complicated twists and loops.

Behind me, the door creaked open. I was expecting Savina, but when I glanced up, it was Shelle, the same yarn wound around her fingers in the same flowery pattern.

"No," I whispered. Our eyes met, and then a bright ray of light flashed from the small window above the bed.

She was gone.

๛

"Hans!" I screamed, barreling down the narrow steps. "Hans! Savina!"

Hans grabbed me as I hit the bottom landing. "What the— Greta, what's wrong?"

I held up the yarn, still wrapped around my fingers, felt the panic rising up from my throat. "She's gone," I said.

"Who?" he asked.

"Shelle."

Savina hurried over to the steps.

"I found her things," I said. "In the wall. Just like with B.J. She's not—" But I didn't know how to finish.

"She's not real," Gideon said, coming up behind his sister.

"She was," I blubbered. "But she's dead. Just like he was. I found a piece of bone."

Hans shoved past me, thundering up the stairs, though the ceiling was so low that with his height, he had to angle forward and pummel through the door.

Gideon followed him, taking the steps more carefully. Savina and I glanced at each other. Her face was so perfectly white that you'd have thought she was the one who was actually the ghost. I reached out to touch her, just to be sure. Of all of us, the hunger seemed to have hit her the hardest.

"Come on," I said, taking her arm.

By the time I reached the top, Gideon had all the things from the little nest out on the floor. Savina started to say something—maybe a prayer or meditation or song—something with words that repeat.

"Do you know who she is?" Hans asked me. "Well, was."

"I think so," I said, my voice small. "The second victim. Shelby. I should have figured it out as soon as B.J., well, Benjamin went away. But I wasn't thinking clearly. Anyway, let me get my book."

I stumbled back down the stairs and through the house, looking for my bag. Right on the floor where I left it, its contents spilling out.

As I hurried back up the steps, I noticed that everything was completely silent. No one crying or moaning or anything. "Guys!" I said, my voice ratcheting up a notch.

"Here," Hans answered in a whisper as I crested the landing.

They were all standing around the chest, just staring into it. The padlock lay at their feet, rusted and broken open.

I didn't want to look. I just wanted to go back down the stairs, back through the woods, back home to my safe little house with Mama. But I couldn't. So I stepped forward. I knew the chest wasn't holding a body; we would have smelled that. "What is it?"

"Clothes," Hans said. "Her clothes. Just like she was wearing. Folded up neat."

"This bone is a shard," Gideon said. "Like when they cremate people, sometimes there's a little shard left. Like this."

Silent tears dripped down Savina's face.

"Where's the other girl?" Gideon asked. He turned to me. "What's her name?"

"Missy," I said, then looked down at my book, frowning. "Melissa."

"Missy can be a nickname for that," Savina said quietly.

"And where is she?" Gideon asked.

Our gazes flitted around the little circle. None of us knew. Savina pinched her lips together and said, "Eating a piece of the house, no doubt. They all were. They didn't see it as a house though. Remember what Shelle said—that she just ate a piece of candy off the mantle. We thought the problem was us, but, well, I mean, there's no end to problems right now…" She trailed off.

Hans was already heading down the stairs, Gideon following him closely, in his lumbering way.

We heard them barrel out the door, looking for Missy.

Savina looked at me. I turned, and she followed me slowly, back down the stairs.

But we didn't get past the kitchen to help look for Missy or Melissa or whoever she is. Was.

Because there, on the counter, sat the basket of eggs. And the gray-blue one was cracked wide open.

"They're haunted," Savina said. "The eggs. They're bringing the ghosts."

And under literally *any* other circumstances, I might have argued. But at just that moment a fourth egg began to rock back and forth—a soft sway turning into a solid tremble turning into a hard rocking movement. A crack splintered up one side of the olive-green egg.

No, Savina mouthed, no sound coming from her lips.

And then we heard it—not a door or screaming or crying. But singing. All the way through the woods. I leaned toward it, realizing I hadn't heard any music since we'd gotten here. Unless you counted the distant birds.

The song was old, one Mama sometimes hummed, one that would still come on the radio here and now.

"'Wonderwall,'" I murmured. "Is that what it's called?"

Savina didn't answer. She was too busy backing up close to the wood stove, her eyes wide, her face even paler if that was possible.

"Greta, we can't let her in."

I glanced at the eggs, and didn't feel sure. There was something about them, like something important was happening with them, with us because of them.

"No," I whispered, as the singing came right up to the door by the living room. "We're finding them. We're setting them free."

"I don't want to find them," Savina said, as a solid knock tapped against the door.

"I'm not sure that's a choice we have," I answered. "When we find them, the spirits go away. If we don't, they stay. And we stay with them, for as long as we're in this house."

"Which means forever," Savina whispered.

The door creaked open. "Hello," the voice called out.

I gave Savina one more look.

"Hey," I said, walking into the front room.

And there she was, just like I'd expected. The girl my own mama had once known. Although looking at her, it was clear that the picture in the newspaper was an old one. Her face was a little more angular, her figure a little more full. And it seemed she'd traded her geometric shirt for some grunge jeans and a flannel shirt.

"Hey, baby," she said to me. "You got a phone in here? I am sooo lost."

I shook my head, my lips glued together. She looked so alive, so happy, so thrilled to have found the house, to have found me in it. How do you tell a girl like that that, not only do you not have a phone, but that she is actually dead and has been for twenty-six years?

"Mmm, this place smells good," she said, setting something down on the little broken bench. "Just like Grandmama's house at Christmas. Is that a candle or what?"

"No," I stammered. A Walkman—that's what she'd set down. Headphones with a little machine that plays tapes. Mama had pictures of herself wearing one.

"Mmmm, something good must be cookin' then. Even better. My name's Risa," she said, holding out her hand for me to shake.

"Greta," I answered, slowly extending my own hand. From the corner of my eye, I could see Savina's shadow darkening the door into the kitchen. She shook her head, but I ignored it.

"Your friend the cook?" Risa asked. Larisa, I thought, remembering her full name.

We both looked at Savina.

"Actually," I began. "There's really not a lot of food. This place just smells good because, uh, because…"

"What you talking about, Greta girl? There's something real nice right here." She moved past Savina—who practically glued herself against the wall to make room—into the kitchen, and like we knew she would, she pried a chunk off of a thick beam in the center of the room and popped it into her mouth. "Mmmm, honey crisps. Just like Grandmama used to make. I sure miss her."

Savina stared in horror as Larisa continued to nibble at the beam. I, on the other hand, felt my stomach rumble, my mouth salivate. I couldn't wait for them all to leave so I could get my fingers on that beam. Honey crisps. That sounded amazing.

It was then that Hans and Gideon banged into the kitchen,

looking like wild men. Hans' hair all greasy and sticking up at angles, his face sweaty. "We can't find her," he started to say, his mouth moving faster than his eyes. Partway through, he realized another girl was standing in the kitchen, right in front of us.

"Larisa," I said, by way of introduction. "The fourth."

"Fourth what?" Larisa asked.

"The fourth… person we've met here," I said. "I guess it's a place people find when they're lost in the woods. We did too. It's not really our house."

"Well, whose is it?" she asked, her eyebrows tipping together in concern.

"We don't really know," I answered. "We think it was, um, abandoned."

"Then who made the honey crisps?" she asked.

Hans shared a look with Savina and she nodded almost imperceptibly.

"Anyway," Hans cut in. "We were actually looking for another girl who was here. Did you see anyone when you were coming in?"

"Nope," Larisa answered with her never-ending cheer. "Just a whole lotta trees and mushrooms and stuff."

"Yeah," Hans muttered. "You got that right."

And Larisa, she just laughed, like Hans was the funniest guy on earth, not some grumpy older brother. Like we were all just best friends, hanging out in a cool old house we found in the woods.

"Anyway," Hans continued. "You just get some of those, uh, honey crisps, did you say? And we'll be right back."

He gave us all a look. A boss of the world look. A look that said, 'Meet me outside.' As we left, I grabbed the basket of eggs, hooking it over my arm as we headed out the door.

CHAPTER 18

HANS

Day 4, afternoon

This was more than mushrooms. It was probably more than LSD, not that I would actually know. But I couldn't imagine anything trippier than what was happening right now.

"We've got to leave," I said, as we walked, Savina by my side, Gideon and Greta trailing after. "Find our way out, I don't know. Something."

Greta stared at me like I'd lost my mind. "We already tried that," she said. "Multiple times."

"Oh, I'm sorry," I snapped back at her. "Then I guess we'll just stay in the house with a bunch of ghosts."

"They vanish," Greta answered. "They vanish when we find what remains of them."

"Are you serious?" I asked.

"I mean, yes," Greta said. "And don't pretend it's any less crazy than trying to find our way through the woods again."

And then Gideon, his eyes drooping like he hadn't eaten for days, which, oh wait, he hadn't, came to her defense. "Is she wrong?"

I ran my hands through my hair, feeling the sticky dirtiness of it.

"I want to leave," Savina said in a small voice. "I think I'd rather die in the woods than go back to that house."

"Savina," Gideon began.

"No," I replied. "Let's try that. Not the dying part," I clarified. "But the looking. Savina and I will look for a way out. You and Greta can stay and do, like, a séance or something. Find the remains, whatever."

"You don't have to be mean about it," Greta said.

And I didn't. But I felt mean. Ragingly hungry, itchy from the fever and the welts that were popping up along the seams of my clothes. Hives, I assumed. Savina didn't look much better. Honestly, I felt like if we didn't get her some food soon, she was going to be too weak to go anywhere.

"Savina…" Gideon said again.

"I won't go back to that house," she answered.

Gideon pinched his lips together in a way that seemed to want to argue. But he didn't. "Take some water."

"You can have my water bottle," Greta said. "We've got the mugs."

Greta

WE WALKED to the well like a funeral procession, most of us looking half dead. Hans was sweating and scratching. Savina dragging like she wouldn't be able to put one foot in front of the other for much longer. Gideon's eyes were shot with blood, rimmed with the beginnings of jaundice.

And I…I had nothing. It dawned on me in this slow kind of

way that ever since I'd tasted that bit of the house, I'd actually felt pretty good.

Which seemed bad somehow, but I shook it off.

Gideon pulled up the bucket full of fresh, clear water. We all seemed to think about how impossible that was, but we took it anyway. It was the only thing keeping us alive.

And then, from the house, we could hear the singing. Larisa belting out Ace of Bass strong enough for it to go through the walls.

Savina blinked like she was hoping to wake from a nightmare. Me, I kind of liked the music.

We turned to walk out of the clearing, into the woods along a line of mushrooms, when I saw it. "The flashlight," I said.

It was sticking out from behind a cluster of trees. Connected to a sleeping Melissa. She had a chunk of shingle in her other hand. Looking at it, my mouth watered.

"Should we wake her?" Gideon asked.

"No way," Hans said.

"The flashlight," I murmured again. "That's what we need to look for; that's the thing connected to her.

"Well, you guys have fun with that," Hans said. "We're going to look for a way out of here."

"Don't go," I said, annoyed at how desperate and pleading I sounded. "I think if we find them all, we'll get out."

Hans shook his head. "It's getting to you, Greta. The hunger, the anxiety, the exhaustion. The only way to get out is to find the way out."

It was getting to *me?* What about Captain Grumpy Desperate? But I stopped arguing. I always stopped arguing.

Gideon took Savina's hand. And maybe because she looked so white and limp, he didn't argue or plead like I did.

"Listen," Hans said. "We'll meet back in two hours if we haven't found anything."

"You have no way to keep time," Gideon replied.

But Gideon and I knew what no one would say—they wouldn't need a way to keep time. They'd be back no matter what.

Maybe deep down Hans knew it too, because he added, "Try to find some food. To keep your strength up." I heard what he didn't say, but must have thought as he looked at Savina. *If we come back, we're gonna need some food.*

"I'll look for food," Gideon said, turning to me. I knew what he didn't say to me too. *You look for the flashlight.*

But where? If I were a killer hiding objects connected to my victims, where on earth would they be?

CHAPTER 19

HANS

Savina didn't make it even a mile. She was panting and stumbling her way through the underbrush, which was only getting thicker. I passed her the water bottle and as she reached out to take it, she tripped, flying forward into my arms.

A cartoon moment.

Except that I thought she was dead, the way she went limp, sinking heavily to the ground. That took the cuteness right out of it.

"Savina," I said, fanning her, loosening her shirt around her neck, until I realized she was shivering. I'd been so hot for days. We must have caught something, and fevers hit people in different ways. She was ice. I was fire.

I took the flannel shirt off my waist and draped it over her body.

"Hey," I said. "Are you okay?"

"Do I look okay?" she asked, and even then, she had this little smile.

"You know, you really don't."

"Hans," she said, sort of rolling into this little ball. "I promise that if we ever get out of these stupid woods, I will never tell you not to listen to your mother ever again."

"I don't know," I said, tucking the flannel tight around her. "If I had listened to my mom, you wouldn't have me here rescuing you right now."

"I mean, that *is* nice," she said, but her voice was softer.

"Do you need a nap or something?" I asked. "Here, at least drink some water."

She took it and even her lips were shaking. "I'm so cold," she said. "I'm not sure I should fall asleep. I mean, it can't be hypothermia, because it's—I don't know—summer out here. But I'm so, so cold."

"Maybe just take a little nap," I said. "I'll look for some berries or something."

"No," she answered. "Don't go away. Please. The woods are just too..." She flicked a finger toward the trees.

"Deep," I finished for her as her eyes closed.

"Wild." Her fingers wrapped around my hand, and when they did, I knew we were in trouble, because her hand was freezing. Colder than normal fingers. Practically the fingers of a dead person. I rubbed them, trying to get some circulation back into them.

And then, because I was burning up, I scooted beside her and lay down, trying to give her as much of my heat as I could. It seemed like it should have worked, the perfect symbiotic relationship—her icy body sucking up all my heat. But somehow, even as we lay there, tight together, she stayed ice, while I held fire.

We fell asleep anyway, that's how tired we were.

When I woke up, the sun was hanging lower, and she wasn't moving.

I cursed, rubbing at her hand, then shaking her shoulder. "Savina!" I said, placing my hand against her, feeling for breath.

It was there, the smallest lift.

I let out my own breath and placed a finger on her neck to check her pulse, which was almost too faint to feel.

Ahead of me were only trees. They seemed knitted together, getting darker with every passing minute of the day.

And then a little thing glinted on the path, a flash of silver. I crawled toward it, expecting it to be nothing more than a trick of the light.

But it wasn't. It was a tiny corner of a wrapper—one of Greta's granola bar wrappers. And on the tree just past it was a marking, grown fat and thick from growth in the last few years, but still legible—the little 'H' connected to the 'G'—our hieroglyphics from when we were kids. From when we'd just moved in because Dad had left. And the move had seemed sad but the woods seemed wide and fun and full of possibilities. Somehow over those years, I'd walked away from that openness, back to the closure of the house.

"Savina!" I said. "We're close. My property—"

But when I turned back, I couldn't see her. "Savina?"

I rushed back and found her, still not moving—she had somehow rolled to some underbrush. "Savina?"

I crouched beside her, holding a hand close to her lips, feeling for her breath. The only thing I felt coming off of her was cold.

I didn't even think about it. I tipped her head back, opened her mouth, intending to breathe for her—all my heat into her mouth.

It wasn't sexy like in the movies. It was terrifying, truly terrifying.

But before I could resuscitate her, her chest lifted and she exhaled. I realized that she'd been breathing the whole time and that I'd overreacted. Just like Mama said I always did, jumping when I needed to step more carefully.

I kept my lips close to hers anyway. My heat to her body.

"Hans," she whispered, her lips almost tickling mine. "I think we have to go back."

"No," I said. "We're close to my house. I just found this tree. When Greta and I were little, we would play in the woods and—"

She stopped moving again. "Savina," I lifted her up, tipped the water to her lips. "I think I can get us back home. Then we'll go for them."

"Do you know the way?" she asked, her voice soft.

"Yeah," I said, though it wasn't fully true. "I found this piece of Greta's granola bar wrapper." I turned toward it, just as a breeze picked it up and it floated away.

But the breeze couldn't blow the tree away even if it wanted to. And I knew it was just beyond where we were. "There's this tree," I began.

"One tree?" Savina asked. "But do you know the *way?*"

I looked into her eyes—the deepest brown in the world—and didn't answer.

"But we *do* know the way back to that old cottage," she said.

I shook my head. "We don't need to go back. We're so close."

"But we know the way," she said, tipping her head in the direction we'd come from.

I closed my eyes, not wanting to see. But it was there, the line of smoke—the line of smoke that Gideon had kept going day and night. How could no one else see it? How could they not find it?

"I want to see Gideon," she said.

"I know," I said, "but then we'll all just be stuck there again. In that house."

"We're stuck here," she said.

"No," I replied. "We're close."

"Do you know he almost died when we were born? Gideon. I was first, all healthy and strong and big, especially for a twin. He came next and Mama had to push so much longer. That doesn't usually happen, but she did, and then when he came he was small, twiggy, and blue."

"Savina, shhh," I said, wrapping my hands over her cold fingers. "Just rest."

"I am," she said. "My first memory—ever—in my whole life is being at the doctor's office when we were three or four and the doctor saying something about how I must have sucked up all the good stuff. It was probably just meant to be a joke. Certainly, it wasn't meant for my ears, but my ears caught it anyway, held it all these years. That guilt. That strength. I'd get asked to homecoming and Gid would ask someone, some girl, and she'd say 'no.' The one time someone actually said yes, she came out to me the next day, saying I was the one she'd actually wanted. That was awkward." Savina let out a little laugh, her breath still cool.

I stayed close, trying and trying and trying to give her my heat.

"Let's go at least look at the tree," I said. "Maybe I'll be able to see my house. Greta and I used to leave marks on trees all over the place—some close, some far. Maybe this one is close."

"Go check," Savina said.

Reluctantly, I set her hand down, scooting away, in the direction I thought the wrapper had been, toward the tree. But I couldn't find it, not the tree, or any others with the markings. Just trees with fungus, trees with mushrooms.

I darted from tree to tree, deeper into the forest, until I could barely see Savina. But there, in the deep, cool shadows of the trees, I still felt hot, hotter in fact. I placed a hand on a tree, my hand pressing against the spongy fungus. Mushrooms, everywhere. That was one thing I was determined never to eat again, no matter how desperate we got.

"Savina!" I called, thinking that maybe I'd lost her.

"We know the way back," I heard her say and she was there, not far from me. Not far, but still hidden in the trees.

"Keep talking," I said.

"Gideon always came up behind. He always dragged," she said. "But not really. When things were hard, I would crumble. I would cry or pitch a fit. But he was always calm, always steady. He was stronger," she said. "Even though everyone—doctors, our parents, every teenager alive—thought he was weaker. He's still stronger," she said, as I made my way back to her. "So we have to go back. I have to see him."

"I don't want to go back," I answered.

"Me either," she said. "But we're going to. Because we can't go forward, can we?"

"How are you going to walk?" I asked.

"You're going to help me," she replied.

And then I saw them, a little stand of blackberry bushes, the berries just starting to ripen. It looked like not a single bird had touched them. "Okay," I murmured.

I stripped the bushes—took every berry and fed them to Savina. A few I shoved into my pockets for Gideon and Greta, though it seemed disgusting and I knew they would mush. I also knew, in some dark corner of my heart, that we wouldn't be able to find that bush again, just like I couldn't find the tree I'd just seen.

"Do you think we're hallucinating it?" I said suddenly. "All of this, the tree I thought I saw and stuff."

"By stuff, you mean the dead kids we saw as ghosts?"

"Maybe," I said.

"No," she said. "But you know what your sister said—about how we have to find those kids. I really don't want to, but I think she might be right. I never really believed in ghosts. But we saw them, those kids; we found that stuff. I think they're drawing us to them, or maybe they're drawing Greta to them. I don't know. But for whatever reason, those kids are trying to be found. And I don't think they're going to let us go until we find them."

"Then why are we sick?" I asked.

"I don't know," she answered. "But we have to go back."

I nodded. What else was there to do? I took her arm and forearm, helping her to her feet. She wobbled. But we walked. All directions seemed to have become the same, but the woods led us there, in the direction we needed to go.

And it wasn't home.

CHAPTER 20

GRETA

Gideon had found more mushrooms, that was all. "I know your brother…" he said, his words faltering like they did. "I know he said not to eat more, but I figured we could eat them before they got back and if *we* got sick, well, then we'd know."

It felt rude to point out that Gideon already looked pretty sick. "Good idea," I said. "We'll just start with a little. What variety is this?"

"I think they're oyster mushrooms, but I can't be sure. You don't have to eat them, Greta. I will at first."

Truth be told, I had all of zero desire to eat more spongy mushrooms when the banister was calling to me, but no way was I going to let Gideon eat them on his own. Though I really did hope he knew what he was doing and we didn't get sick. Especially since I was really feeling okay, good even. I broke a small piece off of the mushroom. A bit for him, a bit for me. "On three," I said, smiling.

"One, two…"

"Three," he ended for me, almost laughing as he stuffed the piece into his mouth.

We both chewed the springy flesh of the mushroom, then swallowed, waiting like it was a potion that would hit with some sort of magical bang.

Nothing.

"I think we're good," I said.

He nodded, and we ate a little more. This time as I chewed, I imagined the silky sweet scent of the banister, browned butter with hints of tangy fruit, like sour orange. I couldn't believe we'd all run our hands up it without realizing.

When I opened my eyes, I realized the mushroom was gone. I must have swallowed it. Plus, Gideon was looking at me funny. "Did you like it?" he asked, like he hadn't. "It looked like you liked it."

"It was okay," I said carefully.

He nodded. "We can save the rest for them."

We exchanged a look. A look that said they should be back soon. But also a look that said, *What if they aren't?*

Both of us tossed the look away, me shuffling toward the attic steps. "I haven't found it yet, the flashlight. Or anything. I'm going to check upstairs."

He nodded, then glanced around. We hadn't seen either girl since Hans and Savina had left. "I'll go back to the woods and see if I can find more food," he said.

I hoped he wouldn't go far, but I was too focused on the banister to worry for long. I hurried to the attic steps, stopping at the banister and picking bits from the part nearest the wall—the part where no one would notice.

"Mmmm, now don't that look good," Larisa said, her booming voice making me jump.

I had to shove down the urge to shush her. "Excuse me, what?" I asked.

"What is it?" she asked, as though she hadn't heard. "Licorice, or something different?"

"Different," I said, my voice mostly caught in my throat so it just came out in a squeak. "I think it's just wood, honestly."

She popped an eyebrow—popped it high. "Now, if you don't want to share, just you say so," she said.

"Oh, no," I mumbled. "Yeah, here, it's all yours," I answered. "I've got to check something upstairs."

I left her behind me and heard her tearing pieces off the banister like they were strips of candy. "Mmmm, just like a fruit roll up," she called up the stairs. "Only better."

When I got to the attic, I realized I hadn't been there since we'd found Shelby's remains. The trunk was closed, but the hole in the wall was still there, open and empty. Hans had moved all the things we'd found to a pantry shelf in the kitchen, so that when the search parties found us, we could show them.

I saw a little broom in the corner, and grabbed it, sweeping up the remaining dust and debris, wondering how much was ashen bone and then trying not to think about it. If I could just sweep it away, the room wouldn't feel so scary, so lonely.

In fact... I opened the window to let a breeze blow in, then dumped the dirt into a little waste bin near the bed. It looked a lot better. I turned a circle in the room.

All this time, we'd been sleeping downstairs in that hot, miserable room, suffering and getting sick. Why not just sleep here? We could all come up together. That would make it nicer, safer too. With the floor clean, it seemed easier to forget about Shelby.

I fluffed the pillows, then turned down the blankets, planning to—I wasn't quite sure—maybe hang them out the window so the sun could clean them and I could whack the dust out. Or maybe just to give them a little room to breathe right there on the bed. Whatever it was I'd intended to do, I forgot. Because there, at the top of the bed near where the pillows had been was a mound, a mound in the shape of a flashlight. I couldn't call Hans or Savina. "Gideon," I said, but I knew my voice was barely a whisper, my hand reaching toward the sheets, even though the rest of my body was screaming at it not to.

I closed my eyes, grabbed the sheets, and pulled them off. The slender flashlight looked older than the one we'd seen, the batteries now corroded, the leakage crusting a bit at the bottom. I wrapped my hand around it, realizing that her old fingerprints would mingle with mine. And who else? Who else's fingerprints had been on it? The man in the woods, or someone we hadn't met yet?

"Gideon," I called louder. But he wasn't the one who came, just like I'd known he wouldn't be.

The girl climbed the steps, looking sleepy in a pair of pajamas, holding a little bear that she hadn't had before. Lifting the flashlight she held, she pressed the small button at its base and swung the light in my direction. It blinded me, and then she was gone.

"Gideon," I said the third time. And this time, finally, I heard his lumbering steps, hurrying as much as he could hurry, up the stairs. They creaked under his weight.

"I found her," I said, holding up the flashlight.

He made a face, a strange face that I couldn't read, all wrinkled and solemn. I realized then, that he was about to cry. "That's good," he said. "Because I did too."

I RACED AFTER GIDEON, to the edge of the wood at the backside of the house. "I was looking for more edible mushrooms," he said, as he strode ahead of me. "Not the ring of toadstools around the house. Anyway, I was digging through this really nice, loamy soil. And then my hand hit something."

"You sure it's a mattress?" I asked. "A full mattress?"

"Oh, it's full alright," he said.

We stopped at the edge, suddenly. He'd dragged the mattress

out of the dirt, at least partially, and I could see the filthy corner like it was growing out of the soil.

"Somebody stuffed the body in," he said. "Then buried it. It's mostly bones now, bones and clothes and a little bear."

"That's so sad," I said.

He nodded, his face taking on that wrinkly look again.

I patted his shoulder awkwardly, wishing Savina was here to comfort him properly, or maybe to give him someone to comfort so he didn't need it so much. He squatted to the ground, away from my touch. My hand hung there for a second, even more awkwardly.

"Guess I'll have a look," I said.

"It's not pretty," he said, looking at the ground. "She..." he began. "The skeleton is intact, wearing clothes."

I had started to step forward, and stopped. Maybe I should just wait for Hans. He was better at that sort of thing.

But Hans wasn't here, and what if Gideon wasn't right anyway? What if it was just some old jacket or something that someone had abandoned in the woods? What if he'd gotten spooked and just imagined the bones, the clothes?

I took another step forward, my mind barely knowing what my feet were doing. Until I was there, at the edge of the mattress. It had been cut open, then sewn shut, but the weaker threads had deteriorated with time and broken open. Dirt was spilling out of the mattress. Just dirt.

I lifted a flap, and then screamed.

THE SOUND of my voice must have echoed through forever, or that's how it felt at least. How could they not hear us? The search parties. How could they not see the smoke, the horrible, incessant smoke?

I stumbled back from the skull, dirty and brown, the polyester bear tucked into the skeletal arm.

Gideon was beside me, dragging me away. "It's okay, Greta. It's okay. Let's just go back."

And I must have been crying because my face was wet and hot and felt all broken.

"Come on, I'll get you a mushroom and some tea."

"I don't want mushrooms," I sobbed.

He practically dragged me to the well, pulled up the bucket of cool water, splashing me in the face. "I shouldn't have let you look."

"Two more," I said. "There are two more children. Larisa is in the house or somewhere *right now.*"

"Y'all talking about me?" a voice said.

I wanted to keep my back to her, to pretend she didn't exist, but Gideon was turning, slowly. Eventually, I did too.

"I brought you some of them honey crisps," she said, holding out bits of wood for me.

"Oh," I said, glancing down at the mulch-like pieces, my hand moving up in slow motion to take them.

"I saw you eyeing them and all."

I looked into her eyes and somehow she didn't look as distant as the other kids had seemed. "Larisa," I began.

"Risa," she corrected.

"Oh, yeah," I said, closing my fist around the mulch, which felt sticky in my palm, more like crisps than wood chips.

"How you know my real name anyway?" She took a step closer.

I took a step back. "Uh, my mom," I replied. "She said you were in a school play or something."

"Musical," she answered. "*Wizard of Oz.* They cast me as Dorothy, and boy, it caused a fuss in town."

"Why?" I said.

She rolled her eyes.

"Oh," I said, realizing. Her skin color. The south. Twenty-six years ago. Even now it might cause a fuss among some of the people.

"The thing was—is—I could sing it. But a few folks thought if I was gonna be Dorothy, then we should be doing *The Wiz* or something—something more for folks like me. As though a black girl can't wear a blue dress and sing."

I squinted at her, not quite listening. Had she started talking about herself in the past tense, and then corrected it?

"When was the show?" I asked. "I don't remember Mama saying."

"Just last week. Did your mama go?"

"Yes," I said, figuring she probably had. "I think she did."

And then Risa started to sing again, a song from the show, her voice soulful and sweet, like it really was cresting the rainbow.

And then she started skipping, this time singing the song, "Follow the Yellow Brick Road."

"Follow, follow, follow, follow." She danced her way back toward the house. "Don't go wasting those honey crisps, girl," she called over her shoulder.

I felt them in my hand, crumbling, like real cookies would have. Even though it was just chips of wood from the supporting beam in the kitchen.

All of a sudden, I glanced up at Gideon.

Yellow brick.

I remembered the floor in the kitchen. Surely she wasn't giving us a hint. The others had barely even known their names.

Taking Gideon's arm, I dragged him back to the house, into the kitchen. Yellow brick. A little circle of it around that beam that smelled like honey crisps.

"Nah," he said.

But bits of the mortar were crumbling. I grabbed an old

butter knife from one of the drawers and started chipping away at the cement.

"Do you think the body's in there too?" he asked.

I shrugged. It could be. Weren't serial killers always hiding bodies in floorboards and stuff? "Don't know," I said.

"I'm gonna look around the property, see if there's anything…" He didn't finish. Just let the sentence dangle there as he looked through the kitchen window, then hurried outside.

I might have glanced up too, except at that moment a whole line of mortar broke away so that I could wiggle the brick. Back and forth, more pieces of the cement giving way, even bits of the brick crumbling. Like cake.

I pulled a bit of the wood chip from my pocket and popped it into my mouth. Sweet with that earthy honey taste. Then lifted what remained of the brick.

And…nothing.

No body. No secret compartment. No ancient Walkman, which I admit is what I was expecting to find. And I guess it made sense. After all, none of the rest of them had given us hints about where to find them, not so directly at least. So of course she hadn't either.

I slumped onto the floor, thinking, just as something feral echoed from the woods. Half shout, half sob. And for once, it wasn't Savina.

"Gideon!" I screamed.

His wails carried through the trees, across the yard, filled the house. Gideon who hadn't screamed or cried since we'd gotten here. There was only one reason for that sound.

"Hans!" I called, rushing from the house. "Savina!"

I followed Gideon's voice, out along one line of the fairy ring, where Hans was dragging from the woods, carrying a body.

No, no, no.

Gideon was with him, helping him, sobbing like a baby.

I hung back, my mouth sealed shut. Was this it? Was Savina the sixth victim? The final egg?

I STEPPED TOWARD THEM.

"She's alive," Hans grunted. "Just—she can barely stand up—did you guys find some food?"

He laid her on the ground as Gideon pulled mushrooms from his pocket, passing them to Hans.

And Hans, he didn't say anything about how we weren't eating mushrooms anymore. He just broke them into bits and slid them into her mouth.

She chewed, or tried to. And I noticed, all of a sudden, that I was the only one not doing anything, not helping. And that was dumb, because I had a feeling that of all of us, I was the one who could help the most.

"I'll make some tea," I said.

"Just bring some water," Hans shouted, his voice sharp.

I nodded, rushing inside to get her little mug, pouring some water from the bucket. But before I brought it, I dug into my pocket, sprinkling some of the crumbs from the honey crisp beam into the water. It wasn't much, not enough for the boys to notice. But I hoped it was enough, enough to help her revive.

I ran out of the house with the mug.

Gideon tipped the drink into Savina's mouth, cooing the whole time about how great she was doing and how strong she was and how she was going to be just fine.

Hans, on the other hand, was glaring at the mug. And then at me. "Gross, Greta. There is dirt or something in that cup. Here —" He passed it back to me. "Go get some fresh water from the well. Rinse this out, then refill it."

I scurried away to...do his bidding. A thought that didn't make me feel very warm and fuzzy. I hated it when he bossed me. I hated it when he didn't say thank you. I hated it when he didn't appreciate or even notice the things that I did.

After all, while they were gone, wandering in the woods and getting sicker, Gideon and I had found the relic of a flashlight, along with the horrible third body. What had Hans done? Dragged his not-girlfriend into the woods against my advice, and brought her back nearly dead.

I hauled the bucket up from the well, leaning over to grab it. I set my hand down on the edge and there—right under it— among all the gray, dull bricks, was one made of yellow—a yellow brick—just like those in the kitchen. I jiggled it and it gave, wiggling away from the others like it was never meant to be there anyway. I supposed that it wasn't. Underneath, in a small space where the mortar should have been, was an opening. Not big. But big enough for a cassette tape.

This one was labeled, "Mix tape."

I gazed at the tiny words printed on it, the names of songs crammed together in neat print. I didn't even bother to call for Hans or Gideon. I knew they weren't the ones who would come.

I expected her to skip to me, but she just walked, not singing this time, the Walkman on her ears as she glanced at me, opening it up. A glint off the plastic of the tape, and she was gone.

I stood, staring at the nothing in front of me, the green trees, the wide-open endless sky.

"Greta!" Hans called, angrily jogging to where I was.

I held up the tape so he could see it, but he just bent his eyebrows together. "Not now," he said, rushing back to Savina with the water.

But Savina was walking toward us, a little wobbly still, but walking. And I knew why. That water Hans had thought was so gross, those few crumbs she'd gotten, the "dirt," were giving her strength, just like they'd done for me.

"It's okay," she said, her voice soft. "I'm feeling better. Those mushrooms must have helped. And the water. Thank you." She gazed up into Hans' eyes as she took the mug from him, as though he'd been the one to bring it out to her first. And Hans—instead of snarling and scowling like he had just done with me—he smiled back, reaching down to touch the side of her jaw with his thumb. They stayed there for a moment, just gazing at each other, until Gideon came up beside me, his face puffy and red. "What is that, Greta?"

I glanced down at the unappreciated tape in my hands.

"Mix tape," he read. "What does that mean?"

"Mama said it was the 90s equivalent of Spotify," I answered.

"You found her," Savina said. "The fourth girl."

"Larisa," I clarified. "And, yes. Also, Missy, in case you were wondering. We found her stuff, and her body." I shuddered.

"Mattress," Gideon said. "In the woods."

"And the last one—what was her name—Risa?" Savina said, taking the tape from my hands. "Where are her remains?"

"Larisa's not the last one," I said, feeling the words go bitter in my mouth. "Just the most recent we've found. And I don't know."

"You found this in the well?" Hans asked, finally deigning to speak to me.

"Not exactly in," I said. "Hidden under a brick." *A yellow brick.*

"So do you think the killer threw her in the well?" Hans said.

"Wouldn't that have poisoned it?" Savina asked, standing up much straighter, but still holding onto Hans' hand.

"It's been a long time," Hans answered. "It would be clean now. We can lower Greta into the well and have her look around."

"Are you even kidding?" I asked, my voice pitching up, much like Mama's did when she was angry.

"Well, no, I'm not kidding," Hans said. "You're the smallest and you've already found several of the remains. I didn't think it'd be a big deal."

"Well, you didn't think correctly," I snapped. "I am *not* going down there."

"Greta, you've got to," Hans said. "We can't very well put Gideon down there, and I'm too tall."

And we couldn't send his precious, delicate Savina down, even though she wasn't much bigger than me.

"I'm not doing it," I said. "It's dark and small and damp. And who knows how well the muck might have preserved the body. I don't want to—"

"It's not in the well," Gideon said. "No one who lived here would have ruined their water source. Even to hide a body."

"Yeah," Savina said slowly. "Even if they killed her there, they would have pulled the body up right after and buried her somewhere else."

"You'd have to be strong to haul a body up out of here," Hans said, reaching out to tug at the rope.

"Kind of like that old man twenty-six years ago."

"Yeah, I guess," Hans said. "But he would have been, like, fifty or something."

"But a woodsman."

We looked at each other, then to the ancient woodpile, which was in direct view from the well. That wood would have supplied the fuel for the wood stove in the kitchen. An ax still rested on the decaying chopping block, rusted and handle-less.

"This is so messed up," Savina whimpered. But the boys were already headed to the pile that must once have been wood, but was now mostly a mound of mulch and dirt.

"Buried, do you think?" Hans asked.

Gideon shook his head, staring at the rotten woodpile, easily twenty-six years old. He pointed. Hans dug.

The bones were scattered, splintered, and broken. But they were bones.

Savina started to cry, those fat tears streaming down her face. And I should have done what Gideon did for me, should have taken her by the hand, splashed water on her cheeks, told her it would be okay. Instead, I said, "Oh my gosh. Could you maybe not get hysterical for once? This is hard enough without that."

And then I stomped away to the house, leaving the boys to glare at my back.

"Greta!" Hans called, all those sharp edges to his voice. But I ignored him. It *had been* hard enough. And I was tired. Tired of sleeping in the hot living room. Tired of pretending to like the gross vegetables. Tired of finding every single victim.

I banged the back door shut behind me, and then stopped on that thought. I *had* found every single victim—maybe not the bodies, but the relics. I glanced at the basket of eggs. Was it because I had rescued the eggs? Four of them now fully broken open, completely empty. Two to go. *Two.* How strange.

Hans shot through the door, on a rampage. "Greta, you can't act like that. This is hard for everyone, not just you."

And I just, I couldn't. I turned my back on him, tearing up the stairs to the attic, ripping off a chunk of brick from the wall once I was out of his sight, and shoving it into my mouth. Red velvet cake. I let the sweet crumbs sink into my tongue, then flopped onto the bed, the bed where a dead girl had once slept.

But I didn't care anymore. I closed my eyes.

Hans didn't come after me.

And before I knew it, I'd fallen asleep.

I COULD HEAR them downstairs when I woke up the next morning, their voices faint. My belly full, my body rested, maybe for the first time since arriving here.

I sat up, stretching my legs, my arms.

I still wasn't ready to face them, half embarrassed at how I'd acted, half annoyed at how they'd acted. I wandered through the attic, blowing dust off of things, shifting and folding blankets.

Before I knew it, I was cleaning it even more than I had the other day—using a rag to dust, shining the metal mirror, sweeping then crawling along on the floor and scrubbing up dirt as best as I could with a dry rag. Just like I used to do when Mama and Hans would fight—finding productive things so I could ignore the harsh banter they shot back and forth.

By the time I was finished, I couldn't hear the voices anymore. Which was fine by me. I was pretty pleased with how the attic had cleaned up—almost homey now.

I figured Savina could sleep here. She'd have lots of blankets, and it would be more comfortable. She was definitely the weakest of the four of us, and it really had been scary to see her like that yesterday. I mean, no wonder everyone had freaked out. A trickle of the embarrassment returned.

"Hans," I said tentatively, calling down to him, ready to apologize. Always the one to reach out first. I shoved the thought down, and made my way into the kitchen.

It was empty. Just like the living room. The garden, the shed, the yard.

"Hans!" I shrieked, rushing back toward the house.

I knew he'd been mad, but he wouldn't have left me. I knew he wouldn't. He was my brother. He loved me.

But then I remembered Daddy, opening the front door, closing it behind him. Never coming back. And not just that— after all, lots of men left their wives, walked out and got apartments—but those daddies still came for the weekends, picked up their kids, taught them to fish or play ball or took their girls shopping for dresses. Not ours. He'd called a couple of times on our birthdays, and sometimes sent a $20 bill for Christmas. But that was it. Daddy hadn't just left Mama. He'd left all of us. And Hans still adored him.

I dragged back to the kitchen, opened the door quietly, just like I had the night I'd snuck out of our house, let it shut without a sound, reached up to rub my neck. I hadn't thought about the scratch for days. It was no longer scabbed, just a slightly raised line that I'd been ignoring since the night we got lost. But now, under the stress, the old scratch throbbed. I figured there was something psychological to that, some sort of brain science behind it.

The house was as quiet as I've ever heard it, no cuckoo clock, no snoring, no creak of the floorboards, no whispers, definitely no laughter, not even any tears. Nothing.

Until the egg in the basket beside me began to shake. Gently at first, and then harder.

I watched it—brown with black speckles. It rocked, rolling from one side to the other. Until the tiniest crack appeared in the shell. And a lonesome musical note carried across the trees.

A trumpet.

CHAPTER 21

HANS

Day 5

We hadn't gone far.

But Gideon had found a creek. He'd heard it when he'd been out looking for stuff, which I considered impressive. I felt like all I could hear was my own breath and the incessant crackling of the fire we'd lit.

Gideon noticed lots of little things that the rest of us missed. Greta did too.

I glanced through the dappled trees, back at the house, to see if she'd come out. Not yet. She must have been tired. Which made sense. I'd honestly never seen her lose it like that. It had always been me and Mom fighting, while Greta did—well, whatever it was she did. Cleaned stuff, I guess. Sometimes even my stuff. Yeah, I'd noticed. I just never said anything, never thanked her. Which was kind of a jerk move.

I sighed, casting another look at the house through the trees. I'd apologize when we got back. I figured she couldn't be too mad we were gone, since *she* was the one who had stormed off to sleep in that creepy attic in the first place.

Now we were following the stream because, in Gideon's words, streams meant fish. And *all* of us could really use some fish.

I wasn't so sure *this* stream meant fish though. It was tiny—as in the width of one of our forearms. But just a few feet ahead of us, it pooled in this little drop off, which was only a few feet wide.

Gideon shuffled to it, then knelt down.

"Bingo," Savina said, dipping a hand into the water.

"Seriously," I said, hurrying up to them, making sure we could still see the house through the trees. That would be ironic—if after all this, we got lost in the woods with Greta stuck in that house. But I could still see the sun glinting off the roof like it was hard candy.

The thought hung there for just a second before Gideon said, "See them?"

And I did. But the fish were—not shockingly—also tiny. Little slips of silver darting through the water. "How will we even eat them?"

Gideon shrugged. "Probably just cook them whole and pop them in our mouths."

"Like sardines," Savina said, though her voice was more of a question than an answer. "We can just chew the bones when they're that little, right?"

It was pretty clear that none of us knew the answer, or what we were doing at all. Including how on earth to catch the speedy little fish.

"So do we make a fishing pole from a stick or something?" I asked.

Gideon shook his head, grabbing unsuccessfully for a fish with his hands. "We need a net."

I looked through the forest, wondering if we could fashion

some vines or something into some type of net. It seemed like it'd be too hard to be worth the dozen miniature fish.

"Your shirt," Savina said, looking over at me. "We could use that."

"For a net?" I asked.

"Sure," she said. "It's porous. It'll let the water out and keep the fish in."

And I won't pretend that I wasn't a little pleased she suggested that I take off my shirt. "Sure," I said, taking it off as manfully as I could without looking stupid. "Here."

I handed it to Gideon instead of Savina. I didn't want her to know how sweaty it was, soaked day and night.

"Your back," Savina said, glancing at me.

I bit my lip. I knew it had been itching, knew I'd broken out in some kind of heat rash, but I had no idea what it actually looked like. "Is it bad?" I asked, trying to keep my voice light.

"What is it?" she asked.

"Just…just a heat rash, I think," I said. "It's been so hot here. I broke out in those hives a couple days ago."

She nodded, her head tipping up and down slowly, like she was trying to understand what heat felt like. "I'm still cold," she said quietly. "Better than yesterday. Thank you for helping me. But cold again today. It's awful."

Gideon didn't say anything, but he didn't look much better than either of us. His face was yellow-ish and pale like Savina's, but sweaty like mine. And his eyes—when he wasn't helping with something—they went hollow as if nobody was home inside. It was kind of scary the way he would stare.

The fish swam in circles, like they didn't understand how they'd gotten trapped in their little pool. A lot like us. The thought made me feel just a little bad when Gideon dipped my shirt into the water, scooping up a bunch of them. Not bad enough though. Because we were starving. Savina's cheeks had even gone gaunt. It had been five days.

In fact, the only one who seemed okay was Greta. Which I was happy about, except for the moments when it made me a little mad—only because it reminded me of my own stupid fever and even stupider hives. After all, Greta was the youngest, the hungriest. She was supposed to be the weakest. Why was she the one doing okay, and kind of holding everything together?

Gideon let the water drain out of my shirt, then dumped the cache of fish into Savina's hands. And even though I got the impression Savina wasn't usually the type of girl to hold wriggling fish in her hands, that's exactly what she did. They flipped and flopped and she didn't even wince. I wondered if her mouth was watering like mine, at the sight of them, at the thought of eating them.

Gideon scooped again. Screw ecology and leaving things to reproduce and stuff. We were taking every last fish in that pond.

Just as he finished wrapping my t-shirt up around the remaining fish, Gideon bolted up. "You hear that?" he said.

"Hear what?" I asked, noticing that one solitary fish was left swimming in the pool, looking distraught and lonely.

He shook his head. "I don't know. It almost sounded like music."

CHAPTER 22

GRETA

Edgar was easy to find. I just followed the notes that reached up and out at the end of every phrase. It was a song I knew—they played it on movies sometimes for funerals. *Taps.*

I could see him sitting on a stump just past where the partial fairy ring opened up to the woods. The leaves from the trees framed his face, making him look like an elf with a magical flute, not a boy with a trumpet.

I stopped near the edge of the wood, where I assumed he couldn't see me. And for a long time, I listened. He played jazz songs I mostly didn't know except one by Frank Sinatra that Mama liked. And then some classical pieces that made the skin on my arms rise up in goosebumps and finally one from *The Music Man*, which Mama always sang.

When he was done with that one, he put his trumpet down and without looking at me, he said, "Hey."

I cleared my throat, surprised he knew I was there, but also not. "Hey." I took a little step forward, not wanting to go too deep into the woods. "I'm Greta."

"Edgar," he answered.

"And what are you doing here?" I asked. "In the woods."

"I always come here," he said, like I was the intruder.

To be fair, that was totally true. I *was* the intruder.

"The neighbors don't like it when I play in the apartment."

"What apartment?" I asked.

"Willow Halls," he said.

And in a small town like ours I should have recognized the name, but I didn't. Finally, I remembered that a few years back Mama had taken us to a place at the edge of town where they were knocking down an old building. She'd figured Hans would want to see. And he had. We'd watched the wrecking ball crash into the brick, the walls crumble in clouds of apocalyptic dust. It had been a nursing home, and a lot of the people had gotten sick before they'd condemned it.

"I thought that was for old people," I said, taking a gamble.

"Assisted living," he said. "I lived there with my grams."

"And she was old?" I asked.

"Duh," he said.

And normally, maybe I would think it was rude to pry, but seeing as Edgar was thirteen years dead, I figured I didn't have too much to lose. "So where were your mama and daddy?"

"Dead for one—overdose," he said, holding up one finger. "As for the other—" He held up a second finger. "I don't freaking know."

I made a little noise that I hoped sounded compassionate, although maybe it really just sounded squeaky.

"Grams had been taking care of me since before Mama died anyway," he said. "Mama wasn't good for much. Just drinking and cussing and finding new boyfriends."

"You say that or your grams?" I asked.

"Both," he answered. "Two peas in a pod, me and Grams."

"How long you been livin' with your grams?" I asked.

"Thirteen years," he said.

"Older than me," I answered.

"Yup," he said, putting the trumpet back to his lips.

"How come the neighbors don't like your playing?" I asked. "It's beautiful."

He shrugged. "Trumpets are loud. And old people are old."

"Doesn't bug your grams though?" I asked.

"She likes music," he said. "Plus, she's practically deaf. Trumpet is the perfect instrument for her."

He started to play another sad song, which I was pretty sure I'd heard before. And maybe I should have interrupted him, but I sure didn't want to. So I sat there while the minutes rolled on, listening to him play. Song after song. None of them much sounded like marches though.

"I thought you were in the marching band," I said, like we were peers, like I was a girl a few grades down from him.

"I was," he answered. "Am."

I squinted. There it was again, the past tense, just like with Larisa.

"First chair in honors band too," he said. "But that never makes the papers."

"You've made the papers?" I asked like I didn't know.

"Few times," he said. "Always that stupid picture of me in my uniform."

"Bet your grams loved it," I said.

"She did," he answered, looking into my face for the first time. Had the others done that, looked into my eyes? "Grams had every newspaper article framed on the wall. Always talked to the neighbors about me too." He gazed off into a little patch of the forest where young trees and scrub were growing. "But she couldn't hear them talking about me, complaining loud through them thin walls. I could though. So I usually came out here to play. It was the perfect spot."

"Did they ever tell you not to?" I asked. "Come out here?"

"Who's they?" he asked.

"Just...anyone," I said, thinking of the police in our living room.

"Grams didn't like it," he said. "She was always worried I'd get lost out here. That didn't sound too bad to me though. Sometimes I wanted to. Grams only had a few years left and when she died, I knew I wouldn't have anyone left. Where would I even stay?"

Knew. Past tense.

"But everyone loves your music," I said, careful to put it in the present tense.

He shrugged.

"You got a lot of awards," I added, thinking about the article in the paper, the tributes on the internet, all of them mourning his lost potential.

"You ever wonder if people would miss you if you were gone?" he asked.

"Yeah," I murmured, thinking of Daddy leaving, then Hans with Savina and Gideon. "Yeah, I do."

We both looked off into the trees. No birdsong today. It was hot, the sun high in the sky.

"But people would miss you if you were gone," I said. "What about Mr. Newsome?" His band teacher, according to the paper.

He smiled, just a little crack of a thing. "Yeah, I guess he'd miss me," he said. "If I was gone. He always said I had a lot of potential. Even said he'd give me a letter of recommendation for college, when the time came. College, ha. That feels like a pipe dream. Grams is, like, the brokest lady in the world. But Mr. Newsome, he'd said he thought I could get a scholarship."

He'd said. Edgar wasn't even really hiding it anymore, as though he was at least a little aware that he was gone. I thought of Larisa with her song, her song that was a hint. As though the more recent the deaths, the more sentient the souls were.

"Yeah," I replied. "From what I've heard, I think you probably could have." Now I wasn't hiding it either.

"Thanks, Greta," he said, the first of the five to use my name. "I'm not sure you're right, but it definitely feels good to hear all this stuff."

And then he hopped off his stump and started to walk farther into the wood. I wasn't sure I wanted to go deeper into the wood, but I followed anyway, like he was pulling me after him with a string.

He stopped at an old tree, one with a big 'V' in the center like it had been struck by lightning and then grown up in two different directions. The perfect tree to climb.

"I used to set my music up in that bough," he said. "It formed a natural music stand."

"*Used to?*" I asked, wondering what he would say.

"Before I had it memorized," he answered. "After I memorized it, I would just sit here, playing, no neighbors to hear me and complain, no Grams to not be able to hear me at all. Just me and the woods."

"I'm sorry," I whispered.

"Sorry for what?" he asked.

And then I saw it, grown into the wood, the glint of the instrument.

He looked at it too, then back at me, right into my eyes. Held the trumpet to his lips.

"Did you know?" I asked. "That you were gone?"

He didn't answer, just gazed into my eyes, blowing that long last note, as I reached out to touch his trumpet, encased in the split trunk of the tree. A flash of light reflected off of the metal.

And then it was just me and the tree. I crawled up to the spot where he might have once rested. Sat there—I wasn't sure how long—remembering the notes he had played, his sad, sad voice, how he said, "Thanks, Greta."

I didn't get down. Didn't want to find the rest of him.

I was sure it was around here somewhere—the body. Everyone else had been near their object. And Edgar, I wasn't sure he'd be fully decayed. I didn't completely understand the science of decay, but I'd once read that it varied from case to case, depending on how many elements you'd been exposed to or protected from. And I had no desire to find the remains of the boy I'd just talked to.

After what could have been forever or no time at all, I heard my name—Hans' panicked voice. I knew I should respond, but couldn't bring myself to open my mouth, to make any sounds at all.

When Hans ran past me, I didn't even stop him. He had to stop himself, do a double take, then backtrack. "What on earth? Didn't you hear me?"

I didn't answer, except to point at the metal in the tree.

"The last victim," he said.

"Edgar," I said. "That's his name. You should call him his name."

"You talked to him?"

"He was closer," I said, not looking at Hans. "Less like a character or the avatar in a game. More like a boy. It was almost like…"

"Like what?" Hans asked, as we heard Gideon's dragging walk catching up to us.

"Like he knew he was dead. None of the others did, but he seemed just more… there."

"Maybe that makes sense," Hans said. "Since it was the most recent. You know."

I nodded, without answering. I could see Hans casting his eyes around.

"I don't know where the body is," I said.

"Why don't you head back?" he said. "Gideon and I will find it."

"No," I said. "I'll wait. I just don't want to look."

Gideon came through the clearing. "Greta?" he said, his voice tipped up in a question.

I pointed to the silver trumpet while Hans filled him in.

"Ideas?" Hans asked when he was done. "About, you know?"

"The body," Gideon said.

I stared at the horizon, sitting on the tree, imagining Edgar playing his songs, at first looking into the sheet music on the bent bough, then…

It connected to another branch, which touched another branch, little knees of roots poking through the ground. "What type of trees are these?" I asked.

"Cypress," Gideon answered.

"They're usually by a body of water," I said. "Something swampy."

"There's nothing swampy around here," Hans replied.

"Not anymore," I said. "But it's been thirteen years. Look at how the trees surround that little area."

"The killer threw him in a swampy section," Hans murmured, walking toward it.

"Swamps preserve bodies," I said. "I read…"

Gideon found the shoe, just sticking out of the once-mud, among a cluster of weeds.

"I'm not digging him out," Hans said.

"I don't think we have to," I answered. "He's here. And we know it."

CHAPTER 23

GRETA

Savina was waiting back at the house, napping in the rocking chair, by the fire.

She stirred when we came in.

"Hey, sleepyhead," Hans said in his sweetest voice.

Savina blinked her eyes open. I had to grit my teeth in order to avoid rolling my eyes as the two of them gazed at each other all gloppy-eyed.

Gideon tossed a few leaves onto the fire, sending a fresh plume of smoke up the chimney. We'd talked about bringing the fire outside, but the big pieces of wood were still waterlogged, though mostly I think at this point, everyone was just too sick to do the work it would take. So the fire stayed, so hot, inside the house.

"You know, I cleaned the room in the attic," I said as a fresh wave of heat filled the room. "You could sleep there in a real bed. It's nice."

"For a dead girl," she answered. And I knew she wasn't trying to be snarky, but it felt snarky.

I thought I'd try advertising the attic one more time. "We could all go up together. It's nicer."

"No thanks, Gret," Hans said.

I shrugged my shoulders. Their loss. I'd sleep up there myself if no one else wanted to. It was nice. *I'd* made it nice and they didn't even appreciate it. In fact, they'd rather sleep in this horrible hot room with the hard, sticky floor, and the cuckoo clock going off at midnight every night, then waking them again in the morning.

"We found the boy," Hans said. "The trumpet player."

We? I wanted to ask, but Gideon sort of corrected it for me. "Greta found the trumpet," he said. "And the old swamp where the killer dumped the body."

"A swamp?" Savina asked, sitting up.

"Old swamp," Hans said. "It's dried up now, but, well, we found a shoe."

Savina pressed against her temples. "This place."

Gideon went to the kitchen to retrieve the basket of eggs and sure enough, the dark speckled one was broken all the way open and empty.

"Only one more to go," Hans said, nodding to the final egg, still intact and not rocking.

"But there were no other deaths," I said.

"That we know of," Hans answered.

"We would have heard," I replied.

"Unless it happened that night," Hans said. "That last night. We haven't heard anything since then."

"But," Savina said. "If the body was here, wouldn't it be, um… fresh? Wouldn't we start to smell it?"

"Depends on where it's hidden," Hans said. "Like, that kid in the swamp—"

"Edgar," I interjected.

"Okay…Edgar," Hans said. "No one would have smelled him. Who knows what else is out there?"

"How will we find the person?" Savina asked. "For all the others, we knew they were gone. Thanks to Greta, we knew who they were." She smiled at me, and I gave her a pinched return smile.

What no one said, or maybe even dared think, is that it was probably one of the other partygoers—less lucky than we had been. Someone Savina, Gideon, and Hans knew. Maybe even someone I knew.

"We'll know when the egg tells us," Gideon said, glancing down at the smallest egg, a bright blue with mottled dark splotches.

Hans cast a glance at it, then stared back at the fire. "So, what do we do in the meantime?" he asked. "We can't seem to get out of this place. Do we just wait?"

I opened my mouth one more time to say that we could go up to the attic, that it would be nicer there, but thought better of it halfway through and said, "I'm going to clean."

"Clean, Greta?" Hans asked.

"Yes," I answered. "It's what I do." I turned away from them and the hot living room, and went into the kitchen, then up the stairs to the attic.

I STARTED AT THE TOP. That was how Mama had taught me to clean. Top to bottom, so any dust or dirt you knocked off would get cleaned up last when you got to the floor.

Which meant I began at the top of the wardrobe. Wet cloth to layers of dust. I'd tidied the attic before, but until now, I hadn't done a deep cleaning.

From the wardrobe, I moved down to the doorframe, then to the ledge of the little window.

I'd meant to air out the blankets the day I'd found Missy's flashlight in the bed, but then of course, I'd gotten distracted.

Today there were no more dead kids left to distract me. I stripped the blankets and sheets off the bed and hung them out the window, shaking them clean. I figured I could probably wash them another day if I wanted. In a tub of well water. Though what to use for soap?

I realized with a tiny amount of horror that we hadn't used any soap at all since we'd gotten here, even on our trips to the "ladies' room." I walked over to the little basin by the makeshift mirror and there, in that cupboard, I found a handful of tiny soaps, homemade from the looks of it. And beside it, a beautiful hand towel, embroidered with birds and flowers.

I set the soap and towel next to the basin, then snuck downstairs and brought up the bucket of fresh water in order to fill the basin. Tada. Hand washing station.

Which made me think of how dirty my t-shirt was. And I didn't even want to think about my underwear.

Tomorrow, I'd go out to the well with the soap and clean my dirty clothes. If, that was, I could find something else to wear.

We'd found Shelle's things in the trunk. No way I was opening that again. Ever. But the wardrobe in the corner—I wandered to it, hoping not to find other dead kids' clothes. Or serial killer clothes for that matter.

I cracked open the door, expecting a barrage of cobwebs and more dust. Instead, I found a perfectly tidy closet with two aprons hung neatly, alongside a blouse and skirt. They certainly didn't look like the clothes of a serial killer, more like those of a twelve-year-old girl. And they couldn't have been the clothes of one of the other children. They were too old-fashioned.

Hans would have told me I'd gone nutty from heat or hunger to take those clothes. And maybe I had, but they smelled fresh and clean, just like the soap by my basin. I took them off the hangers and since no one else was upstairs, I slipped out of my old clothes and into these new ones. They were surprisingly comfortable—light, soft, easy to move in.

And because I was still cleaning, I tied a clean white apron around my waist.

Perfect.

That day, I scrubbed all the furniture, then made my way downstairs.

The next day I tackled the kitchen—arranging all the cutlery, pots, and dishes.

"Greta?" Hans said when he saw me that morning in the old clothes.

"Busy," I answered, curtly.

"Where did you...?"

"I'm cleaning my clothes," I answered. "Soon as I'm done with this."

"The kitchen looks nice," he ventured, still staring at my clothes.

I didn't respond, focusing instead on a bit of brick that Larisa had nibbled on. It looked almost like cornbread. "I found a book upstairs, a book about wild greens. That might be useful," I said.

"Yeah," he answered, sounding a little tortured.

"I'll get it for you when I'm done here," I replied.

That night they went hunting for wild garlic and onions. While they were gone, I feasted on thick cornbread brick and candied bacon cupboard.

The next day I found linens. Folded and put away. I unfurled a lace tablecloth and put it on the table, hung some towels around the kitchen, dug out a vase and plucked some wildflowers from the yard to put in it.

Savina was sleeping in the front room, so I made tea for everyone with bits of a candy cane doorframe sprinkled in. This time I got the water really hot so that the crumbs practically melted into the water.

"Dinner is served," I said, presenting it to them on a little tray. And not with the original clay mugs we'd found, but with a delicate porcelain set that I'd discovered tucked away at the very back of a top shelf.

"Wow, Greta," Savina murmured, her skin looking tissue-paper thin. She didn't even seem to notice my dress, though Hans hadn't stopped staring at it.

"Mmmm," Savina groaned happily when the tea hit her lips. "This is sooo good. What did you find to put in it?"

"Just some leaves I found with the tea set," I lied. "Won't fill the belly, I guess, but might help us all feel better."

"That's for sure," Savina said. "I honestly feel better already."

Gideon was staring at her. I understood why. She looked better too.

"I'll make more tomorrow," I said.

Hans hadn't tipped his to his lips yet. He was still staring at me. "Greta, are you okay? I know we didn't want to sleep in the attic, and I guess I still don't, but are you…?"

"I'm great," I replied. "Now, drink up."

Hans obediently tipped the drink to his lips, though I didn't see him swallow. I narrowed my eyes at that. Why did he have to be so stubborn? But, fine, whatever, if he wanted to die on a diet of wild mustard greens, that was his choice.

"Did you add sugar?" Savina asked.

"Nah," I answered. "Just love."

Hans put his teacup down, and I could see that it was still full.

❦

OVER THE COURSE of the next few days, I washed my old clothes as well as the blankets in a big tub I'd found in the shed, then hung them to dry on a makeshift line. I swept the kitchen floors, which hardly felt sticky to me anymore. And then I tackled the old brick oven, taking ash out by the bucket, then sweeping it clean, before adding fresh firewood, in case anyone ever managed to kill a bird or catch a big fish that might need to be cooked. In fact, I noticed a little hook at the top of the oven, and hung a cast iron pot there. It was perfect. It was…fun. Like playing house. Times a million.

Though I did wish everyone else was feeling better. I'd made them tea every morning and night. It helped. Well, everyone except Hans, though tonight I'd finally seen him take a few sips. Good thing too, since the hives had crept up his neck and were starting to overtake his chin and cheeks.

Still, those few tea crumbs weren't enough to keep their faces from growing gaunter. Both of the boys were holding their pants up with ropes now and Savina's lips were cracking and bleeding.

But what more could I do? If I told them to eat the house, Hans would lose his mind and probably stop drinking the tea again. I just had to keep quiet and do my best to get them strong.

As it was, they were starting to slip, starting to starve. I saw it in the desperate way they looked for food each morning, but then slept the rest of the day, saw it in the hungry way they now looked at each other.

Which is why it wasn't entirely surprising the next morning when Gideon snapped.

Hans was nibbling on the green end of an onion.

"You took too much," Gideon said.

"I didn't," Hans retorted, slurping the end bit up just like a rabbit.

"You did," Gideon said, stepping toward him, almost lunging.

"I'll make tea," I said, but no one seemed to hear me.

Hans stepped closer to Gideon, his chest puffed out in a way that looked almost primal. "Didn't," he said, his breath terrible from the onion and two weeks of not brushing his teeth.

Gideon lunged then, and if Savina hadn't stepped between the two of them, I'm not sure what would have happened.

She held both arms out—little white toothpicks.

Gideon ground his teeth and backed off.

Hans stepped back too, his eyes almost sinking into his face. "I…" he said. "I'm…"

I thought for a moment that he was going to apologize. I wasn't sure I'd *ever* heard Hans apologize—not to me, not to Mama.

But instead, he shook his head and said, "We're going to die if we stay here. We've got to go out."

Gideon grunted, his back to Hans, but it was a grunt that sounded more like agreement than disagreement.

"All of us?" Savina asked.

"All of us," Hans answered. "If we die, we'll die together in the woods, instead of in this hot, horrible house."

Savina cast me a glance—me in my old brown dress, with the white apron wrapped tight around my waist, the little blue kerchief over my clean hair.

Savina—beautiful, perfect Savina—didn't look nearly as well. Her lips had chapped into bloody lines, her skin white and flaking off at various points along her scalp and in the creases between her fingers. "Okay," she said. "Together."

All three of them nodded in that moment, their heads moving in unison. And I realized something, something I guess I'd realized for the past week, but hadn't managed to put into words.

Nobody had asked me. Nobody at all.

CHAPTER 24

HANS

Day 14

I made the tea the next morning, served alongside the last of the little fish that Gideon and I had tried smoking in the fireplace a week ago. Before Greta had cleaned her way through every inch of the house. How did she even have the energy?

The fish were horrible, by the way. Almost inedible. Almost. In a moment of irony, I hoped that we wouldn't get sick from them, but then I remembered how sick we already were and figured it didn't matter too much.

The tea wasn't much better, bitter and grassy. Greta's tea always tasted like mint, or lemon rind, and somehow sweet, but it made me nervous. I wasn't sure why; maybe it was that I wasn't sure where she was getting the herbs for it. Or maybe it was her creepy pioneer outfits that she'd also found buried in this house. *Buried.* Wrong word choice. Wrong, wrong, wrong.

I glanced out of the kitchen window. The sun looked exactly the same as it had at 6:15 every morning since we'd come here. Exactly the same sun, hanging in the same place in the eternally blue, eternally hot sky.

But it had been two weeks. I'd been keeping track, every day. And several weeks into June, the sun should have been coming up earlier than when we'd arrived.

But it didn't.

I looked at the copper teapot, charcoal staining the bottom from our fire. I hated that fire.

Savina wandered in, looking rumpled and ghostly as usual. She splashed water from the bucket onto her face. She smelled better than me and Gideon, but not by much. "You making 'breakfast' this morning, are you?" she said, air-quoting the word 'breakfast.'

"Yeah, well," I muttered.

Gideon stumped in, not looking at me. We'd both been avoiding each other since the night before.

I handed each of them a cup of watery tea that I'd put a few of the sage leaves in.

Gideon choked when he took his first gulp, but he didn't say anything. Savina took a cue from that and sipped hers, her lips pressed tightly together as though she didn't want to let the liquid into her throat.

I took one last glance at the everlasting sun of this place. "Are you guys ready?" I asked.

"What's to get ready?" Savina answered. "Our suitcases?"

I grimaced a response. "Gideon?" I said.

"Yeah," he answered. "Let's get out of here."

We nodded, united, gazing out the window.

And then we all saw her, Greta—out in the yard, humming and hanging linen napkins up on the line she'd created. I took in the white apron, the fresh pink handkerchief tied around her hair.

"What is she *doing?*" Savina murmured, reaching up to her own dirty hair.

I glanced at Savina, flakes of dandruff at her scalp, dried bits of blood at the corners of her mouth.

"Laundry?" I answered, a little stupefied myself.

Greta gathered up a blazingly white sheet, shook it out, and then glanced toward the window, giving us a little wave and a smile.

Just as the final egg began, ever so slightly, to wobble.

WE ALL LOOKED at each other, our gazes meeting for a brief second before we turned to the egg. It wasn't shaking wildly back and forth or anything. In fact, if anything, it was trembling.

Savina was the first to tear her eyes off the egg, looking through the freshly-cleaned kitchen window, waiting for the knock at the door, for a scream, or for a kid to come singing through the woods. No one came. And still the egg trembled.

She stepped closer to the window, her gaze finally settling on Greta—taking in her clear, rosy face, her old-fashioned clothes, her bare feet, tan and solid against the earth.

Gideon turned to gaze with her—his own face waxy, dark ruddy bags under his eyes. He glanced at Greta, his eyebrows dipping together, before he shot a look back at his sister.

There was something in the look that passed between them, something I didn't get.

"Hans," Savina asked, still staring at Greta, who had gathered up her empty basket and turned toward the house. "Was Greta with you the whole night when you came to the woods?"

"What do you mean?" I asked.

"When you came to the party, were you together the whole time?"

"Pretty much," I said, still not understanding.

"So you snuck out of the house *with* your little sister?" she asked.

"Well, no," I answered. "I snuck out and she must have heard me, because by the time I got to the fence at the edge of our property, she was there."

"She was already there?" Savina interrupted.

"Well, yeah," I said.

"Even though she left after," Savina said.

"I mean, yeah," I answered, not liking the feeling that was creeping up my spine. "She knew the woods better than me, so she beat me to the fence post."

Both Gideon and Savina were staring at me now with sad, sad eyes and some kind of twin telepathy.

"And you said that the last two kids who Greta found were a little more aware than the first ones?" Savina asked.

"Well, Greta said that," I answered.

"And what did she mean?" Savina asked.

"That they just seemed to be more with it—like they remembered their names easily and the last kid was playing all those songs he knew and could talk about the band and stuff."

"So they were just more aware?" Savina asked. "Like, the closer the deaths were, the less *gone* they seemed, right?"

I looked to Gideon and he averted his eyes, staring at his shoes.

"I mean, yeah, I guess," I answered, looking out at Greta as she made her way to the house. Greta who wasn't sick, Greta who had seemed attuned to those other kids, found their personal effects, Greta who…

At just that moment, she stopped by the side of the house, right where she thought we couldn't see her, but there was her hand—those strong, healthy fingers. They flicked off a piece of the windowsill, just like…just like… My mouth went dry.

"She's eating the house," Savina said in a whisper, as we heard Greta's hand on the doorknob, the creak of a turn.

"What are you saying?" I hissed.

"I'm saying that Greta is dead," Savina answered, just as the door swung open and the last egg began to rock in earnest.

CHAPTER 25

HANS

Greta walked across the threshold into the kitchen.

"Look what I found," she said, holding up a bushel of sunflower-looking plants. "Jerusalem Artichokes. You can eat the roots—per that book they taste like potatoes—so you should like these."

You. You should like these. Why not her? Why didn't Greta need to eat like the rest of us? Why wasn't Greta sick or hot or thin? Why weren't her pants as loose as Gideon's, why wasn't her hair as oily as Savina's, her back as itchy as mine?

I thought of her face when I'd seen her that night on the last day of May—that night that seemed like forever ago. *I know what you're doing*—that's what she'd said when she'd accosted me by the fence. Just waiting there, like any bratty younger sister.

And I knew she was fast; I knew she knew the woods well. But it really was awfully fast that she'd gotten to that post, especially since I'd checked on her and heard her breathing just before I left.

I left.

I left my little sister alone in the house with an unlocked

door on the final night of a month when every thirteen years a serial killer struck.

I left just like my father had, only this time it wasn't just a broken family that had been the consequence.

I felt the bile rise in my throat; I felt the room sway around me. "Greta," I moaned. Gideon caught my arm as my vision blurred and I staggered.

"I'm right here," she said, rushing over. "Are you alright? Here, just eat these." She shoved the root-like things into my hands, but I didn't take them, couldn't grip them. "I'll make you some tea," she said, racing to the stove.

"The object," Savina said, coming to help Gideon hold me up. "What do you think it was?"

I didn't have to think. "Her backpack," I whispered.

Greta turned, this sort of slow-motion thing. "Are you talking about *me*?"

"Where is it?" Savina asked.

"What?" Greta said, coming over to her, with a mug in hand.

"Greta, I—" she said.

"It must be somewhere in the house," I said. "Check upstairs."

"I don't need my backpack," Greta said, her voice angry. "Not with all this stuff I've found in the house."

Gideon was already making his way up the narrow steps.

"Why do you want it?" Greta asked, trying to hand me a cup of water with a bunch of crumbs floating in it.

Savina took it from her, and I—I just stared. "Greta," I said. "I'm so, so sorry."

"Sorry?" she asked, a little shock in her voice, like she'd never heard the word come out of my mouth. Maybe she hadn't. "Sorry for what?"

"Found it," Gideon called down, and then we heard his lumbering steps.

"I shouldn't have left you that night," I said. "I'm so sorry." I looked at the floor, the tears splashing from my eyes onto the bricks that sucked them up like cake.

"It's okay," she said. "I found you."

I looked up, smiling at her. "Yeah," I said. "Yeah, you did. It's been good to be here with you. I never deserved a sister as good as you. I just…" The tears choked me again, and I heard it, the egg wobbling against the basket as Gideon's feet hit the bottom step.

"Wait," Greta said.

"I'm so sorry," I repeated, looking into her blue eyes, wanting them to be the last things I saw before she…

"No," she said, stepping away from me. "No. I'm not." She glanced at Savina, who looked down. "No. I'm right here. I'm…"

Gideon came up behind her, holding the little backpack, which looked more tattered and old than I remembered.

"I love you, Greta," I said. "I hope you know that."

"I'm not…" she said, stomping her foot as the egg hit the side of the basket with a loud crack. Gideon held up the backpack and Greta opened her mouth in a wide 'O.'

Just as the front door slammed open, smacking the wall behind it with a bang.

We all jumped. Even Greta.

CHAPTER 26

HANS

We saw her through the doorway. The woman. But not a woman like I'd expected to see belonging to this ancient house with its ancient stove and the ancient clothes that Greta had found. No. This woman didn't look much older than thirty. She had her hair up in a messy topknot and was wearing jeans and a tank top with a unicorn on the front of it. Also, she was carrying a paper grocery bag, filled to the brim with food.

We all stared, stunned.

My mouth watered.

She stopped when she saw the four of us. She didn't scream or pull out a phone to call the cops, like someone else might have if they'd found four smelly, nasty kids in her house. She just tipped her head to the side, like a little bird, and said, "Well, what have we here?"

Maybe I should have suspected then, but I couldn't see past the overflowing bag of groceries she had set on the counter—apples, bananas, hamburger buns, all spilling out the top.

Apparently, I wasn't the only one.

"We got lost," Savina said. "Days ago. Weeks." Savina's eyes welled up, and the woman bent her eyebrows together in concern.

"Oh, honey. How awful. I'm so glad you guys found the house." She glanced around. "It's not much. I inherited it from my great-grandmother. But I like to come here a few times a year. Just to get away."

Savina nodded. We all did.

I mean, that made sense, didn't it? A woman who came out every once in a while to take a little mini vacation. I wanted it to make sense.

We must have all been staring at the grocery bag, because all the sudden the woman's eyes got huge and she said, "Oh my gosh. You guys must be starving."

And now the tears spilled out of Savina's eyes, though she cried silently. Gideon reached over and put an arm around her shoulder.

I glanced at Greta, and noticed that—as opposed to the rest of us—she wasn't staring at the groceries, but at the woman.

I saw her open her mouth, and I wanted that food so, so badly that I willed her not to say the thing I knew was going to say.

"Ma'am," she began.

Stop, I thought at her. But I lacked the twin telepathy that Savina and Gideon shared.

"Ma'am, I don't know if you know this—" Greta continued.

And I appreciated that she had at least that level of tact.

"—But there have been several murders on or near this property. We found the bodies while we were here."

"Murders!" the woman said, and even though her voice sounded serious, I could see her lips turn up at the edges, like she was trying to suppress a smile, a laugh. She didn't believe us. And I should have come to Greta's defense, should have pointed out the objects we'd found, said something, anything..

But I couldn't seem to tear my eyes off the bananas poking

out of the bag, couldn't seem to open my own mouth to get any words out at all.

"We found these, um, items," Greta said, her voice wavering. "We put them in the empty pantry."

"Yes, oh dear, you kids must be so hungry. Let's get you some food and then we'll figure things out."

"No," Greta said, stomping her foot and rushing to the pantry. "Look."

She opened it, and I saw it then, through the woman's eyes. A rock, some yarn, a broken flashlight, an ancient cassette tape. Old junk anyone could have found anywhere in the woods. Just…trash.

The woman's eyebrows rose—she was trying to keep her face neutral. "Oh," she said.

"These things," Greta said, faltering, glancing at me. "They belong to those kids who got murdered. Every thirteen years. Of course, the trumpet's still in the tree. But the rest of it is here. And we found the bodies too. Well…" Her voice trailed off. She glanced at me, like she was asking for help.

But what was I supposed to say? Just five minutes ago, I'd been delusional enough to believe that my sister was dead and that we'd been hanging out with her ghost for two weeks. I wasn't exactly prime witness material. Plus, we hadn't actually found the bodies, not really. We had found some things we thought were bones and an old shoe stuck in the dirt. I'd never gone to see the mattress so maybe there really was something there, but at this point—hungry and hot and sick as I was—I wasn't sure I was willing to bet on it.

"We even found a dead man," Greta said, looking a little desperately at me. "Out in the woods. We think he lived here. Or came here. That maybe he was the killer."

The woman made a face, her forehead wrinkling. "That is… awful. Where…where is the body?"

Greta swallowed. "I'm not quite sure. It's easy to lose track in the woods. Not far from the house. We could see the house from where he was, but—" She stopped talking. "I don't know exactly."

And she must have realized what we'd all suddenly realized —that we hadn't seen the old man's body, or smelled it, since we'd come here. Even though it had been quite close when we found it.

"Maybe an animal came and got it," Greta said, looking down at her bare feet.

"Oh, that *is* terrible," the woman said, her eyes growing misty. "And it explains some of the trauma that would have made you, um, find these…things." She nodded to the pantry where the stuff was.

"We even found bones," Greta said. "In the garden. We put them in a big sack."

The woman nodded and then added. "You know, I did bury a dog of mine in that old garden almost ten years ago. Perhaps—"

Greta's scowl cut her off.

"Listen," the woman said, keeping her voice level and serious. "I can tell that you guys have found some stuff that is really upsetting. But I also see that you're ravenous. How long did you say you'd been stuck here?"

"Fourteen days, ma'am," Gideon piped up, looking at his shoes.

"Oh, no," the woman said. "There's not a drop of food in this house. I can't have mice getting in while I'm gone, so I clear it all out. What have you been eating?"

Gideon swallowed. "Mostly greens, ma'am, some mushrooms."

"And you couldn't find your way home?"

We all shook our heads, even Greta.

"Miss—" Savina began.

"What did you say your name was?" Greta interrupted.

"You can call me Gigi," she said.

"Miss Gigi, do you have a phone?" Savina continued. "Our parents will be worried out of their minds."

"I'm sure they are," the woman replied. "But—well, I'm so sorry. I don't bring a phone on these trips. That's kind of part of the point in me coming here. To disconnect."

Savina's eyes grew dewy again.

The woman started taking things out of her bag. "Here," she said. "Start with the bananas. I'll make us some supper in a jiffy. And then we can figure out what to do?"

"Did you hear about us?" Greta asked, taking her banana, but not opening it. "Our disappearance. Seems like it would be all over the news."

"I'm sure it must be," Gigi said. "But I'm not from around here. Not even close. And although I'm sure it's hit the national news if you've been gone for fourteen days, the truth is that I try not to watch the news." She shrugged her shoulders and looked around the house as if to say, *Look where I choose to come for vacation.*

I'd torn into my banana, almost too hungry to peel it first. It was the most delicious thing I'd ever eaten, the sugar hitting my tongue like a drug. Gideon and Savina looked equally enraptured, but Greta just stood there, her banana unpeeled.

"Aren't you hungry, dear?" Gigi asked.

"Not especially," Greta said, looking into the woman's eyes.

Gigi looked into her grocery bag and pulled out a bag of potatoes. "We'll make an amazing little stew. I've got some beef in here somewhere. A stew would be better with lamb or something else, but for now, ground beef will just have to do."

"And where is your car?" Greta asked, still completely uninterested in her banana. I was staring at it, my mouth thick with saliva.

"It's in this little parking area outside the woods. Just over four miles away."

"Is there a path?" Greta asked, and I was sure she'd completely lost her mind.

"I know the path," the woman said with a smile. "Let's get you guys fed and then we'll figure something out."

Greta saw me looking at her, well, at her banana. She passed it to me. I didn't even question it, didn't even insist she keep it. Instead, I broke it into three pieces and doled the other parts out to Savina and Gideon.

Gigi pretended not to notice, busying herself with the potatoes. "Well, look at this," she said, digging through a drawer. "Someone's tidied the place up." She cast a glance around us. "Thank you."

I was sure that would soften Greta up, but she continued to scowl.

The woman pulled out a peeler, holding it up triumphantly. "Tada! You guys go rest. I'll get the fire going in this old stove and we'll eat, then make a plan."

We all wandered toward the living room, looking warily at the fire, which was mostly just coals and ash now. It didn't feel nearly as hot as it had.

"Do you need any help?" Greta asked the woman, surprising me yet again.

"No, dear, not yet. You just go on in with your friends, and I'll take care of this."

Gigi pulled some kindling from a little compartment beneath the brick stove, along with a package of matches. We hadn't even seen it there, the little metal door.

"Come on, Gret," I said.

"I'm not tired," Greta replied, just as the woman said, "Oh, it looks like someone found my old backpack." She picked up the pack Gideon had brought down the stairs. "I left it here accidentally last time. Now off you go, guys. If you look inside that bench, you'll find some card games to play."

Sure enough, the top of the bench opened, revealing several

used packages of playing cards and one battered box of Uno. It felt so modern in the old house that I had trouble putting it all together.

Greta snagged a package of playing cards and began to shuffle.

"What do you want to play?" I asked her, sitting cross-legged on the floor and feeling better than I had since the first day we'd gotten here.

"Solitaire," Greta answered.

"Come on, Gret," I said. "This is awesome. We're going to eat. We're going to go home. She has a car."

"She could be a *killer*," Greta hiss-whispered.

"She is definitely not the right age," I hiss-whispered back.

"She doesn't have to be," Greta replied. "And even if she isn't, she doesn't believe us."

I thought again about the old stuff in the cupboard, how plain and common it looked. Truthfully, I wasn't sure I believed us either. We'd been so tired and so hungry. Savina and I had had fevers practically since we'd gotten here, and Gideon was jaundiced or something. What if we'd all just…gotten caught up in the idea that we were solving these murders when really, we were just finding random junk. After all, I was currently arguing with the sister I'd almost accused of being dead. Which seemed absolutely impossible with her standing right here, being alive and bratty.

Though she still hadn't eaten. And she was wearing those creepy clothes. "Gret, go and get changed. We'll be going home soon. You probably should arrive in the clothes you left in."

"These are more comfortable," she replied, dealing herself cards for solitaire. "I'll change when I need to."

I grabbed the other battered box of cards and went over to sit by Gideon and Savina. "Uno?" I said, holding up the game.

"Sounds perfect," Savina answered with a smile.

I flopped into a cross-legged position on the floor and there, underneath the bench, I saw one of the boots peeking out from behind a leg. They hadn't vanished like I'd thought. Someone had just pushed the bench and the boots had gotten shoved to the back, leaving the mud behind. No one had been coming and going—sneaking in and out. I'd just been hungry and paranoid and, well, not looking very well.

In the other room, the wood from the brick oven had started to crackle, but it didn't feel smothering or hot. In fact, the sound was soothing. And soon enough smells started to drift into the room, potatoes cooking in butter, meat with salt and thyme, onions sweetening as they caramelized.

CHAPTER 27

HANS

We feasted.

Even Greta took a bit of the stew, though she ate daintily while the rest of us scooped food into our mouths like starving lions. Still, watching her eat made me feel even better about her 'being alive' status, and even less sure of my own mental stability in the last few weeks. It'd been rough.

"Eat as much as you want," Gigi said, mostly watching us. "But don't eat too quickly or you'll make yourselves sick."

Motherly.

"Can we go to your car when we're done?" Greta asked, spooning the last drops of stew into her mouth and then rinsing her bowl in the bucket, as though she'd been born to live in 1930.

Gigi looked out the window, at the darkening woods. I did a double take. How long had we been playing Uno? How long had she been cooking? How was the summer sun already fading?

"I know you guys don't want to hear this," Gigi said with a sigh. "I know you must be eager to get home, but I'm not sure how much I trust myself in these woods at night. I always hike in during the day. I've even heard rumors there are bears. I know this is just awful," she said, placing her spoon in her own small bowl. "But if we can just wait until morning, then we can make our way to my car. My phone is there and we should be able to sort this out as soon as morning comes."

And I admit that it *was* disappointing. Though with a full stomach, it was slightly *less* disappointing. Besides, we'd already been gone for fourteen days. What was one more night?

"Now, where have you kids been sleeping?" she asked, scooping a final mushroom into her mouth. I glanced at my bowl. I hadn't noticed a single mushroom in my own bowl and I was relieved. After this involuntary stay in the woods, I wasn't sure I ever wanted to see another mushroom again.

"Living room," Gideon answered with his mouth full of soup, face fully focused on his bowl.

"On the hard floor?" she asked.

"Not Greta," Savina said. "She's been sleeping upstairs."

"Highly recommend," Gigi said. "That's where I stay."

"I'll get my things," Greta said.

"No need," Gigi responded. "I'll just pull out the old cot."

"You really don't have to—" Greta began.

"I don't mind," Gigi interrupted.

"With all due respect," Greta answered. "I'm not sleeping upstairs with someone I don't know."

I almost choked on my ground beef.

"Of course," Gigi said. "That's not what I meant. I meant that I'd drag the cot down here into the kitchen. This room will still be warm from the fire, and cozy as anything."

"You want it to be warm?" I asked.

"Well, I don't want it to be cold," she responded with a laugh, then looked at my sweating head with a bit of concern. I just looked back down into my soup, shoveling another bite into my mouth.

"I'll clean up," Greta said.

"You don't have to—" Gigi began.

"Oh, but I do," Greta said. "Call it a coping mechanism."

And I saw it, the little flick Greta gave the countertop with her fingernail, picking a piece from it, and then popping it into her mouth—almost too casual to notice.

I swallowed the strange lump that formed in my throat, forcing the last drops of my soup down. "Can we leave as soon as the sun comes up?" I asked. "In the morning."

"Not a moment later," Gigi responded.

BUT WE DIDN'T. Because in the morning, Savina was too sick to move.

CHAPTER 28

GRETA

The woman, Gigi, tore through her grocery sack and came up with a bottle of Tylenol. "This should help," she said, looking at Savina's white, glassy face.

And it should, of course, but there was something off about that woman. I didn't trust her. Which might explain why I suggested that I make Savina a nice tea instead.

"Tea is a darling idea," Gigi said. "And I know it's all you kids have had to work with the last few weeks, but I think Tylenol will act a lot faster."

I pinched my lips together, sucking in my indignation. After all, I might not like this woman, but a person couldn't really argue with Tylenol.

Besides, *why* didn't I like her? She'd come to the house, finally found us, made dinner, promised to take us home. Now she had medicine—actual medicine. What more could I ask for than that?

Especially when Hans looked so awful—his face flushed, his hair matted in sweat. Gideon's skin wasn't much better, sallow, the whites of his eyes practically yellow.

"Maybe Tylenol all around," Gigi said, tucking back a lock of hair and mumbling about how she didn't know what to do and if only she had her phone and we couldn't go to the car now, not with everyone running a fever.

"Greta," the woman said to me. "Would you go draw some cool water from the well?" She pursed her lips, like she was thinking. "We've got to get these fevers down before we can move anywhere. But I've got to use the woodstove to cook and it gets so hot in the day. Your brother and friends are still half-starved and I didn't bring any convenience foods with me. Convenience isn't really why I come here."

She rubbed her own temples like she was trying to push back a headache. "This sounds a little unconventional, but I'm thinking maybe we can take a spare cot and some blankets out to that shed. Everyone will be cooler in there. If we can just get their fevers to break, then we can all get to my car. As it is, the girl can't even walk."

And it was true. I wasn't even sure Savina would make it to the shed, much less some lady's car that was four miles away. The boys were barely better. In fact, looking at Hans' skin, red hot and pocked with hives, I felt afraid—really afraid, which was different than lost-in-the-woods afraid I'd felt when we got here, and more like I-can't-lose-everything afraid.

If taking them to the shed would help, then I'd get them to the shed.

"How soon do you think we can get to the car?" I asked, though I was already folding up the cot.

Gigi clipped her hair into a quick bun on the top of her head. It looked a little more severe than it had the day before, a little more down to business. "Soon, I hope," she said.

But even though we set them up really comfy in the shed, right by the high windows where a cross breeze would blow, even though I hauled water for them all day, running cool washcloths over their faces and along Hans' back, even though Gigi cooked three square meals, they looked even worse by the end of the evening.

"Greta," Savina said, as I ran the cold washcloth over her forehead for the thousandth time. "Do you think we're going to die here? In this place?"

"Of course not," I said, wringing out the washcloth and dipping it into the bucket again.

"If I die," Savina said, as though she hadn't heard my answer. "Please tell my dad that I love him and that I'm really, really sorry. Tell Gideon too. And that I never would have made it this far without him."

I glanced over at Gideon, who was asleep, his face practically yellow, though his chest still rose and fell in a nice, regular rhythm. "You can tell him," I said quietly.

But we both knew that he wouldn't hear her if she did.

"What a stupid way to die," Savina said, gazing through the tiny window into the starry night sky. "And just as we were about to go home." This time, she didn't cry, just stared.

Hans was staring too. He reached out a finger and touched Savina's hand. She wound her pinky around his. "I'm glad you've been here too," she said to him.

And usually I would roll my eyes and look away. But tonight I just stared at those white entwined fingers. "Just give me a second," I said. "Maybe…" I chose my words carefully. "Maybe Gigi has some other medicine we can try."

I went back to the house, like I was going to go in and ask her. But I didn't. In the darkness, I knelt down, right by the steps, and plucked a chip of stone from the base of the house. I popped it into my own mouth first. Cinnamon. Yes, that would do. I peeled off three more chips, pill-sized. And brought them back. "Just hold these on your tongues," I said, making them open their mouths so I could drop the "pills" in. "And let them melt."

"Tastes like cinnamon," Savina slurred, as the bit of candy house sank into her tongue.

"Yeah," I said. "Yeah, Gigi said it would."

CHAPTER 29

HANS

Day 16

I woke up feeling better than I had in days, even better than I'd felt when Gigi made that first stew. Whatever the medicine was that Greta had given us, it'd worked wonders. Hopefully enough wonders to make our way to Gigi's car. We didn't have to be all the way better, just well enough.

I staggered to the house, still ravenous. And through the little back kitchen window, I could see Gigi, feeding sticks into the fire of the brick oven.

Dawn was breaking and in the dim light with my eyes still adjusting from a night in the shed, her hair looked gray, her shoulders stooped and old. But then in the silence, I heard the tick of that hateful cuckoo clock, the squeaky chime, and then the creak of the little door Gideon had tried to fix. 6:15. The light shifted, the bright morning sun breaking through the trees and into the kitchen. I rubbed my eyes, my face, and there she was same as always—a woman in blue jeans and a t-shirt, cooking breakfast.

Getting lost for over two weeks and nearly starving to death did weird stuff to your brain, that was for sure.

And body. I felt a trickle of sweat peel down my back. I was glad *I* didn't have to stand in front of that fire, preparing some eggs on a cast iron skillet.

The scent of butter and sage floated to me through the windows and my mouth watered.

I dragged up the steps, through the back door, and into the kitchen.

Gigi turned to me, this look of alarm breaking across her face. "What are you doing out of bed?" she said, her voice rising.

"I'm feeling a lot better," I replied, backing away.

"This is a critical situation," she said, shooing me out the door and following me as I staggered backwards. "Back to bed. We've got to get you guys well enough to hike FOUR miles through these woods."

"But I'm feeling—" I began.

"I'll have Greta bring you breakfast," she said, stomping to the shed to make sure Gideon and Savina hadn't also gone rogue.

Through the gated door, I could just see Gideon sitting on his cot, rubbing his head, a little pink finally in his cheeks. Gigi strode over and tucked a blanket over his legs, though it felt a little more military than motherly. Savina was still sleeping— her breath steady, not shallow or labored as it had been. Gigi stood over her for a moment, gazing at her as though counting the breaths.

"I think we can go today," I said, stepping into the shed and looking at my friends. "We're feeling a little better. Better enough."

Gigi ran a hand through her hair and, for a moment, her eyes seemed to fog over, giving me a glimpse of that older woman I'd imagined earlier. "It's a difficult hike through the woods. Rocky inclines and creeks to cross. I just…What would we do if one of you couldn't make it? Let's give it another day to fatten you up." She reached out and squeezed one of my fingers. "See, you're practically sticks."

And we *were* thin—that's for sure. I could barely keep my pants up and Gideon wasn't any better. I didn't know about Savina, but her arms *were* like sticks, even her fingers bony. I thought of her pinky wrapped around mine—she'd been trembling. And talking about dying.

"I think we can make it," I repeated, even though I was feeling less sure. But we had to make it. Our chances for recovery would be so much better in a hospital than an old house.

"One more day," Gigi said. "If you guys continue to recover at this rate, I think that you can make it then."

And with that she left, shutting the gate behind her.

But there was something strange about it. Instead of the one click as the latch fell, I heard two clicks. The fall of the latch, followed by a thicker, more decisive sound.

I walked to the door of the shed. I hadn't thought much about the door before that. Now I noticed that it was full-length, from the top of the shed all the way to the floor, with cast iron grates narrow enough that animals couldn't wriggle through. I'd thought of the grates as thin and decorative, but looking at them now, touching them—it was clear that they were dense and strong. I gave the door a little shake, trying to open it.

Though I had known—known when I'd heard that second click—that I wouldn't be able to.

Sure enough, there, connected to the latch was a thick, iron lock.

CHAPTER 30

GRETA

"I saw you lock the door," I said, confronting Gigi at the front door.

"What door?" Gigi asked, all big, innocent eyes.

"The gate to the shed," I answered. "I saw you. There's no reason to lock the gate."

Gigi sighed, sinking into one of the stools by the table, like it was just too much to stay on her feet. "Greta," she said. "I know this is hard to understand, but your friends are very, very sick. Hans came out this morning, half delirious, stumbling around, thinking he could make the hike today when he could barely get up the two stairs into the kitchen. Think about it. What if he came out, delirious, and wandered into the woods at night, thinking he knew where he was going, thinking he could do it? He could die out there."

"But if we all went together?" I pushed. "Today."

She shook her head, her face lined with wrinkles, which made her look older. "Here I can care for them, feed them. What if we got halfway there and someone collapsed? What would we do then?"

"We'd carry them," I answered defiantly.

"What if they all three collapsed," she asked, the wrinkles digging into the edges of her face. "Who would carry them then? Just you and I?"

I pressed my lips together. "Why don't I walk to the car?" I asked, poking a long stick into the fire and stirring the embers. "Or care for them while you do?"

Gigi nodded, as though she was considering. "I'm not sure it would be safe for you to do the hike without me to guide you. But maybe tomorrow if they're still not well enough, I could go, call someone, get some help."

I stared into the fire. As far as desperate plans went, it would have to do. "Tomorrow," I said. "If they're not better."

"Of course," she cooed. "And we've got the rest of the day to fatten them up, get them feeling better. Three solid meals."

I nodded. That did seem to be what they needed.

"I'll teach you how to use the oven in case I have to go tomorrow," she continued, placing a hand on the brick, her long nails pressing against it. "After all, you want to be sure they get breakfast, lunch, and dinner." Gigi tipped her chin toward to the fire. "Though it looks like you're a natural."

I tossed in the stick, watching it ignite, then burn bright against the coals.

"And whatever you do," Gigi said, as the stick turned to dust. "If I have to go, you mustn't let your friends out. Or they could wander, lost, into the woods."

HANS

I picked at it, the lock. With my hands. All morning. I'd trusted the woman—Gigi—trusted her perfectly. Even though she lived in this house, in these woods. Even then. Because she had food. And wasn't some ancient, shriveled old woman. I'd trusted her.

Now I was locked in a shed.

I tore again at the lock and this time it caught a piece of my finger and broke the skin. I didn't even care. I'd tear my entire hand off if I had to in order to get out. And I didn't care if the woman said I was delirious.

All at once, I sat back, slumping and cradling my hand in my lap. It was bleeding on my pants, my shirt.

If we didn't get out, which one of us would she kill?

The familiar sweat pricked up along my back, trickling over the thick, itchy welts. Greta was the one in the house. Greta was the one who had had the guts to defy her. Did that mean Greta would be the one she killed first?

I crawled back to the lock, digging at it with my fingers until my nails broke, until my fingertips were raw.

"Hans!" I heard Greta's voice and my heart sped up.

She was running toward me awkwardly, trying to balance a tray of food. "Hans, stop!"

I fell back, so relieved at her voice, at seeing her all pink-cheeked.

"What are you doing?" she shrieked, looking at my hands.

"Trying to get this lock off," I said, smiling kind of goofy at her.

"Stop it," she snapped. "And stop looking at me like that. You're bleeding, you idiot." She set the tray down, swiping her hands through her hair, her face a plaster of worry lines. So much like wrinkles.

I tipped my head to the side, looking at her. "You have food," I said. "So you can open this thing. You'd have to, to give it to us, right?"

Greta looked down at her bare feet. "Only she's got the key. Here, eat." She slipped the food through the slats of the gate, piece by piece since she couldn't hand us the whole tray. Baked potatoes, boiled eggs, a few grapes.

"You," I said. "You don't have the key?"

"No," she repeated. "Only she does."

"But you can get it," I said. "Sneak it off of her. We've got to leave, Gret. We're feeling better."

Greta glanced through the slats. Gideon had gone back to sleep, and I wasn't sure Savina had ever woken, but her breath was steady and deep.

"See!" I said triumphantly.

She looked back at me, the lines digging deep into her face. "Hans," she said slowly. "I need to go get you something for that hand. I think I know where some wrappings are. Don't do that again, okay?"

"Right," I said, my voice wavering slightly. "Because I won't have to, because you'll get the key, right? We need it, Greta. Something is wrong. Way wrong."

She looked at me, right into my eyes. And then away, to the side. "I'll see what I can do."

Greta

I DIDN'T TRUST the woman. Never had.

Unfortunately, right now my worry over Hans trumped my distrust of Gigi.

It'd taken me a long time to clean up his hand, holding it through the slats of the door. The skin of the fingers was torn to bits, the pointer and middle with flaps of skin ripped clean off. I'd cleaned them with well water and a bottle of alcohol I'd found upstairs in the wardrobe, near the chest, the chest where we'd found the clothes of the second girl. What was her name again? Somehow with all the stress, it had slipped my mind.

When I'd gone back into the house, the rag I'd used to clean Hans' hand had been covered, every inch, with blood—blood from him picking away at a lock he could never break like he was, indeed, delirious. Just like Gigi had said.

I'd wrapped his hand in clean gauze, but I'd probably have to clean it every day to keep it from infection. After all, he didn't need an infection on top of everything else.

When Gigi saw the rag, she lifted her eyebrows, that was all. Like she knew what had happened.

I tossed the bloodied rag in the bucket of water by the washbasin and together we watched the clear, clean water go dark. "I'll get some fresh water," I said, gripping the handle.

Gigi only nodded.

On my way out, I glanced at her dwindling bag of food. "What do we do when your food runs out?" I asked.

"I've got more in the car," she said. "Canned goods and stuff. I was going to go back to get it."

I nodded, ignoring the little itch in my brain that said it

seemed strange to leave food in the car at the end of a four-mile hike, so she'd have to go back for it later. Though how much could she carry at once? Especially when she'd walked in, carrying a grocery bag like she'd popped out of a 1950s TV show. Which was also odd. Where was her backpack? That's what she should have had; it's what I would have used. But then again, this was a bit of a Spartan vacation for her, so maybe walking four miles back to the car, then lugging a bag of canned goods another four miles back, was right up her alley.

For lunch I brought out tin cups of fresh water as well as more baked potatoes and some hard cheese Gigi had dug out of the bottom of the grocery bag—a paper sack. It *was* odd, that sack, wasn't it?

Savina and Gideon were up this time. That was good. Sitting in the straw, their gazes hollow. They did *not* look like kids who could make a four-mile hike, even with help.

Hans, on the other hand, was wild-eyed. "Did you get it?" he asked, and I noticed that his bandage was discolored—brown with old blood, but the tip red with fresh blood.

"Are you still bleeding?" I asked. "You didn't pick at the lock again, did you?"

"No," he said, his left hand shoved deep in his pocket.

"Hans," I said, my voice tense.

"Did you get it?" he repeated.

"No," I said. "I haven't even seen it." At least that was true.

"Well, *someone's* gonna have to open this door at some point," Savina said, from her spot across the room. "'Cause if we're stuck here, I'm going to need a bucket."

"Of water?" I asked. "I brought some…"

"Just empty," Savina interrupted. "An empty bucket." And I saw it in her eyes. *Ladies' room.*

I nodded.

· · ·

IN THE END, though, it was Gigi that brought a bucket—two of them. She slipped across the lawn just after midnight—her hair looking white under the moon, her skin translucent and thin. She'd opened the gate without a sound and set the buckets inside.

And I knew, watching her, that Hans was right about one thing. Something was wrong. Very wrong.

THE NEXT MORNING, before dawn had clambered through the windows, I crept into the kitchen, hoping to search for the key.

But Gigi was already awake, sitting near the fire—the lengthening flames reflecting off her skin in angry red and orange streaks, ash floating onto her hair, lining it in gray. Or maybe it was just dry shampoo.

Despite the heat, she sipped a cup of tea, the little crock of honey refilled.

I opened my mouth to say something and then closed it again. Her feet were tucked under her chair, bare now, like mine, her clothes looking a little tattered—a loose skirt and blouse instead of the jeans and t-shirt.

"Do we leave today?" I finally blurted.

She didn't answer, just kept sipping.

I cleared my throat. "Gigi," I said, and she almost seemed to start, like she hadn't noticed me. "Are we ready to leave today?"

And something about the way she looked at me, her eyes glazed, her mouth bent, I almost thought that Hans and the others were dead, that they'd all died in the night. My heart slipped into my guts, but then she said, "They're too thin." And it seemed like the wrong thing to say. It should have been *too sick, too weak.*

"Not ready at all," she added. And with that, she set her mug down, took up the ancient box of matches, and struck one, dropping it into the oven where a pile of straw lit instantly.

We both watched the fire, mesmerized for a moment.

"One of them is my brother," I said, though I wasn't sure why.

"I know," she answered. "I had a brother once too."

And I couldn't be sure, but it didn't seem like she quite knew why she'd said it either.

CHAPTER 32

GRETA

$\mathcal{H}$ans' fingers were raw again when I took them breakfast, but he was weaker, flushed bright red, the welts broken out along his hairline.

"Hans!" I snapped. "Stop it."

"How can I?" he snapped back. "When you won't get the key?"

"How can I get the key when you won't stop acting like you've lost your mind?"

"Me?" he said, reaching a hand to the lock.

I swatted it away.

"You're the one in there living with her, all buddy buddy. When did you start trusting her?"

"I didn't," I said. "Don't. It's just that she said…she said you were delirious, and look at you—picking that thing until your hands bleed."

He sank back like I'd slapped him, slunk into a feral sort of squat.

I closed my eyes. "Hans," I said, composing myself. "I'm trying. But you have to stop. She'll never let you out if she thinks you've gone mad."

"I'm not crazy," he said, staring at the floor.

"I know," I murmured, though I didn't quite. He was definitely acting unhinged. "But I haven't even seen the key." Which was true—as I thought about it, it was strangely true. I hadn't seen the key on the counter or with her things. I hadn't seen her slip it into a pocket, even on the night she'd brought the buckets. Nothing.

"Please, Greta," Hans said, his eyes bloodshot and pleading.

The shed stank now, I could only assume from the buckets. And this morning, all I had to give them were baked potatoes.

"She's going to the car today," I said. "For more food and for her phone. That's what she said. Help will come."

"Greta," Hans said, looking at me with his crazy eyes. "Promise me something."

I pinched my lips together.

"If she doesn't go. If she makes up some excuse or something, you've got to find the key. Okay?"

"Okay," I answered. And this time, I meant it. Of course she would go. It was the only logical thing for a logical person to do. And with more food and her phone, we would be saved. And if she didn't go, well, I tried not to think about that, that's how desperate I'd become.

As soon as I got back to the house, she was gone. Hours she was gone. It gave me peace, knowing. She'd gone to the car, just as promised. She wasn't crazy. And neither was I. And Hans was only a little crazy, because he was so sick.

SHE WASN'T BACK at dusk.

I took the last three potatoes out to the shed, but everyone was already asleep anyway, so I just set them inside the bars. They could have them for breakfast.

And then I walked, front to back, along the line of mushrooms, waiting, watching. Maybe Gigi had gotten lost in the woods herself, or was sending a search party back so people could carry Savina out if she couldn't walk. Or maybe she'd abandoned us to the house.

I wrapped an old sweater around my shoulders. I didn't like it, the dusk.

When I went back in through the door to the kitchen, I noticed a small wrapped lump on the table—a last bit of food I hadn't noticed before—maybe a wedge of cheese. That would help if Gigi didn't come back soon.

I unwrapped it to find not cheese, but a slab of cake, sweet and soft with powdered sugar sprinkled on top.

When had Gigi made a cake? And how? A silver fork lay beside it, along with a folded note. "For you, child. You've been working so hard."

Yeah, right, like I was going to eat this cake. Not when the others needed it so much more than me.

I began to wrap the bundle back in the tea towel when a bit broke off. It reminded me of the house, that piece. Without thinking I popped it into my mouth. Delicate, with a perfect crumb. Vanilla and a hint of something richer. Almond maybe, or maple. A touch of fruit. The taste of the forest spun into sweetness. I figured one more bite wouldn't hurt. We had plenty to go around. Plenty. Then they would eat, they would grow stronger, and we would leave. I lifted another crumb to my mouth. Just a touch, a taste.

Outside, the night turned quieter and darker, as inside I nibbled into the cake, my thoughts growing heavy, my eyes, my body.

I woke to the midnight chime of the cuckoo clock. Crumbs all around me, which seemed like it should matter though I couldn't remember why.

I stood, dusting the crumbs to the floor, then trudged toward my room when I caught sight of a woman outside. A woman. That seemed important.

She trudged across the lawn, wearing an apron, her pockets stuffed, and carrying a basket.

All of it felt like a riddle, but where had I heard it, and why couldn't I remember?

I pressed a hand to my head, trying to clear it, as the woman walked through the door.

Of course. The woman.

"Did you get the groceries?" I asked, looking at the woman, her hair distinctly gray in the light, her eyebrows bushy and bristly, her teeth yellowed like the moon. I swallowed. "Or…" I put a hand up to my head, trying to push the pressure away so I could think straight.

I heard something then, a soft weeping coming from the shed, crying that was so familiar—the same sound we'd heard when we got here. A girl. Savina. She was sick.

The phone. Of course—that's what we needed. "Or the phone?" I asked.

"Whatever for, child?" the woman asked, and I realized that her name had slipped my mind. "I got something better. These delicious berries, fully ripe, and eggs plucked from the nest of a quail. How lovely."

The eggs were indeed lovely. Gray with black speckles. Although the thought of eating them wasn't. And why was that? What did they remind me of?

"I think I might be getting sick too," I said, still holding my head.

"Nonsense, child," the woman replied. "Not when you can eat whenever you want or need. I trust you found my cake."

I looked down at the ground, trying to grab my thoughts,

which broke into thousands of pieces. "I don't feel well," I repeated.

"I'll make you a little something that will help you feel better," she replied.

Something bulged through her the pocket of her apron, but I couldn't remember why that mattered so much.

"You need to eat, child," she said. "One thing about the woods, we must always remember to eat. First the sweet, until you crave the meat." And with that, she crushed a berry, which smeared like blood over one of the eggs.

I JOLTED AWAKE BEFORE DAWN, my head thick with dreams. The strangest dreams. Outside everything was dark, black, save for a curl of white smoke that continued, constantly, into the sky.

I stumbled down the stairs, stopping at the bottom one, noticing the little light in the kitchen.

Gigi—yes, that was her name; of course, that was her name —she was back, but not asleep. Instead, she stood by the fire, the fire that was still burning in that oven large enough to smoke a deer. I peered from the steps through the doorway. Her hand was on her pocket, an old hand, wrinkled and papery, the veins protruding like mountains.

For the smallest moment, a thought flew into my head and I imagined myself coming up behind her and shoving her into that fire—the red flames turning to hot charred welts on her skin. It would be easy, quick. I could get the key then. And save Hans.

Imagining it, a jolt ran up my back to my neck. I rubbed it, sinking down on the stairs, leaning my throbbing head against the wall, a wall that smelled so good.

And then the cuckoo squeaked. 6:15am. My eyes flashed open, the sun streaking through the kitchen windows. My body ached from head to foot and I cricked to a standing position, trying to unfold all the bent places while slips of dreams—of nightmares—slithered through my consciousness.

The fire from the brick oven crackled, and my stomach rumbled. That cleared my head a bit. Tentatively, I made my way into the kitchen.

Gigi was making eggs on a cast iron pan, right over the flames—the yolks just barely firming up.

"Grab me that bit of cheese I've grated," she said.

I obeyed, my dreams still digging against my head.

She took the cheese and sprinkled it over the eggs. But something about it looked familiar, almost like it wasn't cheese at all, but grated bits of wood from the overhead beams. Which was ridiculous, of course.

The eggs smelled perfect, delicious. Why was it I didn't want to eat them? What was it I was supposed to do?

The woman's hair was brown and glossy, tucked into a loose bun with curly bits falling out around her face in a pretty way.

"Your hair," I began, not sure how to end the sentence.

Her only answer was to tuck a lock behind her ear.

"I had the strangest dreams," I said.

"You know," she answered, turning to me with the pan. "Sometimes I do too in this house."

But then I saw it, behind her, the cupboard with the eggs— my eggs—all cracked open. Except one. I walked to it, then trotted, scared that she had used the last one. And she couldn't because there was something we needed to do.

"Something wrong?" she asked, as I pulled the basket out. They were all there, even the last one.

I sighed, relieved. "Oh, no. I just—" I cleared my throat. "I was worried you might try to cook this egg."

"Oh, I could never do that," she said, looking over at the egg with the hairline fracture up one side. "That egg is rotten."

"How do you know?" I asked.

"You don't spend as much time in these woods as I have and not know a thing like that," she said. "Now, have a seat and we'll eat some breakfast together."

"What about the others?" I asked.

"Others?" she said, looking down at her plate.

"In the shed," I answered.

"Oh, we'll bring them what's left."

Gigi pushed the plate toward me, a silver fork on the edge of it, which reminded me of a dream from the night before—a dream I couldn't quite grab. I pushed the food away, my stomach growling. And something about that helped me to remember, bits of memory fighting through the fog in my brain.

The other five eggs, they had cracked, and we'd found things. *I* had found things. But this last one. I squinched my eyes shut, trying to remember. This last egg had been shaking. When that had happened before, children had shown up. Dead children. But this time when it had been shaking, no more children had shown up.

Only this woman.

And me.

I remembered that too, the way Hans had thought something horrible, thought that I was dead.

"You're the final victim," I said, looking up at her, my head suddenly clearing.

"Victim of what?" the woman asked.

"The murders," I said, pointing to my basket. Maybe she'd lived here when the killer had first come along. Maybe he'd killed her to clear the place out so he could use it. And if she was an adult and alone, then no one would have missed her and the killing would have gone undetected. "That's what the egg means."

"I told you," the woman replied. "That egg is rotten, no good at all. You really should throw it away."

"No," I said, looking into her eyes. "No, I need to find something." The relic. *Her* relic.

Because for the egg to crack, for it to release her, and for it to release us, I had to find the thing. The thing that connected her to the murder.

"What you need to do is eat," the woman said, gazing into my eyes.

I shook my head. "I'm not hungry."

And for a moment, I thought that Gigi smiled. And for a moment, I remembered the yellow teeth, the blood-red crush of a berry against an egg. But only for a moment.

"But of course you're hungry, dear," Gigi said. "I can hear your stomach growling. Just have one little egg. With this lovely *sweet* cheese."

The cheese did smell both lovely and sweet. I plucked a bit of it off of the eggs. I would just have a small taste, one teeny little bite.

CHAPTER 33

HANS

Day 18

I waited all morning for Greta to show up with, well, with something. I was hoping for the key, but some breakfast would have been a decent consolation prize.

Gideon was lying on a bed of hay, groaning. Savina was even worse. Turned to her side on the little cot, eyes wide open, face practically translucent—the veins visible through her pale skin. The only thing that occasionally made her eyes flit was the sound of her brother, but she had stopped speaking to him, stopped making any sounds at all.

I wasn't sure how much longer she'd live.

This was more than starving, and I needed Greta. Needed her. And something about waiting for her made me wonder how many times she'd needed me and I hadn't been there. Which was a strange thing to wonder when you were dying. Or maybe the most natural thing in the world.

Several hours after noon, I saw the swish of Greta's skirt through the grate, relief jolting me to my feet.

"Greta," I hissed.

She glanced my direction, looking surprised to see me. Her eyes wide. Almost like…almost like she'd forgotten about us. Which was impossible. Like, it felt more impossible than when I'd thought she was dead.

"Greta," I hissed again and she hurried over. "Did Gigi go to her car? Did she get her phone?"

"Phone?" Greta said. "No, no I don't think so."

I banged my head against the bars of the door, cursing. "Okay, then did you find the key?"

"The key?" she asked.

"Yes, the key," I said, shaking the locked door, sweat pouring down my face, stinging the hives that had multiplied overnight.

"Oh," she murmured, then shook her head.

"Some food then?" I asked, nodding to Savina and Gideon.

Again, that surprised look on her face. She glanced at Savina and Gideon. "They look terrible," she whispered.

"They need to eat," I murmured back. "Please go find us some food."

"I'm not sure it's good," she said. "Last night I ate something, and it made me not feel quite right, and then this morning, the cheese. I…" She paused and I waited, but she didn't finish.

"Greta," I said. "At this point, anything is better than dying, which is what some of us might do if we don't eat. Please."

She nodded. "Okay, I think I know…" She stopped. "Man, I'm glad I skipped lunch, but it looked so good. A stew." She licked her lips.

"Food," I said, watching the way her eyes had glazed. "Is there any stew left?"

"I'm not sure," she said. "But I can find something. Just wait here."

"There's not much I can do but wait here," I grumbled as she scurried away.

Watching her leave, I wasn't a hundred percent sure she would come back. Greta, the most reliable person I knew, and I wasn't sure she'd be back. Something was wrong—that look in her eyes, like everything was slippery, like thoughts left before she could grab them. Had the woman hit her? Did she have a concussion? She had looked okay—no bruising or anything.

But then she was back. With a plate of food. Not good food, not stew or potatoes or beans, but food—crusts of toast, bits of scrambled egg, some vegetables peels and ends from what must have been their lunch stew.

She passed me pieces through the slats. "I'm not sure you should eat it," she was saying as I separated the scraps into three piles and placed them by Savina and Gideon's sleeping spots.

"Lately, when I eat," she murmured, "well, never mind."

"Greta," I said, "you have to find the key." I stuck a scabbed finger into the lock and tried to wiggle it.

"So help me," Greta said, her face clearing, "if you tear open that scab, I won't let you out at all."

Now that sounded a lot more like the old Greta.

"I'm just feeling it, the lock," I said. "It's probably an old key, like one of those skeleton keys."

"Have you seen it?" she asked. "Seen her use it?"

"No," I answered. "She always comes when we can't see a thing."

Greta nodded as though remembering something.

"Key," she said, her face fogging up at first.

"It's an old one, I think." I shook the grate for emphasis.

Greta peered down at the lock. "Skeleton key?" she said.

"Yeah, an old one," I answered.

"Old," she murmured. "An old key. An old woman. A time long ago."

I rubbed my head, which only made my hives itch. "Are you okay, Gret? Did she hurt you or something?"

She shook her head. "Hans, that key. I think that might be it."

"Of course it's *it*, Greta. How else are we going to get out of here?"

"No, what I mean is that the key might be even more important than you think."

"I'm not sure anything could be more important than what I'm thinking right now," I said, glancing down at my small amount of food and then back at Savina and Gideon, who still hadn't woken up.

"What I mean is that the key..." Greta said, her face fully clear, "it might be *the* thing. This woman—I think she's the final victim. Which means I just have to find her thing. Her relic. And I'd bet—" Greta examined the door again. "—I'd bet that key is it."

"Wait?" I asked. "You think she's the last victim?"

"More like the first," she said. "I think someone killed her to take this house—way back in the thirties or forties or something. This is going to sound crazy—"

"What doesn't sound crazy anymore?" I grumbled.

"Yeah, I guess," she said, and that sounded like the old Greta too. "Anyway, she doesn't always look like she did the first day. Sometimes she looks...older."

"Whether she was a victim or not," I said. "Finding that key is what you need to do. Can you remember?"

"I'll remember," she said, looking into my eyes, as though she wasn't quite sure why I would think she would forget. "You look like Dad," she said suddenly.

"I know," I said, meeting her eyes and knowing I needed to say something even though I wasn't quite sure what, so I said all I could think to say. "Please, Greta, find the key."

CHAPTER 34

GRETA

I tore the house to pieces, looking for the key. A skeleton key.

I didn't eat. Couldn't. Or I would forget. The thoughts flew from me so quickly now, almost as if…as if…I thought about that moment before the woman had arrived. The moment they had all thought I was dead.

But I wasn't dead. I couldn't be. Because I was so, so hungry when I didn't use the house to feed me.

Which meant that tearing it apart was its own torture. Every piece I broke off smelled delicious. It used to make me feel so good, the house. But ever since the woman had arrived, ever since I ate that cake, something had changed. The house was different. When I ate it now, things got lost, little pieces of me.

Now, instead of me eating the house, the house ate at me.

Every morning. Every night.

But I had to remember. And the hunger made it easier.

The woman. The key.

She made eggs, the middles soft, perfect. Tea that smelled of mint. Toast with butter slathered thick. I didn't dare eat it. She was sneaking me bits of it, the house. And the house made me forget.

So every time she offered, every time she pressed, I resisted, turning down each delicious bite.

And every time I did—a flash of wrinkles across the woman's forehead, creases under her eyes so deep that I nearly felt them under my own.

"I'm not hungry."

"Suit yourself."

And so it went.

Until the morning my hunger drove me, before dawn, down the stairs.

Eggs. They must be easy to find in the woods. That's why she was always making them. So maybe if *I* made them, without her help, without whatever she was putting in them, then they would be fine. I dug through the cupboards, looking for the grocery bag she'd brought when she'd arrived. Completely empty.

I looked through every basket, every box.

Until all I could see was the basket, *my* basket. One egg remaining. A line of a crack up its side. She had said it was rotten. Perhaps it was true. It had started to smell.

Which meant, of course, that even if I'd wanted to, I couldn't eat it. Not when the house smelled so lovely and sweet. Cardamom and nutmeg, cocoa and sugar.

I plunked onto the stool in front of the fire, hot, flaming, smoking. A fire, just like we'd built to call the search parties to the house. None had come. None would come. Hans was right. We would die here.

A bit of the fire flickered blue. I squinted at it. Beneath the flame, beneath the ash, nestled against the hottest coals, I saw it, the shimmering glint of metal, red hot at the bottom, glowing almost white on the top. Curving and looping in the way of old keys, a crooked tooth that would fit into an old lock.

I looked down at my clothes, the clothes of an old woman. I used a stick to move most of the wood and the glowing coals, then wrapped the apron around my hand and reached into the stove. So deep, so hot. But I didn't stop. Not until I felt the key sear into my palm, the heat going through the fabric of the apron as though nothing was there at all. I yanked the key out of the fire, dropping it to the brick, where it cooled, leaving a blackened mark on the floor.

It wasn't the only mark the key left.

My own hand blistered, the shape of the key forming on my palm. But that didn't matter, not when I had found it. At last.

I stooped over to lift the key, cool now. And I could hear her —the woman—coming. As I'd known she would.

I waited, holding up the key.

She appeared in the darkness, looking just like me—old dress, gingham, is that what it was called, white apron with two pockets. And inside one, I saw it—the shape—the shape of the key.

She put a hand into her pocket, gazing at me, at the fire, at the metal in my hand.

And then she pulled the key out. I saw it glint, the way it caught the light of the fire, the flash between the two keys.

I blinked.

And she was... *not* gone.

I SHOOK MY HEAD, blinking again, looking down at the key in my hand.

"Now what have you gone and done?" the woman asked, the sun creaking over the horizon as the cuckoo croaked out its morning call.

She poured water from a pail onto a rag and reached for my hand. I pulled it back.

"How?" I asked. "How are you still here?"

"What do you mean, Greta?" she asked, shaking her brown curls out of the kerchief and over her shoulders. "Let me take care of that hand."

"I don't need your help," I said. "The key. How are you here?"

"Oh, that old thing. It doesn't work anymore. It was an old key, original to the house—my brother used to use it—but I bought a new lock years ago. Now I use this key." She held up her own key, just a regular key, the type you could make a copy of at the hardware store.

"But you won't need it," she continued, holding out the rag—the same rag I'd used to clean Hans' blood. "We'll get your friends. We just have to wait until they're ready."

"You're still here," I murmured again, looking at the key, looking at her pocket. Only now she was in a pair of skinny jeans, a flowing checkered shirt over them, not a dress or apron at all.

Maybe I wasn't just losing my memory; maybe I was losing my mind.

"But of course I'm here," Gigi replied, placing the cool, wet rag over my palm. "This is quite the burn. I hope I have an ointment somewhere."

I glanced behind her to the basket on the counter. The egg hadn't moved or cracked open, not even a millimeter.

Gigi looked over her shoulder. "Oh, my dear, I told you. That one is rotten. You really ought to just throw it away."

I looked up into her eyes, blue like my own, and the tickle of a thought came into my brain, testing my sanity. "Why don't *you*?" I asked, pasting on my sweetest face. "Why don't you throw it away?"

The woman—Gigi—forced a smile, pressing harder against my burn with the rag. "I couldn't very well take it from you, now could I?"

Then I knew. I knew she couldn't. She couldn't touch that egg, or dispose of it.

And in that fact, I found the smallest trace of hope.

CHAPTER 35

HANS

Day 20

saw Greta coming, another old-fashioned dress. But this time when she got to the door, it rattled as she banged against it.

Gideon started. Savina stirred. I'd been holding Savina's hand as she slept. It was always cold now, no matter how hot my own hand was. But I kept holding it and she kept breathing. Gideon would wake sometimes, walk around, look at our surroundings, then at me. But he'd slipped back into himself, the way I remembered him at school. A shadow. But worse. Because now he had no bright sun of a sister to be a shadow behind.

I let Savina's hand slip out of mine and stood up.

"I found it," Greta said, pressing her face against the bars of the door.

I scuffled to her. "Perfect."

"Not perfect," she answered. "It didn't work."

"You haven't even tried it," I said.

"It didn't work to make her go away. The woman had a key; I could see it there in her pocket. She held it up, just like the others had. There was the flash—" Greta stared into the distance, her eyes almost milky.

I wondered if Greta really had gotten sick, just in a different way than we had. Like, in her head more than her body.

"After the flash, they always go away," she murmured. "But she didn't. She said the egg was rotten."

I shook my head. "What egg?"

"The sixth."

"Forget the egg, Greta," I said, frustrated that she couldn't see past her own crazy theory. "We really need the key. Did you get it?"

Her eyes were wild. "If I can find the thing, then she'll vanish," she said. "She'll go away. And you'll get better. And we can all leave."

"Greta," I said, wrapping my fingers around the grate of the door. "The thing we really need is the key. Otherwise, we are going to die."

"No," she said, glancing at my fingers, which were still scabbed from picking at the lock. "The thing you really need is for us to free the final victim. If we can't do that, it won't matter if you get out or not, because you'll die one way or another."

I pulled my hands away, leaning back on my heels, then sinking into a squat.

"You're right," I said, glancing at Savina with her see-through face. "You're right." I whispered it this time. "We're going to die. Even if we get out." The tears came soundlessly, trickling from my eyes. I didn't even try to stop them.

Greta pressed her face to the slats of the gate. "You won't," she said. "I'm going to free the last victim."

I smiled at her from my prison. "Okay, Gret."

"You think I'm crazy?" she asked.

"I think it's hopeless, that's all," I replied, the tears all the way to my chin now, stinging a cluster of hives.

"It's not," she whispered. "Not yet. I'll set you free. You won't die. No one will. But it won't be because of this…" She pulled the key from her left pocket, an old skeleton key, just like I'd told her to find. My pulse quickened.

"It doesn't work," she said. "She has the real one, and it's not old, not a skeleton key at all. She said she'll get you when you're ready."

"Ready?" I asked. "For what?"

Greta shrugged.

"Let me see it," I said.

"It won't work," Greta said, slipping the key into my hand. "Your fingers," she added. "They feel so skinny, like twigs."

I looked at Greta, but she was staring back at the house.

I slid my hand through the iron bars and wiggled the key into the slot. It fit. My pulse hammered. "Turn it," I said, struggling to maneuver it from my angle inside the shed.

Greta stared at the key like it was haunted, but put her hand to it. She was using her left hand. "Greta—" I began, but she ignored me, turning the key. Only it didn't turn, didn't click.

She glanced at me, turning it harder, jiggling, jerking.

When it didn't click, didn't unlock, she just looked at the ground.

I banged on the key, the lock, trying to get the key in deeper, trying to get it to turn, to click.

"Hans," she said, her voice small.

"It's got to work," I muttered, banging both hands against the lock and key, until one of my fingers started to bleed again.

"Hans," she said, reaching up and wrapping both my hands in hers. "Stop."

I stared at her little hands over mine. One of them was dark pink and swollen. "Your hand," I said. "What happened?"

"I burned it," she answered. "Getting the key."

She held up her palm and I could see it then, the red marks at the center—at the place where the circular end of the skeleton key must have rested. It wasn't just a circle, but some kind of design, like she'd been branded.

"Greta," I whispered, looking at the spot on her hand, then back at the key. In my hurry to open the lock, I hadn't noticed the patterning in the circular end of the key—the arrows, the north and south—but the way it had burned into her hand made it clear.

The key, it was a map.

CHAPTER 36

GRETA

To call it a map seemed like a bit of a stretch. More like the type of compass that you find on a map. What was the word for that? I closed my eyes, trying to remember. Oh yes. A compass rose.

Except…

I held my hand up to my face.

Sure enough, there was the 'N' for north. Only it rested at the bottom of my hand, as though the world had been flipped upside down. Of course, I could have just been burned upside down. Except that then the letters would also be upside down. I cocked my head to the side, squinting at the lines as though the directions would change. They didn't.

"It's upside down," I said.

"Yeah, I'm noticing that," Hans replied.

Shelby had said she'd come from the East, but that didn't make sense since the sun had been rising in the other direction. But the map on my hand, it was backwards too, West and East reversed.

Had we been thinking backwards the whole time? Or thinking forwards in a backwards place?

Half a dozen paths ran through my palm, each of them criss-crossing at a center point.

"The house," I murmured, pointing at it.

And then I noticed something—the dots at the circle that was the circumference of the map, the one that held all the paths in. They weren't dots at all, but tiny mushrooms, surrounding the center point.

"The mushrooms," Hans said. "Like at the back of the house—the arch."

"It's not an arch at all," I said, looking into his eyes. "Just the beginnings of a ring. A ring that holds things in."

"What do you mean?" he asked.

"The mushrooms circle this center point. I think that's the house. Even though it's not literally in the center. These paths, they all lead back, back to the house. Like they did for us, leading us back. And the mushrooms—" I said. "I don't think they're decorative. I think they're a sort of fairy ring. They hold us in, almost like, I don't know—a charm or something."

"Fairy rings aren't really magic, Greta," Hans said in this absolutely condescending way that reminded me he was still just a regular older brother.

"We're trapped in a house we can't escape from where ghosts keep finding us," I said.

"Okay, fine," Hans said. "Maybe something a little weird is going on."

"A little?" I said. "I think we've been following the wrong paths all along."

"What do you mean?" Hans asked.

"I think we need to find the line of the mushrooms, see where they take us, and break out of it. Which *sounds* easy."

He nodded, kind of slowly at first, and said, "But probably isn't easy at all. When I was in the woods with Savina, I found one of our trees, Gret. With our initials scratched into it and everything. But then I went back to Savina and I couldn't find it again. But there were mushrooms—lots of mushrooms along the trees."

"The fairy ring," I said.

"Yeah," he murmured. "Maybe. And it does seem like it would have been easy to just sort of…cross over it. But…"

"But you couldn't."

"I mean, I didn't try exactly," he said. "I wasn't thinking about magical fairy rings at the time. But it almost seemed like those mushrooms sort of appeared. Like, after I found something familiar, something that could lead me back. It sounds crazy, but do you think they grew there to keep me in?"

"Nothing sounds crazy anymore," I said.

"So if we can't cross it?" he said.

"We can at least follow it."

CHAPTER 37

GRETA

I started at the back of the house where the fairy arch was. I stepped over it, super simple. No invisible magical barrier, no dark force beating me back, no ogres or wolves blocking the way. But after I'd walked a few paces, I could see it again, another fairy arch, just like the first. I stepped over it and sure enough, about ten feet deeper into the woods, another appeared. Or one was there at any rate. Concentric circles. Or the fairy ring was expanding. Or perhaps it was just very thick.

So it *was* like Hans had said. The ring was growing, or reappearing, or super wide, or at least not letting us out through the simple act of stepping over it. Looking down at the nearest mushroom, I gave it a kick. Like any other mushroom, it broke easily. But I could see under it, dozens of little baby mushrooms waiting to grow up and take its place.

I'd read once that mushrooms aren't really individual plants, but one large system underground that the mushrooms would sprout from. Which meant that I couldn't just take out one mushroom if we wanted to get past the ring. We would have to somehow destroy the underground system.

And this was a very large system.

The line of the ring extended into the forest, as far as I could see.

And so I walked. After all, I hadn't come out here thinking I could kick down a few mushrooms and save us. I'd come out here to follow the map. A map that went on for miles into the dark corners of the forest.

From my line of mushrooms, I could see various paths, like the ones we'd followed our first few days here, back when it seemed a simple thing to make our way back home if we just tried hard enough. Each of the paths bumped up against the mushroom hedge, travelling through as though nothing was stopping them. But I knew that when the paths wound through the ring, they would twist, turning somehow back to the house.

I walked for hours along the fairy line. Until I came to a tree that looked familiar, not because I knew a lot about trees, but because a man-sized mass of moss and leaves rested at its base —man-sized and man-shaped. In a position I remembered, in a position I would never forget no matter how hard I tried. The first time I'd seen that shape, he had been resting against the tree, as though he'd paused for a break. Until Gideon had laid him down, testing him for breath and pulse, declaring him dead.

Somehow he seemed more than dead now, both more and less at the same time. Because he'd become part of the earth, and as such, he'd started to grow with it.

The line of mushrooms, they marched along, rising up through the leaves that covered his body, gray and white dots—some big with enormous brown caps, some small with only white pinheads at their tips. Dozens, hundreds.

And there, on the place that had once been a face, where the man's mouth might have opened in one last sigh, sprouted a singular mushroom. Beautiful and deadly—red-capped with yellow spots.

You didn't have to be a genius—just a kid who lived by the

woods with a protective mama—to know that you didn't eat the mushrooms that looked like that.

Even so, I couldn't stop looking at it. I reached for it, one finger touching the tip, just like Sleeping Beauty with the spindle. I almost expected to feel something, touching that deadly fungus. A wave of nausea, an electric shock, blood pricking to my finger.

Instead, I felt my hand winding around the stem, squeezing it off from the matrix fungus that must have been growing beneath the earth, from its hundreds of brother and sister fungi.

With a sharp twist of my fingers, I plucked it from the dead man's mouth and tucked it into the right pocket of my apron.

I watched the mouth, almost expecting another to sprout up in its place. None did.

I turned to leave, to keep following the fairy ring, when I tripped.

Looking down, I could see the line of a mound that had once been the man's arm. And there at the end of it, in his loamy lump of a hand, sprouted a dark gray mushroom surrounded by white dots of fungi—a singular accent blossom in a bouquet he was holding.

I leaned down, pulling it from the base of the soil, and placing it into my other pocket.

When the six are gone, the rest will live. That was the strange thing he'd written on the note with the eggs.

Behind me, I could feel it—the house—just as we'd sensed it the day he'd died. Looming, calling us back to it. And just like then, I didn't dare turn to look, to see the crooked roof or well-worn door. Just like then, I stood gazing at the man.

But this time, there was no Gideon to turn resolutely, to take a first step. This time, there was just me.

And that didn't seem like nearly enough.

Hans

GRETA HAD SAID that *we* would follow the mushrooms, but that wasn't true—not at all really—because only one of us was free to follow anything. The other one was stuck in a locked shed, with two waste buckets quickly filling, and only a few bread crusts left to eat.

I didn't like it, the useless feeling. Didn't like the hours I spent counting Savina's breaths, or noting the different grades of yellow on Gideon's face. Didn't like the weakness that seemed to have overtaken my body, the weakness that only grew worse from sitting here, not eating, not moving, not doing anything.

There was this saying my mom used to use: If you can't be happy, work.

Oh man, I'd hated it every time she'd said it. Probably because she always said it when I was the most mad or sad and was lying down on the bed in my room, usually with a pillow over my head, refusing to talk. She'd wanted me to get up off my bed, to do something.

I never had. All those times I'd heard her say that, and I'd refused to get up off my bed and go work out, or do my homework, or wash the dishes, or do anything at all.

Now, I swung my legs over the cot, and went to the door of the shed. We still had a few bread crusts, which Greta had left on a skinny, chipped saucer. I poured a bit of water over them, letting them soften, before working them into a paste with my fingers and a cheap, tin spoon.

It wasn't a meal that was going to win any beauty contests. In fact, it looked disgusting, though in my absolute hunger, it didn't smell half bad. I allowed myself two bites, before going over to Savina, who lay there, barely moving.

I settled in next to her, remembering how my mom used to feed me when I'd been sick. I slipped a gentle hand under her head, propping her up, so she would be able to swallow with ease. Her head lolled to the side, and I scooted closer, settling her into the crook of my arm.

"You hungry?" I asked.

She didn't answer.

I took the spoon and gently worked it between her lips, hoping she'd swallow.

It took a minute, but her mouth started to move, working over the mush, then swallowing. Her eyes fluttered, but didn't open, and I gave her another spoonful.

She swallowed that one faster.

From across the room, I heard Gideon shuffle toward me, watching.

"You take some too," I said, still spooning bits into Savina's mouth.

"No," he answered. "She needs it more than I do."

"You need some too," I replied.

"No," he answered. "I don't."

I remembered the story Savina had told me when we'd been in the woods, the one about when they were babies and how the doctor had joked that she'd taken his nutrients. "I think she'd want you to have some," I said.

"It doesn't matter what she'd want," Gideon said. "Because I won't take it. Not until she gets up and makes me."

And Savina, who hadn't moved except to flutter and swallow, suddenly clamped her mouth shut, refusing to let the spoon in.

I glanced at Gideon. He pinched his lips together just as stubbornly, as though he was convinced I might come at him with the spoon like I had Savina.

"I think you better have some, dude," I said. "At least a bit."

"For every bite I take," he said. "You feed her." And then he whispered into my ear. "Double."

I nodded. And we went on like that. Three teens who looked

like a triplet of grannies in the nursing home. At least if the nursing home was an old shed once used for animals and filled with wood chips and decayed straw.

I knew something then, feeding Savina while Gideon tried to eat as little as possible. I knew that I would do anything for these friends. No matter what it took, I would save them.

I offered a spoonful to Gideon and he silently shook his head. "I don't think she'll let us die," he said, refusing another bite. "The woman in the house."

"I don't know," I said. "People who lock kids in sheds are usually pretty far along the crazy-town road."

And Savina, I swear she almost smiled.

Gideon did not. "I think she wants us for something," he said. "Or she would have killed us already."

"But what?" I asked, quieting my voice in the hope Savina wouldn't hear.

"That's kind of the big question, isn't it?"

And with that, he picked up the discarded skeleton key, tracing each line, dip, and dot, moving his lips as he did— memorizing it.

Greta

I WAITED WITH THE MAN—THE mound of a man—until the sun turned to amber over the horizon. The line of mushrooms that ran along his body looked plain now, usual. I patted each of my apron pockets, feeling both the red and the gray.

The children we'd found—I'd found—they had been killed. Out in the woods.

If they'd been as hungry as us, what would be the easiest way to kill them? The killer wouldn't need a gun or a knife. Just a simple stew with the right ingredient.

And I knew of someone who liked to make stew.

I stood up, looking to the house in the distance.

I'd thought the woman had been the first victim, but what if I'd been wrong? The woman hadn't vanished when I found the key. That meant that I had either the wrong relic, or the wrong victim. The question was, which one was it?

CHAPTER 38

GRETA

"You killed them with a stew," I said to Gigi when I finally returned to the house.

Her hair was brown, curly. Jeans tight at the hip with a flare at the bottom, white ruffled blouse.

"Have you been out eating mushrooms, honey?" she said, that sweet, condescending lilt to her voice. She pulled a smooth loaf of bread from a dish towel and placed it on the cutting board near her plate.

"I thought you were the first victim—that a serial killer had killed you to take this house. But you're not the first. You're the last. You killed five children by mixing poisonous mushrooms into a stew. And then you died yourself."

I plunked the two mushrooms from my pockets onto the cutting board, as though they were evidence I was presenting for a case.

She looked at them, and then laughed. The tinkling sound of a young woman, a girl even.

"The fact that you think that shows how very little you know." And with that, she popped the gray mushroom into her mouth, and chewed.

I glanced at the other one.

"Aren't you *hungry?*" she said, her voice taking on a taunting, raspy tone, as the sun sank low and the dying light brought gray streaks into her hair, decaying spots to her teeth.

"I'm not eating that," I said.

"Pity," she replied. "Because this one tastes like apricots." And with that, she brought it to her lips—the bright spores smearing onto her gums in blood-red lines. She bit into it, peeling the skin off the top, then crushing the gills between her teeth before swallowing the stem in a final gulp.

"But how?" I asked. "Everyone knows the spotty ones are dangerous."

"Everyone doesn't know a lot," she replied, lifting a knife from the cutting board and wrapping a gnarled hand around it.

"You can eat them because you're dead," I said suddenly. "You're a ghost like all the others."

"Am *I* the ghost?" she asked, slitting a line through the tough outer crust of the bread.

"Who else would be?" I asked, my face reflected in the smooth metal of the knife.

"*Wenn die sechs weg sind, wird der rest leben,*" she said in perfect German.

"The note?" I murmured.

"Of course, dear. I read the card with the basket. 'When the six are gone, the rest will live.'" And with that, she slid the knife through the soft center of the pale dense bread.

I took a step back, startled by the sound of the knife scraping the cutting board. "I just have to solve it."

She smiled, looking out the window at the sun that sank, the darkening sky.

Her skin had gone thin, her face lined with wrinkles, her eyes gray and watering. "If you like a good riddle," she said, turning back to me, dipping the knife in the bucket of dishwater and wiping it clean with her apron, "try this one: Everything you think you know is wrong. But you're getting closer."

And with that, she lifted the bucket of dirty dish water and dumped it onto the fire, extinguishing the light, throwing us into darkness.

I stood, expecting to be killed, feeling in fact a sharp shot of pain near my neck, as though it had already happened. But instead of a searing tumble, a rush of blood, and my own screams, I simply heard the soft snore of the woman. Gigi—too young a name for such an old woman. She was lying on her cot, fast asleep, the knife discarded beside her.

And then, stumbling through the darkness, I made my way, at last, to my room. *My* room.

I STOPPED at the final step, holding the banister—a banister that wasn't sticky though I knew it was edible. Edible. And sweet. I brought my face close to it in the darkness, and sniffed. What was it that Larisa had said? That it tasted like a fruit roll-up? It smelled that way too. I caught the fruity hints of it—almost like... *apricot*.

"The house," I murmured to myself. "It's made of mushrooms. And just like the fairy ring, it's trapping me inside of it."

I WAITED for Hans by the shed. As dawn crested, as the world came alive. Birds in the distance, dew under my feet, insects creeping along.

I watched my brother and our friends sleep. It wasn't precious, like watching children. I felt like the nurse at an old people's home. They looked gray, gaunt, their hair thin, their bodies rumpled.

At exactly 6:15, Hans' eyelids flew open. "Greta," he croaked. "Did you bring breakfast?"

"I don't have any," I said.

"I thought she wanted to 'fatten us up,'" he mumbled, rolling over in the hay, and pressing himself up like he barely had the strength.

"She does," I said. "Which is why I won't."

He gave me a strange look, a look he'd given me sometimes when I was with Mama—a look with a taste of suspicion behind it. "And the map?" he asked. "Did you follow it?"

"Yes," I said.

"And?" He walked to the door as Gideon began to softly groan. Savina only fluttered, her eyes never fully opening.

"Mushrooms," I said. "It led to more and more mushrooms. Like concentric circles, or just a really thick field of them, I don't know."

"So…nothing," he said.

"Not quite," I replied. "I found the old man, his body. Covered in mushrooms."

"Gross," Hans said.

But it hadn't been. If anything, it had been oddly… beautiful.

"Did he stink?" Hans asked.

"No," I said. "But I picked two of the mushrooms, fed them to her. Well, she ate them at any rate."

He pressed his eyebrows together. "Were you trying to poison her?"

"No," I answered honestly. "But I thought that maybe she'd poisoned the children."

"And did she?"

"Yes," I said. "And maybe also no."

"Greta, seriously, you sound like you're on drugs or something. Talk normal."

"Hans, I've been eating them, the mushrooms."

"Well, maybe that's why you sound like you're on drugs," he grumbled.

"Not from the ground," I said.

"Where else would you eat mushrooms from?" he asked.

"They're in the house," I said. "Mixed in. Different types, different flavors."

"Greta…" he began slowly. "What are you saying? What do you mean?"

"That I've been eating it. The house."

His eyebrows didn't release, didn't let go. "I know," he said slowly. "I saw you once."

"Yes," I said. "And it's somehow trapping me. Now when I eat the house, I forget things."

He looked away so I couldn't see his eyes, couldn't know what he was thinking or wondering.

Savina was sitting up now, staring at me, her eyes as big as moons, set deep into her sickly face. "Hans," she whispered.

"Greta," Hans said, ignoring Savina for once. "You know who else ate the house?"

"They did," I murmur. "The others."

"But you're *not* them, right?" Hans said, his voice rising. "So why are *you* eating the house?"

"I'm not the only one," I whispered. "I've fed it to you guys too, when you needed it. I added crumbs to Savina's cup when you got back from the woods. I sprinkled bits of it onto your tea, your food, so you would live. Every time you've felt the smallest bit better in these woods, it's because I've been giving you pieces of the house. But it's a dangerous remedy—a cure that is the disease. The more you eat, the more you crave. And the more you crave, the more you eat. And now, now that she's here, the more you eat, the more you start to forget."

"You're sick too, Greta," Hans said. "We've got to get out of here so we can get the help we need. We've all gotten sick differently, but…"

Savina stood up from her cot, Gideon watching her with those sunken eyes.

"Prove it," Savina said. "Prove that you've been eating the house. Prove that we've been eating it too. Prove that it has helped."

"I can't," I answered. "It's starting to mess with my head."

"No crap," Hans muttered, running his hands through his greasy hair.

"It's making me forget things. Important things. I can't eat it anymore if I want to get out."

"Well, I want to eat it," Savina said, staggering forward. "I want to eat it to feel like you, to look like you. At this point, I don't even care what I forget."

"*She* wants you to forget—the woman," I said. "Everything. Your family. Your home." I looked into Savina's dull eyes. "And then it doesn't matter to you when you are gone."

Hans leaned his head against the bars, bits of hair poking out. "Maybe it's not us forgetting stuff that you need to be worried about," he said. "Maybe she's getting to you, tricking you into doing things that aren't good for you, that aren't good for *us*."

I reached up and stroked Hans' hair that was sticking through the grate. "We have to keep you thin," I said tenderly. "Because the woman—she's lived in this house too long, and she's bound to it, to the mushrooms, the disease. The craving that's never satisfied. Until you eat ..." I realized suddenly that there was something that would satisfy the craving the house left. "Until you eat…meat," I finished quietly.

"Greta," Hans said, his voice almost cracking. "You've got to feed us. Please, listen to me. That woman is brainwashing you—"

But before he could finish, Savina came right beside him, her legs wobbling like a dying bird. "You're trying to kill us," she hissed.

"She can't kill us," Gideon interrupted, standing behind Savina. "The ones who eat the house on purpose are already dead."

I felt it then, a searing pain in the back of my neck. Hot, but wet. I touched it. Just sweat. "I'm alive," I whispered. "I just…I'm getting so hungry."

"Then eat," Savina said. "After all, you're the only one who can."

Hans looked hard into my eyes. I wished I could tell what he saw there. When I looked back into his, I saw the sky, the ocean, the whole world open up. And then close again.

"We have to find the sixth victim," I said.

"We *are* the sixth victim," Hans answered. "One of us is going to die. Maybe all of us. Then your egg will crack open. Will you be happy then?"

"No," I said. "And you're wrong."

"Am I?" he asked.

"Yes," I murmured. "What if the sixth victim—" But I didn't have a chance to finish, because at that moment Savina collapsed.

CHAPTER 39

HANS

Day 21

Greta had gone too far.

We were going to die, right under her nose, under her *care*. And she couldn't even see it. She was too sick, too wrapped up with her harebrained ideas and conspiracy theories.

I felt for her; I really did. Something was wrong with her mind, just like something was wrong with our bodies. We were all sick.

But that didn't mean I could stand back while she let us starve to death.

"Get her some food, Greta," I said. "Anything. I don't care what it is. I don't even care if you think it's going to kill us."

"I can't," she whispered.

I looked at her then, my eyes sharp. "Yes. You. Can. In fact, you are the *only* one who can."

"Hans," she pled, her eyes wild. "If I do, you'll forget."

"*You've* already forgotten," I said, my voice rising. "You've sat in that house, eating her food, all safe and happy, while we've been out here rotting and dying. Look at us, Greta. Just look." My voice pitched up again and her eyes teared up. Something about that made me even madder. "Don't you even care if we die?"

"Hans," she said, then opened her mouth like she wanted to say more, but I whipped around, turning my back to her and kneeling to help Gideon with Savina.

"We need some food," I said, not looking at her. "I can't let my friends die."

Greta

THEY *WERE* DYING. Hans wasn't wrong. He wasn't wrong about my brain being foggy either. So maybe he was right about it all. But if he was right, then why did everything feel so wrong?

I pictured him and Gideon, kneeling on either side of Savina, trying to get her to come to. And I couldn't fault Hans, not even a little. She had *collapsed.* And it wasn't his fault that I was outside of that circle. He hadn't put me there—well, not exactly, not this time anyway.

I heard his voice again. *Don't you even care if we die?*

Yes, I realized. I did care. I cared about that more than anything else in the world.

"THEY NEED FOOD," I said to Gigi when I got back into the house. "They're dying."

"Wonderful," she replied, spinning on her heel, her curls bouncing on a smooth shoulder. "I've just made supper."

And in fact, a round loaf of bread sat on the counter, a nub of butter next to it. "How?" I asked. She was completely out of food.

She didn't answer. She didn't need to. We both knew the answer anyway.

I cut three fat slices of bread—the same knife she'd used the other night—still flickering with my reflection, then spread a thick layer of butter across the dense crumb. Like frosting a cake.

"A little honey," she said, passing me the full pot. Her fingertips were pink and plump, the nails shining and smooth—filed to a clean, sharp edge.

I took the honey, drizzled it on.

"You're hungry too," she said, looking into my eyes.

I nodded. After all, there was no use denying it.

"But you won't eat bread," she replied. "Not even lovely sweet bread."

I swallowed the acid I tasted in my throat from my days of hunger. "No," I said quietly.

"But there's something else, something you're starting to want even more."

I looked into her blue eyes, her hungry eyes, and nodded. "Yes," I said. "I notice I've started to crave meat."

AND THAT BREAD, which was made—I can only assume—from crumbs of the house, you'd think it would have helped them feel better. And in a way it did. They ate it that night, and an herb-flavored loaf in the morning for breakfast.

Everyone was sitting up, Savina chewing vigorously, though she didn't look anywhere except at the food.

"At this rate," Hans said between mouthfuls, "we'll be able to hike out within a few days."

My only response was to sit down in the grass outside of the gate. I plucked a wild onion up by the roots and nibbled at the tip.

"Mama will be so happy she won't even punish us for going into the woods and coming out…" Hans paused. "How long has it been?"

"Twenty-two days," I said.

"Yeah," he muttered. "And coming out twenty-two days later."

It was a small thing, the forgetting. But Hans had been keeping track of the days ever since we got here. For him to lose that number, to forget it… If they kept eating the food the woman fed them, the food full of mushrooms connected to the house, then it would only be a matter of time before he forgot more than just the number of days.

"I brought tea," I said, my voice as cheerful as I could make it. I didn't look Hans in the eyes. It wouldn't have mattered if I did since he wasn't looking at me.

He was staring into the distance, mapping an impossible escape route.

Truth be told, I was doing the same thing—because I knew now, with my thinning face and sharpening mind, that Hans wouldn't be able to help get them out. Only I would.

EVERY DAY AFTER THAT, I brought them food from Gigi's oven. Savory muffins slathered in a thick garlic butter with herbs. Cornbread and jam, with berries from the woods. Rhubarb cooked into tarts and sprinkled with chunks of thick sugar. One day to two to five. Twenty-seven days total. Until their faces grew plump, their cheeks rosy, their hair shining and thick.

Though I could see the way that their eyes had faded, shallow and dull, though I could hear the forgetting in the thick way Hans said my name, as though the tones were no longer familiar and he had to reach back deep to find them.

A few days later, I dropped a pile of perfect crab apple pastries inside their door. Hans was there in three strides. He looked at my now-skinny frame—the scaly lines of dry skin that ran along my neck and forearms. "Honestly, ...Greta," he said, pausing before my name as though he'd barely remembered it. "How hard would it have been to be doing this all along?"

I nodded as he snatched another pastry from me. When his finger grazed mine, I noticed it had grown fleshy and thick. My mouth watered a little, thinking of plump little pigs, and how nice it would have been to add sausage to this morning's breakfast.

I thought of Gigi, the note, my craving for meat. Only she knew why the house did what it did. And I needed her to tell me.

CHAPTER 40

GRETA

"How did you die?" I said, coming back into the kitchen and facing Gigi.

"Die?" she asked, sipping tea from a clean, white espresso mug. "Why would I be dead?"

"Because you're here. And everyone who came here after us was dead. Simple as that."

"If there's one thing I've learned about this house," she said, "it's that nothing here is simple."

"This is," I said, ignoring the pain in my neck, the sharp tug of the muscles. "The people who came to us were dead. And you were the sixth."

"And why would you think me one of them?"

"Because of the egg," I said. "When you showed up, the last one was rocking. The final egg. They thought it was me. They thought I was dead. And for a second, I almost did too. It was rocking so wildly, and they'd gotten sick and I hadn't. But then you came in, just as it fractured. Like it had with the others."

"And it always did this when a victim came?" she asked, nodding at the cupboard with the dead kids' stuff.

"Yes, always."

"Well, then it could have been any one of us. We were all there. All five of us."

"No," I said. "That's not how it works. We'd all been there already. It would have cracked if we were the victims."

"Unless," she said—and even though I didn't mean to, I leaned in, listening— "Unless there isn't a victim—*yet*. Just a killer."

I leaned back, my hands shaking.

"So I guess the question remains," she continued, and now she was the one leaning close to me. "Who is whom?"

"The victim?" I whispered.

"And the killer." She smiled, her lips cotton candy pink. "If I'm the victim, then I suppose the killer is one of you."

"They've been sick," I said.

"Well, that narrows it down then: Is it me, dear? Or is it you?"

"I'm just twelve," I said.

"Then I guess I'm the killer. And that you're dead."

"I'm not dead," I said, grinding my teeth, the muscles of my neck tensing and sending a jolt of pain from my shoulders to my head, that same searing pain.

"Eat or be eaten," the woman replied, popping a big chunk of candy apple brick into her mouth. "Kill or be killed. Which is it, Greta? Are you dead, or are you going to kill me? Just another copycat in a long line?"

"You're crazy," I said.

"Am I?" the woman asked, the candy apple brick melting in blood-red lines on her lips. "Or is it you?"

"It's you," I said.

"Well, I guess that depends on what choices you make," she answered, her candy apple lips practically dripping.

"I'm a child," I said.

"As I once was," she replied, yawning and standing up as though we'd been chatting about crochet patterns, not killers, as though this was the most boring conversation she'd ever experienced.

"I won't let you kill them," I said.

"Then you might have to kill me," she answered, dabbing at her lips with a white linen handkerchief, the color smearing in streaks of red along the fabric.

I STARED into the fire until it died to ember, then ash. Well past the cuckoo that chimed midnight, and into the morning when the sun struck at 6:15, and the bird slipped into its little door.

Someone had lived in this house. Long ago.

Did that person still live here? Or had they died?

Was she killer, or victim?

And what did that make me?

I realized, at last, that I knew.

CHAPTER 41

GRETA

Day 31

By morning, my hunger gnawed at me, deep and gruesome.

But I wouldn't eat, couldn't eat. Not yet. Not until they were safe. It didn't matter if Hans loved Savina more than me, or if Savina had come to care about food more than home or if Gideon had lost himself entirely. I knew they were there, under the glassy eyes. And I knew I could set them free.

Did that make me a martyr? Or just someone without a lot to lose? Was there a difference?

My brother had already chosen—his friends over me, his freedom over me, that party over me. Again and again he'd chosen other things before he chose me. That didn't mean he didn't love me. Sure, he loved me. Just not as much, never quite as much, as I had loved him.

Which made what I had to do a lot easier.

I prepared breakfast, fat slabs of toast, heavy with butter. I mixed berries and honey in a saucepot, creating a jam, which I spread warm over the bread. Placing it on a platter, a silver platter I noted for the first time. It had been tarnished nearly black when we got here, but now it sparkled and I could see my own face in it—growing thinner, as they grew fat. That would change soon too.

I poured tea into the cups I'd found—how long ago was it now—a month, at least, though it felt like forever.

Peppermint tea, with honey and no crumbs from the house. I didn't need crumbs at this point anyway, not with a full loaf of bread.

As I turned to the door, I saw the key—the modern key— sitting right there on the counter, as I'd known it would be.

I took it, dropped it onto the tray. Today they would be free.

I would stay. It seemed simple now. The house had called me to it, bound me to it. And so I would stay with it.

Earlier that morning, I'd found the little scrapbook I'd made of the other victims. I set the tray down for a moment, slipping the book out of my apron pocket and taking one final look at it —the old newspaper clippings, the kids with smiles and toys and the hope for a future they wouldn't have. And then I walked over to the cupboard and tucked the scrapbook into the bag with the items from the other children.

There. Someone would find it one day.

I picked up the tray and pushed the kitchen door open with my backside. When I got to the shed, all three of them were looking fat and practically glowing—Hans' hair smooth and thick, Gideon's skin peachy and pink, Savina's lips plump and soft.

Even so, Hans paced back and forth, like an animal in a cage.

I set the food down in front of the door and he hurried to it, barely looking at me as he reached through the slats for a fat piece of bread.

His hand brushed the key and a layer of the glassiness

slipped off of his eyes. "You found it," he said, like he wasn't quite sure why it was important, but he knew deep down that it was.

"Yes," I replied. "Now eat up before you go. It'll be a big hike."

And with that, I slid the key into the lock. The gate clicked open—again, so simple—and I let my brother and his friends go free.

Though they *did* eat first. Of course they did.

I WATCHED THEM, standing back like some sort of servant girl. As they finished, Hans looked at me, right into my eyes. But he wasn't really there, his memories blurred, his thoughts with them. "Thank you…" He paused as if trying to come up with my name.

"Of course," I said. "Safe travels."

"Yeah," he said. "Thanks." He turned toward the woods, then paused. "Are you going… anywhere?" he asked, turning back, that fuzzy look like he was trying to grasp at something that kept slithering away. A feeling I remembered. A feeling I would soon know again.

"Not today," I answered.

He nodded.

"Well, if you ever come my way, you should stop by and see us. Mama would…"

And then the thought got lost.

Gideon stepped forward, always the first one, even now. Savina following.

The woods would make them hungry, and in a few days they would remember. But by then things would be done, and they would be safe. The fairy ring would pose a problem, but I suspected it would only be a barrier until the final victim was claimed. And that wouldn't be long.

Hans turned back to his friends, taking Savina's healthy fingers and wrapping them into his own.

I smiled, glad he wouldn't be alone in the woods.

And then I watched them, as they walked along the line of the fairy ring, stepping into the woods, following a path that would lead to a buried man, to a criss-cross of paths, to an old fire pit where a party had once gone wrong, and finally—once it was finished—all the way home.

I watched Hans until his back was a dot of blue t-shirt and then nothing at all, lost to the dark of the wood.

It wasn't until then that I finally returned to the house. My house. At least for today.

I would clean it one last time.

After all, that always cleared my head.

I picked up a broom, just outside the door, sweeping the two steps as I moved toward the kitchen.

I had hoped to stop the murders, hoped there would be something I could do. But when your brother and friends were at stake, what was there, really, for you to do? Except to save them.

In thirteen years, my brother would remember, would think of the night when he went into the woods and came home to find his sister gone. In thirteen years, the police would come around again, warning parents to keep their children from the woods. In thirteen years, it would seem even less likely that the original killer was still alive.

And so, in thirteen years another child would come into the woods.

But I would not be here to see her.

Right outside of the door, I snapped off a sticky bit of awning as I went into the house. Cinnamon stick. My favorite.

CHAPTER 42

GRETA

My thoughts didn't grow fuzzy, not right away anyway. Which just goes to show how long it'd been since I'd eaten the house. Instead, my body perked up, the candy melting sweet against my tongue, just like it had that first time—the house holding me up, at least until it turned on me.

I walked to the far corner of the living room, noticing a tiny pair of black boots under the bench. The perfect boots, I realized, for a girl to wear while she lived in this house. I slipped them onto my feet, surprised at how well they fit, and began to sweep.

By that evening, the house sparkled and I was ready.

I made my way into the kitchen, where Gigi sat sipping her tea, looking much the same as she had when she'd arrived—messy bun, tank top, soft jeans. Though I noticed that her feet dangled off of the chair, bare.

I unlaced the boots from my own feet, slipping them to her.

It wasn't until the final drops of her tea were gone that she finally stood, her back creaking as the chair scraped the spotless floor. She tipped her head to the side, curls falling from the bun as she slid one foot into a boot, then the other.

"You've made your choice then?" she said, lacing the boots tight against her ankles.

In answer, I plucked at the countertop, stripping a line through the varnish over the wood, and popping it into my mouth.

She nodded, moving to the fire and removing the poker. Ginger sparks fluttered at her touch, flying around her face and hair as the coals awakened, hissing. She tossed more sticks on, thin and dry at first, then thick and strong. Until the fire billowed up the chimney, roaring into life.

And all the while, I took bits from each part of the house. B.J.'s pretzel sticks, Shelle's butterscotch, Missy's sugar wafer, Risa's honey crisps. Red licorice strips, sponge cake walls, creamsicle posts.

"Hungry, were you?" she asked, the fire casting shadows into the corners and across her face.

I didn't answer, just continued to eat.

"Well, tonight one of us will eat meat." She tied an apron tight across her body, knotting it like a rope.

"You know," I said, considering a bit of red velvet slab in my hand, then popping it into my mouth. "For someone who built this house, it seems you're just as trapped."

She only smiled, her face still young, though bits of ash had settled into the creases around her eyes. "No one said I built this house."

"Who then?" I asked, as the sun melted into caramel lines and began to set.

"Since you will soon forget, I suppose I might as well tell you." She tossed bits of dried sage into the fire, which smoked with the scent.

"Tell me what?" I asked.

"There *was* a sixth," she said, staring into the flames, "though I'm not sure 'victim' was the right word."

"What was she then?" I said, cracking a piece of peanut brittle from the counter, listening. "And who?"

"She was going to kill my brother," Gigi began, thrusting the poker into the heart of the fire. "He was nearly dead as it was. And she was going to take him, and eat him for supper."

"Who?" I asked. "Who was going to eat who?"

"The witch," she said, removing the poker with its golden-hot tip. "The one who lived in this house. My brother was in that shed, and I was supposed to feed him, to fatten him up. Things from the house, bits of the house. It made him foggy. But the witch was half blind, couldn't see a thing, so I tricked her with a stick instead of a finger. Until one day she couldn't take it anymore. She got the old ax, and said we would eat well tonight. She fired the stove, hotter and bigger than I'd ever seen it before. She was standing in front of it, those blind eyes gleaming practically white. And I just did it."

"Did what?" I asked, though I wasn't sure I wanted to know.

Gigi turned to me, backlit against the bright fury of the fire she'd just built, its flames seeming to lick at her shoulders, her waist, her hips. Almost as though she was challenging me, *daring* me. "I pushed her," she said, turning back to the fire. "It was easy when the choice was between that woman and my brother. The old hag went quickly, just a few screams. And with those brittle bones and that cobweb hair, it took only minutes. I stole the key then. Got my brother. And we tried to leave."

"But you couldn't," I said, staring outside at the dying sun, which matched Gigi's growing fire.

"There was a charm around the house. Every path led us back. For days we walked, nearly starving. Just like when we'd first arrived. Lost in a very different way. And just as hungry. You can guess what happened, I suppose."

"You started eating the house," I said.

"Of course," she answered. "My brother said I shouldn't, that there were other ways to live. But I didn't care. I was too hungry."

"And you grew foggy?" I asked.

"Oh no," she said. "With the witch gone, things had changed, at least for me. But this house, it sustains you for a while. And then it turns on you. Your mind, your heart. That's part of the enchantment. How else would the witch trick children into sacrificing their brothers and friends? Once you've eaten, it's difficult to stop, growing ever hungrier, craving its sweetness more than anything else. Until, that is, you begin to crave other things."

"Meat?" I asked.

"At first, we could stop it, or slow it at least, hunting for what we needed. There were wolves back then, stalking the edges of the property. But they didn't scare me. Kill or be killed, that's what I'd learned from the witch. I hunted several of them before the pack left. And when I did, my brother and I ate handsomely."

"Until you didn't," I said.

"Until we didn't."

"So you killed your brother?" I asked.

"Never," she said, turning sharply, her own face so much like the hiss and heat of the fire that I knew it was true. "But as the mushrooms grew from the dead things of the earth, so grew my hunger. Deep. Insatiable. And I lured them—children. Lost, hungry. Right to this house. They always found it, ate it, and then they were mine."

"Yours?" I asked, my voice weak.

"Yes," she said, looking into my eyes.

"How so?" I asked.

"They grew fat, forgetful. And then it was much easier. So easy. To take them." She sighed. "But not for my brother. Before I killed the first one—that rude little farm boy—my brother left. He said this couldn't be, that it would destroy me."

"But how did he leave?" I asked. "With the enchantment?"

"Same as your brother has and will," she said. "As soon as a victim is claimed, the fairy ring wilts and dies. At least until my hunger for meat grows again, and the mushrooms—blooms of bygone death—with it."

She clenched her teeth together, tight lines of muscle along her neck. "The thing was that my brother kept coming back, trying to claim me, trying to save me. He would wander the woods, find eggs and greens, fight a bear or wolf, at least until the world changed and we had neither bear nor wolf left in these parts. I would see him occasionally in a slip of colored fabric or a pile of mushrooms left at my door. But mushrooms were never enough. Not for me. Not anymore."

The sun sank beneath the line of trees, bathing the room in gray, and with it, the woman's features. Her fair skin turned paper white, lines of blue running along her temples, hands as knotted as primordial trees, pale lips with gullies dug into them, everything ancient except the ashen hair, which hung in two thin braids along her face, so that when the moonlight hit in silver beams, you could almost believe that she had turned to a child again—stoking the fire of an abandoned cottage, and hoping someone would come to find her.

"How long ago?" I asked.

"Surely, you've figured it out by now," she replied, hanging the kettle over the flames.

I thought of B.J., dead in the fifties. Which meant that thirteen years before that…

She lifted a bushy eyebrow, her lips tight lines around broken teeth. The kettle whistled and she poured me a cup of tea, served alongside a slate of chocolate shingle. "The thirties were a difficult time for a lot of people. Some sent relatives off. Some trudged across the country looking for work. Some took their own lives."

"And yours?" I asked, swirling my tea and watching a lonesome leaf get trapped in the whirlpool.

"My mother died," she said.

"And your father?"

"He married again. A difficult woman who wasn't fond of two extra mouths to feed. She was always coming up with schemes for us to go off and make some money. Selling papers or matches, finding bits of glass to exchange for a few pennies. And then, finally, the idea for us to go into the woods, bring back purslane and lamb's quarters. She sent us with that book, the one you found. But I don't believe she really wanted us to find anything. I think she wanted us to lose ourselves."

"And you did," I said.

"And we did."

"You lost more than you thought you ever could," I said.

"So much more, child."

"I'm sorry," I said. And wildly, insanely, I was.

"You will not be for long," she said.

"Because *I'm* the next victim, aren't I?" I said.

"Someone has to be," she answered. "Once you've eaten the house, you either grow hungry and kill. Or fat and forget. Your choice. Eat or be eaten. What a terrible lesson for a child to have to learn."

"Yes," I murmured, holding the bit of chocolate slate between my fingers. "But the victims," I said, remembering something through the growing fog. "They all have a relic, something that lets them go free from this place. Maybe that old woman—the witch—maybe if we could find hers…" I paused, thinking of the little basket full of broken eggs, all cracked open except one.

"Oh, my dearie," the woman said, looking at me through watery blue eyes. "You can't find the relic, at least not in the usual way."

"And why is that?" I asked.

"Because I *am* the relic. The witch lives on in me."

I stared at the fire, which leapt nearly to the ceiling, its heart hot and white. "Which meant that if I killed you…would that break the curse?"

"For me, child, yes. But not for you. Because as you have already figured out, the cure becomes the disease. I might be gone, but the witch would live on in you."

I nodded, closing my eyes, taking a bite of the chocolate shingle, making my final choice. It melted, dark and warm against my tongue.

"That last child," the witch said, wiping streaks of ash onto her apron. "Edgar—he had stopped eating too. As soon as he lost the memory he had for those songs. Then he knew, knew something was wrong, knew he had to stop. But it was too late. He was fat, and I was hungry."

"I'm sorry," I said again, my voice small as the fog in my head grew thicker and I took another bite of chocolate.

"Oh, I know, child. We all are. That's the worst part of it all."

CHAPTER 43

HANS

I woke under the moon, my body aching, like I had the worst hangover on earth. Only I didn't remember drinking a thing. Truth be told, I couldn't even remember arriving at the party.

I dragged my hand up to my head only to realize that someone else's hand was inside of mine, a small, feminine hand. I sat up suddenly, sucking in a breath and trying to get my brain to remember just as she—whoever she was—rolled over groaning.

"Savina?" I said, looking down.

She leaned forward, holding her head in both hands. I almost expected her to throw up, but she didn't.

"Um, are you okay?" I asked.

"How did we *get* here?" she said, more than a little accusation in her voice.

"I don't know," I said. "I don't remember."

She shook her head again. "I feel like I've been out here forever. I *smell* like I've been out here forever."

And, truth be told, she didn't look great. I mean, she looked good because she was Savina and all, but her skin looked pale in the moonlight, her hair a mess of twigs and grease, her clothes loose and dirty along the curves of her body.

"I think maybe someone put something in our drinks," I said, still trying to remember taking a drink, or even making it to the bonfire.

"No one put anything in your drinks," another voice said.

Savina and I whipped around to see Gideon sitting in the dark.

"Gid!" Savina said. "Do you remember how we got here, wherever here is? Oh man, Dad's gonna kill us."

Gideon stared into a place behind us that looked pitch dark in the middle of the night, except for a line of mushrooms that stood out white against the blackness, almost like they were glowing.

"We came from the woods," he said. "We were really hungry and there was something..." He squinted like he was trying to remember.

"And how do you know our drinks weren't spiked?" Savina asked.

"Because I never drink anything at those parties," he replied. "And I'm here too. Plus, I have all these weird memories, like dreams."

"They probably *were* dreams, Gid," Savina said. "Drink or no drink, someone gave us something that wasn't okay. Maybe in our food. Maybe they were smoking it and we inhaled too much. I don't know, something."

I stood up to look at the mushrooms that climbed up the tree —thick, stiff lichen. Something about them reminded me of a gate, a gate I'd wanted to go through with my friends, which seemed like a strange way to think of mushrooms. I reached up and tore one off. It broke in my hand, but there were dozens more.

"I remember mushrooms," Gideon said, watching me.

"Well, that would honestly explain a lot," Savina grumbled.

"No one made us eat them," he continued, staring like he was haunted, then coming to stand beside me. "*I* found them. And we were hungry."

"I still *am* hungry," Savina said. "Starving really. Do you think someone brought some of those marijuana brownies or something?"

"No," Gideon said, slouching along the line of lichen trees. "We're hungry because we *didn't* eat. We couldn't because..." And then he shook his head like he'd lost the thought.

I pulled off another mushroom and another. But there were always more, big, little, a solid clump. Eventually I ripped off a whole section, and it reminded me of something Greta had said once, about mushrooms not being individual plants, but a system. But when had she said it?

And why did it feel important?

My hand settled onto the tree and I felt little lines, different than the normal feel of the bark.

The lines...I whirled around. "Greta. She came with me— followed me—to the party. I don't know where she wound up." I darted in and out of the trees, looking for her.

"You said we were hungry, Gideon?" I asked, racing back.

"Yeah," he said. "We had to eat mushrooms." He kicked one over and there were dozens of tiny ones underneath.

"Gid," Savina said, her voice soft, like she was trying to explain something gently. "I really just think we ingested some-thing we shouldn't have. I know you don't like that, but—"

"No," I said, cutting her off. "No no no no." I tore through the lichen on the trees. I was supposed to help us, all of us. I dug through the lichen, down to the letters—the letters from one of the trees that Greta and I had carved our initials into when we were kids. "She's gone," I whispered.

"She probably went home," Savina said practically.

"She didn't go home," I said, the memories fighting their way to me. "She's the one who didn't go home."

CHAPTER 44

GRETA

I stood in the living room and looked around at the candy house—rock candy mantle glazed in sugar, dots of divinity for mortar, the floor made of a stiff cookie crumb—what did they call it in other countries? Biscuits, yes, that's right. Each pillar like candy canes without the stripes—and a whole slew of flavors from peppermint to root beer. Jelly bean varnish on counters that you could pull off in gummy strips. Fluffy bits of cotton candy insulation behind the walls.

The woman had sent me here to wait and rest while she got things ready for dinner.

A thought slipped through my head that I couldn't quite grab and for a moment I wished I had a hammer to break the sugar house all into pieces, leave and never look back. And then I plucked a lemon drop stone from the corner of the window and wondered why I would think such a thing—why, when I had everything I needed right here in this house, a soft bed, a chair to rock in, and plenty of food to eat. So, so much food.

Although something seemed to be missing, though what it was I couldn't begin to remember, especially when I'd gotten so fat in recent days—had it been days, or maybe just hours? Either way, I felt deliciously, delightfully plump.

Perfect, the woman had said. Her name had slipped from my mind. Such slippery things, names. To hold onto mine, I'd had to repeat it every time I took a bite. *Greta, Greta, Greta, Gret.* Someone had called me that last one, someone sometime though I couldn't remember now.

As for the woman, she just called me 'girl' and we left it at that.

The woman would be needing help in the kitchen very soon, as soon as she could get the fire just right. For some things, she'd said, you need more than a simple flame.

I settled onto the chair with a cup of sweet tea, nearly four teaspoons of honey drizzled into it, then took up a doily from the end table and traced a finger along the threads, the strands like paths, woven and knotted.

Hans

IT WAS easy to find our way back, once I remembered. We followed the white mushrooms in the long line—the long arch —that led us back to the house. They weren't dead, the mushrooms, and that meant—well, I hoped it meant—that Greta wasn't either. We'd grown fat, though looking down I realized not really—just something in our heads had. The woman had poisoned us somehow and then taken Greta.

Though I didn't remember being forced to eat anything. In fact, I remembered being desperate to eat, even though Greta— she hadn't wanted me to. I'd been so desperate to eat that I'd almost hated her for that. But she'd been right. We shouldn't have eaten.

The thing about Greta that sometimes made me so angry, was that she was usually right. And somehow it seemed that I'd forgotten that too.

I saw the smoke at least a mile away, and started to run. Gideon followed, moving faster than I'd ever seen him go, but Savina was struggling.

"Hans," she called, her voice thin. "I mean, 'Hank.'" She rubbed her head.

But I could see the smoke, and I knew.

Savina stopped, hands on her knees as she wheezed. "I'm so sorry," she said. "I don't know what's wrong with me. But can we slow down?"

"We've been sick," I said, crouching beside her and looking into those gorgeous brown eyes, flecks of bronze running through them in the moonlight.

"Why can't I remember?" she said, still looking at me like she didn't quite trust what I was saying, like she still thought we'd all been drugged, or maybe even that I'd drugged her at the party. "Why can you, and not me?"

"Because you were the sickest one," I said.

"Listen, I respect that you need to get your sister," Savina wheezed, "but I just want to go home."

"I understand," I said, standing. "But I can't slow down. I'll see you guys later."

She nodded, her eyes glistening just a bit. "Okay, Gid," she said. "Let's go."

He stood in the shadow, like one of the trees himself, and I saw him swallow.

"Gid?" she said, her voice a question.

"You *were* the sickest," he said, his voice thick. "And you can't remember. But you will. And if you go home, you'll regret it, because you'll remember."

"If *I* go home?" she asked. "You're not coming?"

"No," he said. "I'm going with Hank...Hans. My memories keep batting around like these fragments I can't quite get a hold of, but I remember we were all together. Greta, too. And I don't want to regret. I don't want you to either. We have to try."

"Try what?" Savina asked.

"I can't remember," he said.

Savina ran her hand through her hair and I saw that it was greasy, her face paling. "Well," she said, looking one last time at Gideon, his jaw set against the moonlight. "Then let's go."

CHAPTER 45

GRETA

The woman called me, though she didn't need to. I could feel the heat through the whole house now, feel it in my bones. And although I couldn't remember who I'd once loved or where I'd come from or how I'd gotten here, I knew one thing—that the heat was coming for me, and I would not be able to escape it. At this point, I wasn't sure I wanted to. Those people who had once loved me—they were gone. I felt their misty departures in the fog of my brain, little cold flashes stabbing through the witch's heat.

I walked a straight line to the kitchen, running my fingers across the wood paneling—crisp caramel marbled with candied nuts.

And then I was there, facing the oven, which burned orange and blue with a little heart of white at the center.

The woman had grown old, older than any woman I'd ever seen in my life—her skin maple glaze that wrinkled and cracked, her back bent like a candy cane staff, her hair bits of sugar floss in thin clumps, her teeth cracked and yellow as butterscotch. And her boots—little black slips of licorice, tiny things like a child would wear.

"Come now, dearie, and warm yourself by the fire."

I stepped closer. Sweat beaded at my forehead. Closer. My skin broiled and chapped. Closer. The hairs of my arms warmed as the woman stepped behind me, such a frail creature.

It would have been the easiest thing in the world to spin around, to send her into the flames instead. The easiest and the hardest too. Because if I did that, then it would be me standing there with the glazed paper skin and the wisps of hair, me with the hunched back and the hungry eyes. And though I couldn't remember anything else, I knew this. And I didn't want the hunger of the witch, the thing that ate her, just as surely as the flames would consume me.

I felt her hand against my back, the weight of a butterfly. I resisted for just a moment as I closed my eyes, letting the heat encircle me, my cheeks flush, ash dropping on the fabric of my sleeves.

Her butterfly hand became a mallet and with one whack, she sent me hurtling forward.

"Greta!" a voice shrieked, grabbing at the back of my dress, tumbling to the floor with me, rolling once.

The witch was quick then, but she didn't grab me. She took his foot—the one who had saved me—pulled him by the ankle as though he weighed no more than a sack of flour. She dragged him along the floor, and I hoped that it felt like a cushion of cake, though looking into his eyes, I wasn't sure. Those eyes, so blue, just like mine.

I grabbed his hand, trying to pull him back.

The witch cackled, all of her teeth gone now, the lips turning in on the jellied gums, as though she was getting older with every minute.

"Just shove her into the fire," the boy screamed.

I shook my head.

"Gret!" he shouted. And there it was, that name, my memory returning like shards of cooked sugar.

"Hans?" I murmured, tasting the name.

"Push her in!" he shouted.

I shook my head again. "I can't," I said, plucking at the crumbs of memory.

"Why not?" he shouted. "She's a freaking serial killer."

The old woman dug her nails, long and yellow, into his ankle, drawing blood. She licked her lips—a salt taffy tongue.

"If I kill her, I become her. Just like she did with the last witch."

"Gret, what are you talking about?" Hans said, clawing at the floor. I lost my grip on his hand as she pulled him away.

"I don't want to become her," I said, feeling the tears bite at the edges of my eyes.

"Right, okay, then let's just do what we have to and leave. And maybe…a little help."

He tried to scrape his way along the floor to me, and I grabbed both his hands.

But the witch cackled, dragging him toward her. "The house makes me strong. Much stronger than a weakened boy and a little girl, especially when I've been eating it for so long."

I pulled at Hans, his palms sweaty from the heat, our grip slippery.

He sucked in a sharp breath, then kicked the woman suddenly with his other foot. For a moment, she lost her hold and he bolted up, reaching out to me, but she grabbed his t-shirt, jerking him back to her, forcing him right next to the fire.

"A lovely morsel," the witch said. "And I can hear the others, somewhere in the house. I'll feast tonight."

I stepped toward the witch. Hans' hair was singeing, his fingers blistering against the side of the brick oven.

"The relic," Hans said, suddenly, shoving with all his might against the edge of the bricks and pushing away. I could see the blisters—white on his palms. "What about the relic? That's what you said, Greta. That's what we need to find."

"There is no relic," I said, reaching for the witch, stabs of consciousness returning. She couldn't have my brother. It was the only thing I was fully certain of. Even if she had taken other children, even if it destroyed me—she couldn't have him. "She IS the relic," I said, gripping the woman by the shoulder, my fingers digging into her wafer-thin skin. "She killed the last witch, and became her."

"She's the relic?" Hans asked.

"Yes," I whispered.

Hans looked at me, scanning my dress, apron, my small bare feet. And then landing on my eyes, before glancing back at the witch. "If she's the relic," Hans said. "Then we just have to find the matching relic." His own blue eyes almost black in the blazing light of the room.

He held meaning in those eyes and I tried to grab at it as my hand pressed into the thin shoulder of the witch—all bones and skin. So light, so easy.

"The matching relic?" I said.

The witch had loosened her grasp on Hans. Now I held her effortlessly, though I couldn't help but notice that she watched me with even hungrier eyes than she had before—hungry for something different than food, something even more tempting.

"Yes," Hans said, his voice thick, his face lined. "Where is the piece that matches? A girl who grew old in this house, a girl who would have been willing to kill a witch…"

I looked at my hand on the woman's shoulder. "…To save her brother," I murmured. "Do you know that's why she did it? They were so hungry, and she had started eating the house."

"Yes," Hans murmured, listening.

The witch had let go of him completely.

"And the relic?" Hans said. "Do you know what it is?"

"You mean 'who,'" I said.

"Yes," he said. "I mean 'who.'"

I swallowed, feeling the weight of the witch under my

fingertips, barely anything at all, feeling the heat of the fire in front of us, feeling the freedom it would bring. At least for Hans.

But instead of pushing the witch in, I grabbed her thin arm, digging my own long nails into her, and turned her toward me—blue, blue eyes, just like Hans. Just like...*me*. "You lost him, your father. When your mother died, you lost all of one parent and part of the other. But you had a brother, a brother you thought you could save. Only you couldn't, not when you were so lost yourself. So you set him free. But he came back. He came back with one wish—to free you too. To save you after you'd helped him so much. You figured, though, that you were too far gone to be saved. But he came back again and again. To clear the fog, to try to save you."

I saw the basket of eggs sitting on the table, all of them broken open except for one.

"It's rotten," the witch said, following my gaze.

"No," I said, looking back at her. "Just abandoned. Lost. You didn't like to eat the eggs in the forest. They weren't like wolves or bears. They were babies, and they couldn't defend themselves."

"Eventually I ate the eggs," she said. "Eventually I ate everything, everything I could find."

"Not every egg," I said, taking the final egg from the basket, the thin sliver of a crack up its side. "There was one you kept, the first you saved."

"It was foolish," she said. "I couldn't save it, that egg. It died under my care."

"You couldn't," I said. "But you tried."

"It was so pretty," she murmured, the wrinkles on her face softening. "I knew something like that deserved to live."

"Where is it, Gigi?" I asked. "The final egg?"

"I told you," she replied. "*I* am the relic."

"Yes," I answered. "And *I* am your counter-relic. But you are only part. To be complete, to have all of you, we have to find the things you saved."

"I didn't save anything," she repeated. "It all died."

"Didn't you?" I asked. "Your brother? We already found him—the old man in the forest. But what about the little robin egg?"

"I told you," she practically screamed, shoving Hans away from her. "That egg is rotten. I killed it instead of saving it. I tried—" She was crying now, hot tears that evaporated from the heat of the fire. "—I tried to keep it warm, to make it hatch. And it rotted," she said. "It rotted black from the inside under my care."

She stepped closer to me, the spittle flying from her tooth-less mouth. "As for my brother—he wandered the woods for over *seventy* years—all of his adulthood. He never fell in love. He never had children."

"Didn't he?" I asked, looking into the blue eyes of the witch, little circles of gray at the center, just like Mama's.

Hans saw it after I did. "No," he murmured.

"Our great-grammy, the one who lived in the house," I said. "She lived at the edge of the wood. One summer she got pregnant—quite the news in a town like ours, especially back then. But she didn't get rid of that baby. Had our grammy, raised her all by herself, with stories of a dashing summer fling."

The witch grabbed me, digging her fingers into the back of my neck, such a familiar pain, drawing a sharp dagger of a fingernail through my skin, like a knife. "Stop it," she hissed. "Stop talking."

The familiar cuckoo began to chime.

"You saved your brother," I whispered back, feeling the blood trickle into the collar of my dress, listening to the chimes—two, three, four. "You set him free."

The fifth chime.

Savina and Gideon flew into the room, Gideon holding a

part of the old cuckoo clock in his hands. They stopped when they saw me, face white against the heat of the fire.

"Greta," Gideon said, holding the piece out to me, the little nest with the little bird, cradled in his hands.

Another chime, and another.

"That clock's been broken ever since we got here," I said. "Because even after you couldn't save that bird, you kept the pretty little egg, putting it where you thought it would feel safe. So much a part of you that it began to rule the rhythms of this place. Midnight and 6:15. That's when it would chime. That's when you could see your little egg again."

Eight, nine.

She locked eyes with me, tears forming at the corners. "I couldn't ever save anything," she said.

The tenth chime.

"But you did," I answered, feeling dizzy from the blood that was pouring from my neck. I held the final egg from the basket —the sixth. And then I took the broken egg from under the cuckoo nest.

"I'm more than your relic," I said. "I'm your great-niece."

The eleventh chime struck.

She held out her hand, slowly opening her palm. I lifted the old robin egg from the cuckoo clock, fragile and thin. She stared at me, then reached for it. Our hands met, her sugar-glazed skin hot against my white fingers.

I released the broken egg into her palm, just as the clock struck twelve.

The fire leapt, flashing white, throwing me to the floor as the egg in my own hand cracked open and my vision blurred from white to black.

CHAPTER 46

HANS

Midnight, day 32

e choked on the flames as I pulled Greta from the house, Savina and Gideon crawling along behind me.

All around us, the walls crumbled and melted, everything smelling like burning sugar—sweet then harsh against my nose.

Gideon looped one of Greta's arms over his shoulder, lightening my load and moving us toward the door.

As we passed the tiny cupboard where Greta had put the relics, Savina paused, then jerked it open, hauling out the sack with the things. On her other arm, she carried the basket of broken eggs.

"It's okay," I said, coughing. "Just leave that stuff."

"No," she said, following me and Gideon onto the grass and toward the woods. "Greta would be upset if we left it."

I didn't argue.

All around us the ring of mushrooms molded and decayed,

crumbling into the ground as we hobbled along with Greta—dragging and unconscious—between me and Gideon.

I paused to cough and Savina handed me the lighter sack, taking Greta's arm and draping it over her shoulder. We traded like that, staggering through the woods, following the line of decaying fungi until we came to the trees. The lichen fell off of them in clumps and I saw one of our trees—mine and Greta's with our initials scratched into it all those years ago.

We practically ran to it, and there in the dirt lay a little glint of silver—a discarded granola bar, the top torn off, but the bar still intact, like Greta had just dropped it there, in the dirt.

Then Mom's fence, the faded orange posts.

Just past them, we heard the shouts, the screaming—Mama's voice above them all—calling our names. Instead of answering like a sane person, I started to sob like a baby, like I hadn't cried since the night that Dad had left.

The sun was peeking up over the horizon, not orange like it had been all these weeks, but pink.

I laid Greta on the ground, shouting, as Savina leaned down, holding the wound on Greta's neck closed with her hand and taking Gideon's jacket to try to stop the blood.

She unwound the apron from Greta's waist, using that as well, and I noticed then that Greta was in jeans and a t-shirt—the same ones she'd been wearing that first night. I squeezed my eyes shut, trying to remember what she'd been wearing at the house, and couldn't.

"Mama!" I screeched—using the term I hadn't since Dad had left. "Mama! Greta needs help. We're over here."

Loads of footsteps, what felt like thousands, thundering toward us. And right at the front of the pack, Mama's steps—the sound I'd heard every morning of every day no matter how tired she'd been, no matter whether she was coming home from work or headed to it, whether she was making breakfast or doing dishes, whether she was teaching Greta to read or painting a picture—a secret thing she thought I didn't know she did. I heard her feet—that little shuffle that was distinctly her own—a hard step followed by a quick one.

"Hans," she said, reaching us, and then stopping, her face going white. She swooped down to Greta, helped by a man beside her who scooped Greta into his arms as they ran back, someone else calling for the ambulance.

The three of us ran after, into the fray that was our back yard, a little tent set up by the local police, lights flashing in the driveway, floodlights shining into the woods—officers and rescue parties with bright flashlights treading through the muddy woods.

"Son," one of the officers said, as an ambulance careened up the drive and loaded Greta up. "We'll get another one for you three as soon as they get your sister taken care of."

I shook my head. "I'm fine," I said, staring at the bright open doors of the back of the ambulance and moving toward it. "I need to go with Greta."

The officer took my shoulder, held me back. "We'll get you another truck soon as we can. Your mama's with her; she'll be just fine."

But looking into his face, he didn't look convinced. I looked down at the small notepad in his hand, a date scratched up at the corner.

"Sir," I asked, looking up at the officer. "What day is today?"

"How much you had to drink tonight, son?"

"Nothing," I answered, as he shined his penlight toward my pupils. "Please tell me what day it is."

"It's June first, son. We been looking for you kids all night."

CHAPTER 47

HANS

Savina, Gideon, and I rode in the second ambulance that arrived. The medic in the back bustled around, treating a few scratches and some burns that she kept calling poison ivy. "What on earth were you guys thinking?" she asked. "Going out there?"

"We had to find Greta," I answered. "We had to go back to get her."

She grunted, like she didn't quite believe me as she dabbed a bit of cream onto a burn on my palm. "So she went out first?" the medic finally asked.

I looked into her eyes, dark brown set in a pretty olive-colored face. "No, ma'am," I answered. "She followed me."

The medic dabbed alcohol onto a scrape that ran along my chin.

"Is Greta going to be okay?" I asked.

The medic didn't answer, except to say, "You guys didn't see what happened to her? You just came and found her?"

"We saw," I said, confused. "We brought her back."

The woman lifted an eyebrow and didn't ask anything else.

"Is our dad coming?" Savina asked in a small voice.

"Yeah, baby," the medic said. "He was in the woods looking for y'all when all this happened. They gave him a call real quick."

She nodded as the medic bandaged a scratch that ran up her arm. "And the police? Will they be questioning us?" Savina stared directly at the woman, her jaw set, though I could see the tremble of exhaustion in her cheek.

"Yeah, sweetie," the medic said. "Yeah, I reckon they will."

Savina pinched her lips together, her eyes resolute while Gideon looked down at his hands. Back to their usual roles as soon as we came out of the woods.

Except.

Except that at that moment, Gideon looked up. "Good," he answered clearly. "Because we've got a few things to say."

CHAPTER 48

HANS

Two Days Later

Greta sat propped up in the hospital bed, drinking from a juice box when I arrived. I'd bought flowers, though I'd asked Savina to help me pick them out. "Should we buy candy too?" I'd asked.

"Definitely not," she'd said.

So I'd selected a collection of daisies and cornflowers—all blues and yellows and golds. The colors that most reminded me of Greta.

"Hans!" Greta said when she saw me, her voice sounding slightly drugged and sluggish.

I shoved the flowers awkwardly toward her. "I, uh, we got you these."

"They're pretty," she slurred, a goofy smile on her face.

I looked at the wound stitched across her upper back, just under her neck. The cops said she'd been stabbed, out in the woods, and that they were looking for the killer.

I had told them I expected they wouldn't find the killer because there'd been a fire, but they hadn't considered me a highly valuable witness. Although they *had* treated her for smoke inhalation, which they figured was from a fire the killer had used to lure her. I guess that part was true enough.

"I had the weirdest dreams," Greta murmured. "While I was dying."

"You weren't dying," I said. "We had you."

"You did," she murmured. "But while I was unconscious, I dreamed that we found the killer. And she was a witch."

"Sounds wild when you say it out loud, doesn't it?" I asked.

"Dreams are always wild," she answered. Then, "Hans. It was a dream, wasn't it? Because witches—they wouldn't really be real, right?"

"Anyone who would kill a child is a witch," I answered.

"But real ones," she said, "with candy houses and big fires for children."

I took her hand. "Greta. I didn't save you. You saved me. You saved us all—all that could be saved. And the kids that couldn't be saved, well, you saved them as much as you could."

She leaned her head against the pillow. "Did you have the same dream, then?"

"Yes," I answered. "According to the cops that's exactly what I had. And in my dream, you were the hero."

She squeezed my hand. "You were the hero, too. Because you saved me. I figured you would leave, like Daddy had—no looking back. But you didn't. You came back. For me."

I didn't answer, because my throat had gotten tight. I squeezed her hand.

"You were all heroes," she went on. "Gideon at the house. Savina holding my neck at the end, not a bit afraid of the blood."

When I finally composed myself, I opened my mouth, shut it again.

"What?" Greta said—just like her to notice the details even when she was pumped full of drugs.

"You should probably know that Dad, um, well, he's coming to visit you too."

"He didn't just send a note?" she said.

"He's here," I said. "That night, well, Mama hadn't really trusted me to not go into the woods, so she'd checked my location, and it had been blank. Yours too. She panicked, came home. We were gone. So she called the cops. And then Dad. He drove up as soon as he heard we were missing, straight from Atlanta. He was, uh, with Mama when they found us. I didn't recognize him."

"Is he that different?" she asked.

"He's bigger," I said. "Older. He carried you to the ambulance."

"Does he have a girlfriend?" Greta asked.

"Wife," I said. "She didn't really want him to come, to drive all night, but he did anyway, soon as he heard. That's what he said."

"Well," she said. "Some things are even stranger than dreams."

"There's a lot more," I said. "A lot more to tell, but maybe I should come back later. You're tired."

"I'm not tired," she said. "I've been sleeping for days. You have no idea how boring it's been after my…dream. Please. Keep talking."

I nodded, pulling an envelope from the back pocket of my jeans. "Mama just got a letter."

"What kind of letter?"

I handed it to her.

"Turns out that the property behind our house wasn't owned by a husband and wife," I said. "But by two German siblings. And there was a will found at a makeshift gravesite, leaving it to Mama's grandmother. Or her posterity."

"And since Grammy and Great-grammy are dead…?" Greta said.

"Yeah," I replied. "The 'posterity' is Mama. And, well, us too, I guess. The woods are ours. If we want them."

Greta scanned the letter, sipping at her juice the whole time. "Gretl 'Gigi' and Johan Hansel Schmidt. Gretl," she whispered. "So much like my name. And these people… They're dead?"

"He is," I said. "The sister they can't find, but with her age being what it would be…"

"Nearly one hundred," she added.

"One hundred and two to be exact. And at that age, well, she's assumed dead."

"Assumed?" Greta asked, looking into my face.

"The house is burned, Greta. Burned to the ground."

"And the things," she whispered. "Did the police, did they believe you when you showed them the things?"

"No," I muttered.

She closed her eyes, a long blink, like she was going to go back to her dreams.

"But Mama pushed," I added. "The police all assumed I'd been drunk that night, that I'd been drunk the whole time. Even after my breath came out clean, they figured I was high, or something. But Mama pushed anyway, even though I don't know if she believed me. But she—well, she chose to believe me. Even though I hadn't given her a whole lot of reasons to."

"And…" Greta said, opening her eyes a sliver.

"And so she pushed. And so they looked. Into the woods where Savina and Gideon and I told them. They found some stuff—the mattress, the trumpet, and an old house that had burned to the ground. They're still looking for some of the other things, but they sent your bag of stuff up to Montgomery for DNA testing. They think that's it, the site of the murders."

Greta slumped into her pillow.

"They found the old man too. In a grave of leaves by the tree.

That's how we got this actually." I waved the envelope. "He had the envelope in his pocket. With the will."

"But they didn't find her?" Greta asked. And I could hear the word hanging in her thoughts. *Assumed.*

"The cops are assuming," I said. "But I feel pretty confident."

"And why is that?" Greta asked.

I bent over and picked up a box big enough for a pair of shoes. "Savina feels kind of bad for how she handled some of, um, our time there. She says she's sorry she freaked out so much."

"She was fine," Greta murmured.

"Yeah," I say. "Anyway, she hopes this will make it up to you. As we were leaving, she managed to grab your basket."

I opened the box. Inside lay six eggs. Each one of them cracked wide open, even the pretty robin's egg that had been closed before.

"We freed her," Greta said.

"Yeah," I said. "I think we did."

Greta leaned back, plunking her paper cup onto the tray. "She deserved that, to be freed, even with all the terrible things."

"Mama's coordinating with some people in town—Risa's parents, and Edgar has a cousin in town. They're making a memorial, and Mama thinks it'd be nice to open up the woods, make a nature preserve—she's looking up how to do that. Government stuff, you know."

"Dreams really are the wildest things," Greta said, leaning back.

"Yeah," I said, fluffing her pillow just like Mama used to do for me. "Especially when they're true."

EPILOGUE

GRETA

One Year Later

The woods were buzzing. But not with insects. To be honest, since it was summer and all, they were probably buzzing with insects too, though no one could hear them over the din the construction company was making. Weatherproofing the path they'd built through the woods, tightening loose screws, inspecting and adding finishing touches.

Originally, the construction company had suggested cobblestone, but I knew the woods would eat those up in no time with weeds and mud, so they'd opted to build a wooden path above the forest floor. Walking on it was like floating above the ecosystem that lay beneath my feet. And I liked that.

Tomorrow they'd have the ribbon-cutting ceremony. *Memory Garden.* That's what Mama had decided to call it, after consulting with as many family members of the victims as she could find. Each kid would have a little spot along the way with mementoes of things they had valued.

A miniature baseball field for B.J., a pollination garden for Shelle, a wooden sculpture of bears and dolls for Missy, a small stage where theater or scout groups could come to perform for Risa, and finally, a tree with a music stand in its branches and a brass trumpet etched into the trunk. They'd hired Edgar's old band teacher to direct the creation of that piece of art, and it was my favorite of the five. I stood there, imagining Edgar's music as it had floated through the air. Beautiful and sad.

Five relics for five kids.

Of course, I knew that we were missing one.

Nobody had considered Gretl Schmidt worthy of a shrine.

But I wasn't thinking of the old, insane Gretl Schmidt when I pulled a small porcelain egg from my sack and nestled it among the prettiest cluster of mushrooms I could find.

I was thinking of a little girl and her brother, running through the woods in a desperate search for food, not wanting to hurt even the egg of a little bird. Just wanting to survive, to grow up, to know love. And thinking of the heavy cost all those things had exacted from them, from her.

I settled the decorative egg down in the loam by the mushrooms, away from the path, from what onlookers would see. "I learned some things from you, Gigi," I said to my new little shrine. "We all did."

I pulled a small candle from my bag, lit it, and let it burn down before blowing it out, a bit of the ash drifting along the tops of the mushrooms.

The sixth victim, or the first, depending on how you looked at it.

I stood up, dusting off my jeans, just as Mama's voice floated through the woods. "Greta!" Mildly frantic, like it had been ever since that night when she couldn't find me.

"Here," I called, trotting back to the path that ended at a nature center where people could rest and watch the birds.

She hurried up to the building, holding hands with William,

who pushed his glasses up his nose. "Where were you?" she asked.

"Just watching the birds," I answered, which was—at this moment—one hundred percent true. "You made it real nice, Mama."

"Well, I had tons of help." She squeezed William's hand. "I thought your brother was out here too."

"Probably somewhere making out with Savina."

"Greta!" Mama said. "You shouldn't say things like that."

I lifted an eyebrow at Mama and she peeked out, like Hans was going to pop up from a bush or something.

He didn't. He came up along the path, in a perfectly respectable way, with Savina beside him, and Gideon with them.

"Hey Mom," he said. "Looks like you're ready."

"Can you be ready?" Mama asked. "For the opening of a memorial dedicated to children killed by a madwoman?"

"Not really," Hans said. "Least not when you put it that way. But you're gonna have to be. 'Cause Daddy's coming up later tonight. And a bunch of other people, too. Savina said it made the news last night. All the hotels in town are booking up." He looked at William and gave a nod. "Hello, sir."

"The news?" Mama asked, looking at Savina.

"Yes, ma'am," Savina answered. "And not just local. It's a pretty big story—this whole thing." She nudged Hans.

"It's a sad story," Mama said.

"With the happiest ending possible," Hans added, and everybody looked at me and I looked down at my shoes. My neck didn't hurt anymore, not like it had—a little line of red scar all that remained of that night. A line I could sometimes feel when I brushed my hair or put on a necklace.

Savina cleared her throat and Gideon put an arm over her shoulder, like he so often did when she needed a little extra bravery. "They'll probably want an interview with Greta,"

Savina said. "So if that's something you're not wanting, you should tell them that, real clear, early on."

Mama made a little humming sound in her throat—something she did when she was stressed. "An interview?"

"The news is going to be here," Hans said. "So, probably, yeah." Savina slipped her hand into his and I saw him give her fingers a squeeze.

Mama turned to me. "Do *you* want an interview, sweetie? Or should I talk to the police to make sure you're not bothered?"

I thought of Edgar, Risa and Missy, Shelle and B.J. I thought of two kids starving to death in the thirties and the sugar-charred house that was now just a square of ash in the woods, already being taken back by moss and weeds and tiny baby ferns.

I thought of all the voices that hadn't been heard. And the way I'd been lucky enough to have someone come back for me. "Yeah, Mama," I said. "Yeah, I'd like to."

Mama gave a sharp nod, ever the pragmatist. "Okay," she said. "That's that. Unless you change your mind. If you change your mind, you just tell me, okay?"

"Mama," I said. "I got it."

"And I suppose they'll want some write-up too." She turned to Hans. "Do you want it to say, 'Hank'?"

"'Hans' is good, Mom."

"You kids with the names. You know I can't keep up."

"Oh, I know, Mama," Hans said, leaning over to give Mama a hug. "I know."

And then I hugged her and then she hugged us back. And then she was crying. "Oh, Greta girl," she murmured. "I'm so glad I didn't lose you."

I didn't answer. I didn't know what to say with the white clouds above us and a sun that moved and a brother that cared and a Daddy that was coming and a happy Mama with a new boyfriend.

I didn't know what to say with a whole ecosystem growing beneath our feet, constantly pushing out the old and ushering in the new.

I didn't know what to say when the world could change in a breath and turn on a flame.

So I didn't say anything, just felt the sun and heard the birds and held tight to the people that mattered most in all the world —the people who had looked for me, who had come for me, who had remembered me. Even after I'd forgotten myself.

And then I knew just what I would say when they interviewed me. I'd tell them to remember. A word that sounded easy, but was often hard.

Because sometimes to remember, you spoke. Sometimes to remember, you created. Sometimes to remember, you held still. Sometimes to remember, you let go. And sometimes to remember, you held on.

I held on. And Mama and Hans—they did too.

NOTE FROM THE AUTHOR: Thank you so much for reading! I hope you enjoyed this book. If you did, you can sign up for my newsletter HERE. Or try one of my other books. These two series starters are free! *Grey Stone or The Determiner.*

ACKNOWLEDGMENTS

I want to give a huge shout out to my book club, who read this and gave feedback. (It was an awkward ask—'Hey, want to read something I wrote and then criticize it, but like we're friends and stuff, so if you just hate everything about it, I don't want to know.')

Several of my children also read it and gave me opinions, which I appreciated so much. (Not an awkward ask; your children are always happy to tell you what they think you've done wrong with something; I'm joking; well, sort of…).

And of course, my amazing ARC readers. When you started reaching out telling me how much you enjoyed the book, it lit up my heart. Thank you.

Thank you to my cover artist Queen's Cove Creative, who brought the house to life. And to my editor, Carrie.

And to my husband who always supports my work. Love you.

Finally a thank you to my siblings. You are the best and this book is dedicated to you. Hansel and Gretel is a story about siblings alone in a scary world. You are that for me. And, yes, I would always come back for you (if I had the bad sense to leave you alone with a witch in the first place).

ABOUT THE AUTHOR

Jean Knight Pace is the author of *Click* as well as the co-author of The Determiner Series and The Grey Series. She lives in Indiana with her husband, children, cats, and a variety of wild backyard creatures. In addition to fantasy, she writes non-fiction and sweet women's fiction. You can find more about her at jeanknightpace.com.

www.ingramcontent.com/pod-product-compliance
Lightning Source LLC
Chambersburg PA
CBHW032220050726
47591CB00001B/193